This book belongs
to:

_____

who has the Witches
Gift of

_____

Blood Moon

EARTH

A witch with the Gift of Earth can manipulate plants, animals, rocks, the earth, and the weather. He or she is usually nurturing, stable, and trustworthy. Color: green. Plants: mosses and lichens. Stones: Coal, emerald and peridot.

FIRE

A witch with the Gift of Fire can manipulate and create fire. He or she is usually passionate, emotional, and has a bad temper. Color: red. Plants: bougainvillea, pine, chili peppers, and coffee. Stones: Lava, quartz, and garnet.

A I R

A witch with the Gift of Air can manipulate air or wind and is skilled at recovering
lost items and traveling. He or she is usually
of high intelligence and has a lovely singing
voice. Air witches are also good at hiding,
blending into the shadows. Color: yellow.
Plants: fragrant flowers, dill, and leaves.
Stones: mica and pumice.

WATER

A witch with the Gift of Water can manipulate, control, and sense water in all forms. He or she is loving and calm. Water witches are skilled with psychic abilities, healing, creating potions, and scrying (seeing the future). Color: blue. Plants: water lilies, seaweed, rose, and gardenia. Stones: shells, amethyst, and aquamarine.

DREAMS

A witch with the Gift of Dreams sees the past, present and future in dreams. A Dreamer has a connection to the Otherworld, or the world beyond our own, and a few have the rare Power of Spirits, or the ability to see and talk to the ghosts of the dead. He or she is intelligent, caring and observant. Color: white. Plants: lavender and lemongrass. Stone: moonstone.

M I N D

A witch with the Gift of Mind can sense or feel others' emotions, intentions, and the kind of person someone is. Occasionally, a Mind witch can hear thoughts. He or she is logical, sympathetic, and a problem-solver. Color: purple. Plants: peppermint, anise, and cinnamon. Stones: amethyst and lapis.

First Hardcover Edition: June 2013
First Trade Paperback Edition: June 2013

For information on subsidiary rights, please contact the publisher at rights@jollyfishpress.com.

For general information, write to Jolly Fish Press, PO Box 1773, Provo, UT 84603-1773.

Printed in the United States of America

THIS TITLE IS ALSO AVAILABLE AS AN EBOOK.

Library of Congress Control Number: 2013941581
ISBN 1939967015
ISBN 978-1-939967-01-5

10 9 8 7 6 5 4 3

For my Matt.

Thank you for the endless support, love, and goofiness.

Witches named the full moon in October the blood moon. As winter tightens its grip on the earth, it is a time of death. The barrier between our world and the Otherworld thins and all magic, Light or Dark, is given a rare boost of energy.

On this night, all things are possible.

Blood Moon

The Moonlight Trilogy

I

TERI HARMAN

JOLLY
FISH
PRESS

CHAPTER 1
WANING GIBBOUS

Present Day, June

O n a dull Tuesday night, two weeks after her high school graduation, Willa Fairfield stood at the soda machine filling a glass with Dr. Pepper, absently wondering what movie to watch after her waitressing shift, when she *felt* him walk in.

Warm electricity washed through her body, stealing away her breath. With a short gasp, she set the half-full glass of soda on the counter, almost spilling it. The intensity started in the space behind her heart, radiating outward to fill her whole body in the blink of an eye. She gripped the sides of her head, teetering on her feet, her head spinning, deliciously dizzy. She fought to pull in a full dredge of air as the heat heightened, growing, pulsing.

Willa swept her eyes around the small dining room of the Twelve Acres Diner, expecting to see patrons bending over and gasping, but everyone sat serenely eating, gossiping and carrying on as usual.

She spun around, looking for the source of the unexpected sensation. Everything was the same. Yet her body was absorbing warmth from somewhere, sucking it in like sand soaking up sunshine. The heat throbbed, warming her chest, belly, and pelvis. She pushed a hand to her gut and pulled in a shallow breath. *Am I sick?*

The fever curled inside her, blooming with a zing of energy, leaving her weak and exhilarated at the same time.

Do I collapse to the floor or run around the block?

Willa limped toward the swinging kitchen doors, thinking about the comfy chairs in the break area near the back of the restaurant. She wondered if she could make it without anyone noticing her wobbly legs and flushed skin.

Pulling in half a breath in an attempt to steady herself, she pushed through the doors.

There he stood.

The source.

A fresh burst of heat hit her full in the face as she stumbled back, bumping into the swinging door. He stood next to the time clock, fumbling with his apron, shaking his head, blinking in confusion. Instantly their eyes met and the warmth inside her boiled, bubbles bouncing in her veins, her head spinning even worse than before. The activity and noise of the kitchen were sucked away, leaving her in a void of heat.

He was the only thing Willa could see.

Tunnel vision.

He managed to stumble forward, closing the distance between them. Willa couldn't remember how to draw breath. He pulled all the air away, pushing into the spaces inside her.

The details of his person came into sharp focus. His broad, powerful body towered over her and she gazed up at his face. He stared down at her with a stunning set of chocolate brown eyes, so rich, most people would think they were black—but Willa could see the brown; she was swimming in it. His hair spiraled off his head in short, delicious curls of butter blond, the color of the setting sun. His upper lip glistened with a thin sheen of sweat. Finally, a long, thin nose and squarely set jawbone completed the picture, each piece handsome and right.

"Hi," he said. The weak excuse for a word tripped out of his mouth and Willa gasped at the rich, silky deepness of his voice.

Willa still couldn't find her voice—it was somewhere back by the soda machine. She stared, eyes fixed, body burning, mind confused. *What is this?* She quickly searched her mind. *Did I see this in a dream? It feels like something I would dream.* But nothing came; it was all new.

He took another step forward and searched her face as she searched his. Deep inside her, she knew they belonged to each other. She knew it the same way she knew her dreams—and the ghosts—were a part of her she could never escape.

Is this real? Is it possible?

Then, as though someone had thrown a switch, the rest of the world came rushing back, snapping into place around them. Suddenly, there was a high-pitched flapping sound next to Willa's head. It took her a moment to realize it was talking—Rosa, the hostess, a round, top-heavy woman who tended to talk more than people wanted to listen.

"Oh, good! You guys have met. Willa, this is our new cook, Simon. He's a student at the University. Pre-med. Prestigious, huh?" Rosa put a pudgy, frigid hand—everything felt cold compared to the heat—on Willa's shoulder. "Simon, this is Willa, one of our cute, little waitresses. She'll start at the University in the fall, history major."

Willa didn't say anything and neither did the new cook. It was impossible to look away from him. The entire kitchen staff had stopped working to watch the odd interaction with growing curiosity. A few of the cooks snickered and whispered.

Rosa's eyes bounced back and forth between Willa and Simon. She lifted a hand and snapped her fingers in front of Willa's face. Both she and Simon flinched, and the line of cooks erupted with laughter. "You kids all right?"

Willa blinked furiously and shook her head. "I, uhhh, I . . . don't know. I don't feel good." She looked briefly over at Rosa, but couldn't stand to look away from Simon for long. His eyes poured into hers, and his body leaned toward her only a few inches away. She could tell he was trying to think of something to say, but what words could he use?

Rosa pushed her clammy hand to Willa's forehead. "Whoa! You are burning up. Go home right now. It's a slow night anyway." The hostess put her arm around Willa's shoulders and started to pull her away. Willa resisted, lifted her hand toward Simon, her fingertips brushing his shirt before Rosa tugged her away. Moving away from him hurt—actual stabs of pain in her chest. She groaned.

"Come on. No puking in the kitchen. Let's go, Willa. It's okay. We'll cover for you."

Simon took one lurching step toward her, and Willa almost shoved Rosa away to fall into his arms, but reality pushed back into her head. She finally noticed the gawking stares of all her co-workers. Service had completely halted as everyone watched the cook and the waitress 'have a moment.' Willa didn't want weirdness attached to her; she had spent her whole life pushing it away.

He's a total stranger! What am I doing?

She looked at Simon once more before giving into Rosa's coaxing, accepting the bolts of pain in her chest as she turned away.

As Willa rounded the corner out of sight, the space behind her heart tugged, the confusing connection to Simon straining, fighting to hang on. Guffaws and taunts echoed from the kitchen as Simon took the brunt of the audience's reaction. Willa wondered what he was feeling. Did his chest ache like his heart was ripping in half?

Simon.

Simon.

She rolled the name around in her head, a rough stone in a tumbler. She attached his image and all that she had felt—was feeling—and let it roll and roll, feeling it change. *Simon.* The stone stopped tumbling, now smooth and shiny. A gem. A treasure. She dropped it from her mind and held it against her heart. It fit there, but she didn't know why or how.

THE FEVER GRADUALLY PULLED AWAY from her body, like a wave pulling back from the shore, reluctant, but unstoppable. As certain as the shore misses the warmth of the sea, Willa fiercely missed Simon's warmth. Huddled under two heavy quilts, she shivered and shook, an odd, aching withdrawal pulsing in her core.

Simon.

The newness of his name, of his image, rolled through her mind, lingering there since the moment she left the diner. His eyes like fine chocolate truffles, danced in her memory. The sound of his deep, resonant voice floated inside her like a drug. He had spoken only a single word—*Hi*—but the tone and feel of that word echoed inside her.

It had been an hour since Rosa had pushed her out the back door and she'd stumbled outside, sat on the curb and texted her mom to come pick her up. While she waited, head in hands, she fought the prickling urge to turn back, to run back inside to Simon. Her mom had arrived seconds before her will power gave out.

"Are you okay? You're so flushed!" her mom had declared when Willa dropped into the passenger seat. Sarah Fairfield's baby blue eyes were pinched in concern, her round face tense as she looked at her daughter. In a hurry to get to Willa, she'd come in her pajamas—black, cut-off sweat shorts and a raggedy Twelve Acres Museum T-shirt. Her chestnut hair, a shade darker than Willa's, was mostly up in a haphazard ponytail.

Willa rolled her head to meet her mom's worried stare, almost smiling at her mom's appearance and how she still managed to look pretty. "I'll be fine," was all Willa could manage, the ache in her chest now gripping her throat as well.

Her mom watched her closely all the way home and had personally tucked her into bed, something she hadn't done since Willa was six. After taking her temperature—a boiling one hundred and three degrees—and shoving four ibuprofens into her hand with a cup of ice water, her mom had finally retreated and left Willa in peace.

Willa replayed the meeting with Simon over and over. The electricity of it still bounced around inside her, unsettling, but she didn't want to let it go. She refused to listen to the part of her brain that demanded an explanation. Right now, she didn't care how or why she felt this way; she only wanted to hold on to it, keep it alive.

Simon.

Simon.

Willa didn't remember falling asleep, but she found herself standing in a field of tall grass, a dream taking shape. The field was bleached of all color, a palate of brilliant white that hurt her eyes. She squinted and raised a hand. On the horizon she saw a figure moving toward her. The same heat she'd felt in the diner flared, bringing with it the delicious dizziness.

Soon, Simon stood in front of her, dressed as he'd been at the diner—khaki shorts and a white V-neck t-shirt. His blond curls glowed in the harsh light, his dark eyes locked on hers. She smiled and tilted her head to look up at him; he was almost a foot taller than she. He reached out a hand but didn't touch her. She wanted desperately for him to touch her; although he stood directly in front of her, it was impossible to reach him.

Movement behind him caught her eye. A swirling cloud of coal black smoke tumbled across the field toward them. Simon spun around and placed himself protectively in front of her. The cloud moved like a great beast, rising and dipping as it surged forward, menacing, dangerous. Willa's heart began to pound against her ribs, her hands grew cold. Fear surged up her throat, acrid on the back of her tongue.

She should've run, but her legs ignored the command to move. Instinctively, Willa reached out and gripped Simon's solid, muscular arm, finally able to touch him. As soon as their skin came in contact, a jolt of electricity moved through her, rocking her head back. Simon gasped, feeling the same thing.

The power of their physical connection pulsed out of them in an arc of electricity, white-blue and crackling, curving through the air and connecting with the black cloud.

With a deafening roar, the cloud exploded into nothingness, leaving behind no evidence it had been there.

In the alarming quiet that followed, Willa looked up into Simon's smiling face. He reached out a hand and touched her cheek—a soft, gentle brush of his fingertips—sending waves of warmth down her body.

Willa woke in a mess of sweaty confusion. Disoriented, she pushed off the heavy blankets. Her hair, face and body were damp with sweat, brought on by a sparking heat deep inside her, just like before, undulating and thrilling. *Is this from the dream?*

She pushed her damp hair back from her face and let her eyes travel over the scape of her dark room, finally settling on the window. An odd tickle of instinct burst to life in her stomach. She leaped out of bed and tossed back the curtain, her knees nearly buckling at the sight of Simon standing in a pool of light under a streetlamp. His face was lifted up to her window and his eyes met hers.

Without a second of hesitation, Willa bolted from the room, down the stairs and out into the warm summer night. Only then, on the front porch, did she pause. A breeze tickled her face and raised goose bumps on her slick, wet skin. She wore only a thin, short nightshirt, any pretense of modesty forgotten.

All she could think about was Simon standing only a few feet away.

SIMON HOWARD TENSED WHEN HE saw her at the window and then, just as suddenly, disappeared. What if he'd scared her? Was she calling the police? But a moment later the front door opened and she stepped out onto the front porch.

He didn't miss one inch of her. His gaze started at her toes, nails painted neon pink, and traveled up the line of her shapely, golden legs. Her nightshirt fell high on her thighs and clung to her body like a second skin. Mussed and untamed dark brown hair hung around her shoulders and face. She gazed back at him intensely, stirring up a thousand emotions until they roiled inside him like a hurricane. In the pearly light, a sheen of sweat glistened on her face and slender neck. Being near her, seeing her again made his whole body quiver. He fidgeted, fire bubbling under his skin, the same as before.

Willa.

His shift at the diner had dragged on as if time itself had been buried alive. Every second after the chubby hostess had shoved Willa out the door had caused him pain. He did his job, working quickly, but his mind and spirit were caught up in that first meeting, in the memory of her gorgeous face and vibrant blue eyes. The second the clock ticked over to ten, signifying the end of his shift, he had bolted.

He had to find her before he went crazy. He had driven his black Jeep Wrangler through the sleepy streets of Twelve Acres, passing only a few other cars. The pulsing energy inside his chest guided him, pushing him on. For perhaps the first time in his life, Simon had forgotten about logic. He didn't wonder, didn't even care, if what he was doing was right. He only knew he had to find her. Tonight, he didn't care about consequences.

The heat and electricity inside him had crackled and bounced the moment her house came into view. He stared at the two-story Tudor-style home with its ivy-covered walls, inviting flowerbeds and big paned windows. Somehow, he sensed her sleeping, almost saw her cocooned in quilts on her bed. He'd parked the Jeep and stood under the streetlight for only a moment before she appeared.

Willa.

Now she stood only a few feet away.

He took a few hesitating steps forward, and Willa did the same until they met face to face on the front lawn, under the canopy of a giant ash tree. For a moment, only breath passed between them, their eyes searching each other's faces. Finally, Willa broke the silence.

"I'm glad you found me." Her voice was like music carried on a fragrant breeze. Simon's face spread into a wide grin and he laughed softly.

"Me, too."

He reached out and slid his fingers down her arm, her skin like cream, and then took her slender hand in his. The fever between them surged and the simple touch sent waves of longing through him, including a strange familiarity—the feeling that somehow they were not actually meeting for the first time, but coming back together after a long absence. A reunion.

Willa watched his thumb stroke the back of her hand. Then, lifting her eyes, she searched his face and took a step closer to him.

"I don't understand what's happening," she whispered.

Simon shook his head, lifted his other hand and brushed a few stray hairs away from her face. There were streaks of gold in her dark waves. "Neither do I, but this is the best strange thing that has ever happened to me."

She smiled. "Me, too." She took one step closer and rested her forehead on his chest. He put his arms around her, holding her. Never before had he felt so content, so at home. Never before had he felt so connected to another person; his strange abilities demanded a careful distance. But the threads that pulled him toward her, now busy tying knots, felt timeless, ageless, eternal. As if they had, and always would, exist, and most certainly could not be ignored.

Her mind seeped into his, bits and pieces of happy and confused emotions, but for the first time he didn't care. It didn't feel like an intrusion as it usually did, it felt like a conversation, his heart questioning and hers answering. Never before had he wanted to hear another's thoughts, but with Willa he wanted to know everything. And to tell her everything. A flicker of emotion he didn't recognize burst to life behind his heart and he had no idea what to do with it.

Lifting her head, Willa looked up into his face. She raised her hand and gently stroked his cheek and jawline. He watched her as her emotions flickered through his mind.

The rustle of wings brought them both out of their

thoughts. Above them, a great horned owl landed in the ash tree, adeptly folding his wings back and casting his bright gaze down at them. His coin-sized eyes blinked slowly, the yellow irises almost glowing in the night. He hooted.

Willa smiled and looked back at Simon. "Speaking of strange things."

Simon laughed. "Yeah, very strange. Willa, I . . ." His voice faded away, words failing. Instead, he brought his hands to her face, cupping her jaw. "You're so beautiful, my Willa." The term of endearment slipped out easily, surprising them both. Simon bit his lower lip, suddenly anxious and a little embarrassed. *What are we doing?*

Willa eased the moment by lifting a finger to trace his lips. "My Simon. It's nice to meet you."

Simon smiled, but it quickly faded as he considered her, studied her. Anticipation, eagerness, and . . . peacefulness pulsed out of her and, surprisingly, his emotions exactly matched hers. She held her breath as his eyes moved over her face and settled on her lips.

Simon leaned in closer, his lips brushing hers.

Willa sighed, her breath on his lips, the taste sweet and tempting. Simon kissed her again, deeper, longer. The strength of their connection flared, a febrile shock in body and soul. Simon's hands slipped from her face and wound themselves in her long, waist length brown hair. Her arms now wrapped around him, pulling his body against hers.

A sudden wind raced around them, a whirlwind spiraling upwards. Simon's rational mind stepped completely away, his heart and soul moved to embrace her. The kiss slowed, and soon, they were forehead to forehead, breathless and laughing.

CHAPTER 2
WANING CRESCENT

June 1890

Ruby Plate stood in the dirt road, a half-hearted wind tossing her skirt around her legs and coating her shoes in a thin layer of dust. The shadow of her house—*her very own house!*—fell across her pretty, heart-shaped face. The two-story Victorian structure rose triumphantly from the dirt, framed by a wraparound porch and accented with pitched gables. The clapboards were painted a cheery light green, the same color as the aspen leaves in summer, and the Queen Anne trim sparkled white.

Pleasure and pride swelled in her chest. Beyond her beautiful home were the bold, mighty mountains of Colorado. Twelve Acres, Colorado—she loved the sound of it. And she loved that this small town, tucked in a valley, protected by the mountains and their thick forests of pines and aspens, was *home.*

Finally, a home!

The memories of all the years leading to this moment traveled across her mind like a train down a track, one miserable car after another. Each memory clicked through her mind, loaded with its cargo of pain and emotion, each scar fresh and pungent. The strain on her heart and soul had aged her prematurely.

But now . . .

Now, the nightmare was over and a new road lay before her. It had taken three long, grueling years and more secrecy and death than she'd anticipated, but they did it. The first Light Covenant in America, the joining of two True Covens to harness the Powers of the Earth. The most powerful of witch circles.

It was a triumph to be sure. A triumph spearheaded by Ruby herself. Destiny and desperation had propelled her forward, and, thank the Earth, the others had been looking for something more, for something better, and had been receptive to her offer of powerful good. No true Light witch would turn that down.

From the moment she had read about the joining of two True Covens, the words drifting off the dusty page and threading themselves into her mind, she knew she must try. To find others, to join together, to have power and protection—that was all she wanted.

She'd hidden her powers all her life—the idea of sharing in magic with others was too tempting a course. Ruby knew it might be an impossible task, but the thought of not trying was more painful than failing. She *had* to try.

Charles was the first. It was a chance meeting, late at night in a misty churchyard. She'd been there visiting her parents' graves, and he, walking past, had stopped at the sight of her. A bright spark behind her heart pulled her toward him, and fate unraveled.

Before Charles, her life had always been lonely. She knew she needed to keep her distance to hide her unnatural ability to sense others emotions and sometimes hear their thoughts, but everything with Charles was different because he was just like her. Their connection was silken energy, wrapping her in a heavenly cocoon. For the first time, someone looked at her without pinched eyes or judging smirks. For the first time, someone looked at her with understanding and compassion, and it thrilled her beyond words.

He'd immediately agreed to the idea of searching out other witches to form a Covenant. But forming a Covenant was not enough. They had to hide themselves away from the suspicious and superstitious; the turn of the century was near, but people were still uneasy with witchcraft and magic. It was also important to distance themselves from any Dark threats from the evil witches who might seek to destroy her Covenant.

Once Ruby and Charles had found the other ten Light witches, it was decided that they needed a new place to establish their own way of life in peace and safety. So, they headed west, where there was still open land and people were too busy trying to survive to notice a group of witches.

The twelve witches—six female, six male, two joined True Covens—traveled together and settled their own town, fully independent and hidden away. Or so they prayed. Everything possible had been done to ensure their new peace. Once well established, Ruby hoped to bring others to this place, others in need of refuge and the freedom to practice magic the way it was meant to be.

A whole town of witches—that was her vision.

The first thing they did was divide up the land and build houses. A house—that was Ruby's first priority, her life-long dream, her aching need. A place rooted, stationary, comfortable and unchanging. She'd spent so many years bouncing from place to place, never having a true home. But now . . . here it was, rising out of the earth in front of her, magnificent and perfect, down to the very last detail. It was decadent and luxurious; not at all the norm for a settler's home, but that was one benefit of having magic.

Ruby now walked the perimeter, her right hand held out, the fingers waving through the air, setting the last spells of protection and longevity. The land, long ignored, swelled up around the house, hugging it, happy to welcome and hold the magic. The land promised to do its part to keep the house safe and standing. Ruby smiled, one of her first true smiles in a long time.

She felt, rather than heard, footsteps in the dirt, the thrill of their connection humming in her mind as he approached. Warm hands slid around her waist. "It's done and it's perfect. Don't you think so, Mrs. Plate?"

She laughed, turning her face into Charles's neck. "Yes. Perfect. And I plan for it to be that way for a very long time."

"Oh, it will be. I have no doubt." He ran a thickly calloused hand over her dark auburn hair tied up in a loose, simple bun near the base of her neck

"I've waited a long, terrible time for this. I want peace here. I want children here, grandchildren. I want it protected for as long as it can stand and to always know the joy of Light magic."

Charles smiled, "I believe it will be a haven for our family for many, many generations. This town, Twelve Acres, is a special, magical place."

WANING GIBBOUS
Present Day, June

Archard and Holmes stood side by side, staring up at the sagging Victorian home. Archard half-smiled at the run-down state of the once-great home of the once-great Ruby Plate, the last Luminary of a Light Covenant. It gave him an immense sense of pride to own it, knowing what it once represented, and especially what he would do with it now.

For years, he'd been planning and scheming, trying to find a way to fix the mistake his grandfather was famous for among Dark witches. *The man who almost formed a Dark*

Covenant. The man who almost *erased Ruby Plate's great legacy.* It was an embarrassing family history to own, and Archard couldn't wait to erase it with his own triumph.

But it couldn't be as simple as forming a Dark Covenant. It had to be poetic; it had to be revenge against the people who were responsible. It *had* to include the ruin and degradation of Ruby Plate's legacy. And that is exactly what he was doing.

"I have to *live* here?" Holmes whined.

Archard shot him a warning look and Holmes looked away. Archard stared at the back of the man's bald head. Then, in his crisp tenor voice he said, "It's only until she breaks. How fast that happens is completely up to you."

Holmes turned back and smiled, his lips curving under his heavy black beard. "It'll be quick, I promise."

"Good because I'm not a patient man."

Holmes nodded and folded his arms over his broad chest. "You sent the letter?"

"Yes."

"And you're sure she'll buy it and come?"

Archard smiled now, his perfectly trimmed goatee framing straight white teeth. "After what I did to the others, she'll come running."

Holmes lifted his eyebrows, but didn't question. "Well, let's go in and see the basement. I have preparations to make."

Archard smoothed back his slick black hair, straightened the jacket of his suit, and lead the way into the old house.

CHAPTER 3
WANING GIBBOUS

Present Day, June

History has its very own scent. It is the distinct smell of *old*, of layers of dust, smudges of oils from fingertips, breath from those long gone, and the weight of time. It's the collection of so many other scents that have twined together over the years to become an entirely new smell that instantly invokes what used to be. This smell is smeared thickly on the air in libraries, in ancient houses, in the drawers and cupboards of antiques and, most of all, museums.

For Willa, that smell was the breath of life. She felt most at home in those places where time exhales dust, age, and secrets. The Twelve Acres History Museum, next to her own family home, was her favorite place in the world.

The June morning was already hot and Willa hurried to the museum for her shift of volunteer work. It was hard to think of being holed up in the dark museum after what had happened last night, but she couldn't bail on her work just because she'd had an amazing first kiss. The time alone would be perfect for thinking, for figuring out. And she *had* to talk to Solace.

Housed in what was the original City Hall, the museum was a squat, long, two-story stone edifice with large arched windows. Cheery flowerbeds greeted visitors out front before they walked through the massive wooden double doors. Inside were several dimly lit rooms filled with quaint artifacts. It was the standard collection for a western town, with a few peculiarities thrown in.

Glass and stories. Willa knew and loved every piece of it.

And not just because of the ghosts.

She often wondered if her fascination with history was because of the ghosts, or if the ghosts came because of her fascination. She couldn't remember one without the other. But she did remember the first time she set foot in the museum, that dusty, mysterious smell filling her lungs, the zing of excitement running down her spine.

Even at the age of five, she knew she was connecting to something in her soul, something she was meant to be a part of. Behind the fingerprinted glass, she saw people, not just objects. Each chipped piece of china, each yellowed book, each tattered piece of clothing used to be a part of a life. Each one had been held, used, maybe even loved. Instead of zipping through the rooms like most children, Willa had insisted on going slow and reading every single word on the displays. And even that had not been enough to satisfy her curiosity.

She wanted to know more.

That was also the day she first tried to ask the ghosts about the objects in the museum.

At that age, she was only barely beginning to realize that these people whose bodies shimmered and went in and out of focus were the spirits of the dead, and only she could see them. At two, Willa had pointed out the "almost-there people," as she called them, to her mom and dad, who would immediately hush her and try to distract her with something else.

When she was three, around Halloween time, while watching TV, she saw a cartoon in which a little girl's dog died. The girl cried as her dad buried the small black dog in their back yard. Immediately after the dad finished dumping the dirt back into the hole, a white, dog-shaped wisp rose up from the earth and bounded over to the girl. "Dad!" the girl yelled, "Look, it's Licorice's ghost. Can I keep it?"

A strange bloom of understanding had burst in Willa's young mind while watching the show, and she triumphantly raced into the kitchen to tell her mom. "Mom! I see *ghosts*. That's what the almost-there people are. Ghosts of dead people!" Her mother, a knife in her hand frozen over a potato, had stared wide eyed, the color draining from her face. Little

Willa had waited eagerly for a happy response, for her mom to share in the discovery, but quickly sensed what she'd declared was not as great a comfort to her mother as it was to her. Her mom dropped her head and went back to chopping. "Please go play in your room until dinner is ready," was the only response she gave.

Willa quickly learned not to mention the ghosts to her parents. Even a three-year-old can understand when something scares her parents, and the last thing she wanted was that fear attached to her.

But something about being in the museum for the very first time broke down her usual carefulness. She had wanted to know everything, and the ghosts hanging around the displays, the spirits of those who might have lived the history, would have answers. For the first time in her life, she'd tried to talk to the almost-there spirits of the dead.

Is this your lantern? Can you tell me what it was like back then? Did you read that book? If you're dead why are you here? And why can I see you?

The ghosts didn't answer. Some ignored her completely while others scowled at her intrusion. The next thing she remembered was her mother grabbing her hand, pulling her away, saying it was *time to go.*

But Willa wasn't easily discouraged. She would return to the museum as often as possible, and every chance she got she'd quietly ask a ghost or two her questions. But none ever answered. When she got older, she volunteered at the museum and devoured every piece of town history she came across. By the time she was twelve, she knew as much about Twelve Acres as the museum curator.

But there was something odd in the history of her little town. Whole pages and sections of documents were missing. The curator didn't know why and, as hard as she looked, Willa couldn't find a reason for the missing information or any clue about what had been removed. Her already well-honed historian instincts told her there was a mystery there, one she desperately wanted to solve.

The first and only clue came on a muggy August day the summer before Willa's junior year of high school. It was also the first time a ghost answered back.

August 2008

The air in the tiny museum office was stale and hot. The air conditioning never reached the room, no matter how many times the maintenance man tinkered with it. Willa stood hunched over the worktable, a spread of tools and cleaning supplies laid out before her. She'd been tasked with cleaning one of the oldest artifacts in the collection: a tall silver candlestick. The candlestick stood about twelve inches high and was stunningly ornate. It sat on a cupped, circular base; the surface of the stem was curved, beveled, and handsomely shaped. Inside the cup of the base was carved the phases of the moon. In some places the candlestick was spotted with age and tarnished beyond the healing power of polish, but that only added to its beauty and mystique.

According to the museum catalogue, the candlestick had belonged to Ruby Plate, one of the original founders, and was most likely some kind of family heirloom, as it dated back one hundred years before the town was founded.

Willa put a dab of polish on a soft cloth and wondered how such an item had possibly been left to the museum and not kept by the Plate family—wherever they might be now. Another oddity of Twelve Acres was that no founding families remained living in town—not one relative of the original twelve settlers. Where had they gone? Why did they leave? And where were they now? Just more questions no one had answers to.

Lost in her thoughts, Willa continued to carefully rub away a layer of dust and tarnish on the precious candlestick. Suddenly, the base fell off, clattering to the table. Willa blinked down at the stem in her hand with panicked surprise.

Oh, no. Oh, no!

She snatched the base off the table and fought a wave of nausea at the thought that she had destroyed such a magnificent piece of history. Willa leaned forward, held her breath, and looked to see if there was a way to reattach the base. She paused.

What is that?

For a moment she could only stare down at the frayed, brown edges of something just peeking out of the end of the stem. The quiet of the room seemed to expand. Willa angled her head and brought the stem closer to her face, noticing the coiled layers of paper. She set the base and the stem down on the table with extreme care and proceeded to sit in the squeaky, old swivel chair, rubbing her palms on her thighs.

Do I dare?

Making up her mind, she rummaged in a nearby tool-box. After much clinking and clanking she found what she needed: a slim set of tweezers. Holding her breath she took the stem in one hand and carefully pinched the end of the paper, pulling it gently, wincing as the paper crunched and flaked. With a whisper, the paper came free.

Willa gasped and then lowered the paper to the table. Using a cloth, the tweezers, and the practiced patience of a historian, she unrolled the newly retrieved artifact. Her heart thudded. Written in dark ink and a curving script were twelve names: six women and six men.

Willa's knowledgeable eyes ran down the list.

The town founders. All of them!

If it had just been the names, Willa would have shrugged it off, but next to each name was a small triangular symbol. There were six distinct triangles, repeated twice, once for all the women and again for the men.

To add to the oddness, below the names were four lines of text.

Willa read the words out loud in a hushed mumble. "*All the Gifts we join this day. The Powers of the Earth, the one true way. A Covenant of Light now forged for good. We bind forever, our true path understood.*" Below those words was a date: October 8, 1889.

A finger of heat stroked the back of Willa's neck as a

current of energy moved through the air that whispered of ancient, powerful secrets. She sat flustered in the heat, her heart racing, her mind spinning. She didn't know what the words meant, but she knew how they felt on her tongue, how the air around her was perfumed with energy.

Did the founders have a secret? "So who are you people, really?" she whispered.

"Those are my parents." A wispy female voice came right next to Willa's ear, causing her to jump out of her chair and move away, heart pounding. The ghost of a young girl stood at the table, bending over the old sheet of parchment. She was dressed in a dark purple dress, a straight silhouette that fell just past her knees; her sleeves were short and playful organza ruffles adorned the collar. Willa pegged it as late 1920s, maybe early 1930s. Her hair was light blond, short and waved into finger curls. She looked young, maybe fourteen or fifteen.

For a moment, Willa only stared, wondering if she'd really heard the words. She'd seen this ghost many times before, wandering around and sitting in the rocker in the *Life in Early Twelve Acres* room reading a book. But she'd never spoken before.

"I'm sorry," Willa started, daring one step back toward the table. "Did you say something?"

The ghost looked up, smiling, her round face floating in and out of focus. "Yes. These are my parents." She pointed to two names on the paper: Camille Krance and Ronald Krance.

Willa looked down at the paper and then up at the ghost's pretty round face. "Your parents were town founders?"

"Are these the town founders?"

"Yes."

"Then, yes." She smiled triumphantly.

A rush of curiosity. Willa hurried to ask, "Do you know what this paper means? Why it was hidden in the candlestick?"

The girl frowned and ran a translucent finger over the paper. "No, I'm sorry. I know those are my parents' names—I can see their faces—but the rest is blackness."

Willa watched the girl's face, a ripple of sadness moved over her eyes. "I'm sorry." The girl nodded, her figure shimmering like a mirage. "So, you must be Solace?"

Startled, the ghost looked up. "How did you know my name?"

"I'm a historian here. I've seen your name in the town's historical papers, listed with your parents."

Solace relaxed. "Oh, of course. And you're Willa, right?"

"Right. Nice to meet you, Solace." Willa smiled. "Do you know how you are able to talk to me? No ghost has ever talked to me before."

Solace shrugged and leaned casually against the table. "No, but I do sense that I'm different than the others who are dead and trapped here, I'm not sure why. I've wanted to talk to you for a while—there is something about you—but was nervous you wouldn't talk back".

Willa nodded, a little disappointed. She'd finally found a

ghost who could talk to her, but this one didn't seem to have any answers. She sat back down in the chair and scooted to the table, leaning over the paper. "This was hidden inside that candlestick. I found it by accident when the bottom fell off."

"Oh! That sounds like a mystery. What do you think it means?" Solace leaned in closer.

Willa looked at the symbols again and a strange heat sparked in her body. "I wish I knew. There's something weird about this town's history. It's full of mysteries."

Solace grinned and rubbed her hands together. "I love a good mystery. Have you ever read *Sherlock Holmes?*" When Willa shook her head, Solace said, "Oh, you must. Maybe a few lessons from the master will help you solve your own mystery."

Willa smiled. "Maybe." She scanned the note once more. "I wonder if this date means something significant." She swiveled the chair and rolled to the computer on the desk behind the worktable. She typed October 8, 1889 into the search engine and scrolled through the results.

Solace, hovering over her shoulder, asked, "Anything good?"

"Hmm. Not really. That was the date of the full moon that month. That's about as exciting as it gets."

Solace and Willa went back to the note. Solace leaned close to it. "Something about these symbols is familiar, but I can't remember exactly what. I know I've seen them before, but I can't recall what they mean."

Willa studied the ghost for a moment, thinking about the few facts she learned about the girl, Solace Krance, daughter of Camille and Ronald. In the records, there was only mention of her birth—summer of 1916, if she remembered correctly—but nothing to indicate that the girl had died in Twelve Acres. There was no grave alluding to her name in the town cemetery. Curiosity swelled inside Willa, and despite what Solace had said about not remembering, she asked, "Solace, do you remember how you died? There isn't anything about it in the history records."

Solace frowned, folded her hands, and lowered her eyes to the floor. "No. It's all black."

"Do you think you died here in the museum? Is that why your spirit is still here?"

"I wish I knew," she said quietly, fidgeting with her hands.

Willa could sense that Solace was uncomfortable with her questions, but she couldn't resist. "What was your life like? Do you remember anything about what you did every day, who your friends were, stuff like that? Did you know Ruby Plate?"

Solace turned away, her body nearly fading out of view.

Willa reached out as if to grab the girl's arm, but her hand passed through Solace's form, touching only cold air. "Wait, Solace! Please don't go."

Lifting her head, the ghost stopped, but didn't immediately turn back. "I can't remember *anything*, Willa. There are only a few faded pictures in my mind of my real life. My only solid memory goes back as far as waking up here in this building years and years ago," she lifted her hand to gesture to the room. Finally, she turned to face Willa, her eyes glassy with unshed tears. "I've been stuck here ever since. Like this." She looked down at her shimmering body. "I don't know *why*. I don't know *how*. And I *hate* it!" Her hands flew to her face to hide her emotions.

Willa blinked in shock. She hadn't meant to upset the girl, but in her haste for answers she hadn't even considered how Solace might feel—it hadn't really occurred to her that a ghost could have such strong emotions. Standing, Willa moved next to the girl. "Solace, I'm sorry. I didn't think. You're the first ghost I have ever talked to and my questions got the better of me. Are you okay?"

Solace lowered her hands and shyly brushed at the ruffles on her collar. "Yes. I'm sorry, too." She smiled weakly. "You're the first non-ghost person I've talked to." She lifted her head, her pale blue eyes suddenly bright. "And let me tell you, ghosts, for the most part, are terrible conversationalists. So I'd really love someone normal to talk to, but I can't provide you with any answers. I'm really sorry."

"Don't be. It's okay." Willa laughed. "And I don't know about normal—I am talking to a ghost after all—but I'm here a lot. We can talk as much as you want. I'd really like that, too."

Solace nodded, smiling. "Friends, then?"

"Friends." Willa's heart swelled at the word. Of course, she had friends at school, but none of them knew anything about her strange abilities. There had always been a disappointing degree of separation between her and all the kids at school. She'd accepted it, gotten used to it, but Solace was different. Something inside Willa stirred.

Solace's eyes drifted back to the forgotten candlestick. "Can I help you solve this mystery? If my parents are a part of it, maybe we can also find out some stuff about me. Maybe we can both get answers. Plus, I'm so bored all the time, stuck in this drab museum. I need something more to do than read all the same books over and over. What do you say?"

Willa laughed again, feeling at ease, comfortable. "I'd love some help."

"Perfect!" Solace smiled big. "Sherlock and Watson." She pointed to herself and then Willa. "But you have to promise to read that book because I don't want to work with an amateur."

Willa threw back her head and laughed, and soon Solace joined in.

Present Day, June

"Good morning, Solace," Willa said as she stepped into the *Life of Early Twelve Acres* room, duster in hand, the cheery June sun pouring in the windows. The room was divided into small recreations of different rooms of a typical nineteenth-century home. Sitting in a rocking chair, with a book in her lap, was Solace's ghost. Her body shimmered in the sunlight, fading in and out of view, like a reflection on rippling water.

"Good morning, Willa. Is it dusting day again already?"

Solace smiled, her face diffusing for a moment and then steadying. She kept her eyes on her book, trying to finish the page she was on.

"Every Saturday." Willa was bursting to tell Solace about her night, but she was also nervous to say the words out loud, to make the events with Simon real by gossiping with her best friend.

For a moment there was only the *swishing* of Willa's feather duster and the gentle creak of Solace's rocker. Suddenly, the ghost sat forward and snapped her book shut. "Something is different about you," she exclaimed, her pale, almost transparent eyes pulling open wide.

Willa stopped, the duster suspended over an oil-wick lantern. She looked up in surprise. "What do you mean?"

Solace giggled. "Don't be coy with me, Willa. I can see your soul, and it is absolutely glowing." She sighed and brought a hand to her heart as she continued to gaze at Willa. "Sun and moon, look at that! Like a little sun pulsing behind your heart. It's beautiful." She sighed again. "Alright, tell me what happened to make it so bright." Solace threw her book onto a table, and a second later, seemingly without moving, stood directly across from Willa, her eagerness causing her form to shimmer even more than usual.

Willa laughed and glanced down at her chest, wishing she could see her soul, knowing it would be a beautiful sight because it felt very much like Solace described.

"Please, Willa," Solace urged impatiently, clasping her hands under her chin.

"Okay, okay. Sit down and I'll tell you everything."

Solace clapped with delight, a soft and muted sound coming from her barely-there hands.

Willa took a deep breath and then plunged into her story. When all the details of the life-changing night were told—with many smiles and gasps from Solace—Willa sat back in her wooden chair at the antique table, body tingling from the excitement of it. Telling Solace hadn't taken away any of the magic, in fact, it had only stirred up the feelings inside her into a swirl of wistful hunger for this boy she knew nothing about.

Solace, across the table, sighed deeply and dramatically. "How wonderful! To *feel* each other's presence! Even better than love at first sight. I wish I had lived long enough to experience love like that. Or maybe I did and just can't remember." A shadow of longing moved over the ghost's face before she found a smile for Willa. "Simon. It's a good, strong name. He sounds so handsome. You must bring him here so I might see him."

Willa's smile faded. *Bring him here?* That would mean making him an integral part of her life, making him real. It would mean pulling him out of the dreamy nighttime hours they'd shared and revealing him to the daylight. Until now it all felt surreal, separate from real life, but the reality of it finally hit her. To be with Simon again, to be with him for real, would mean risking exposure.

Her own parents who had known about her abilities her whole life wouldn't talk about or admit to her strangeness, how could she expect anyone else to? Would Simon just be another person she had to hide her secret from? She didn't want him to be, but how could she tell him? *Oh, by the way, I see dead people and have dreams about the future.* This was exactly why she'd never had a boyfriend.

"Willa, what's wrong?" Solace asked.

"I can't have a boyfriend. I can't be in love. I could never tell him about . . . about you and the dreams. He'd give me *that look* and then run in the other direction." She dropped her face into her hands.

The connection to Simon had been so powerful, so strong, but Willa feared revealing her secret would be enough to sever it. She exhaled. *Why can't I just be a carefree teenager like everybody else?* The biggest mystery Willa wished to solve was her own. More than why Ruby Plate might have hidden a secret in her candlestick, or why information was missing from the town history, or why Solace was a ghost in the museum, Willa wanted to know *why* she was like she was. Why did she see ghosts and dream of real events? What did it mean? What was the *purpose?*

Solace was quiet for a moment. "I think you're wrong. I think you can tell him, and he will understand."

Willa scoffed. "Understand? No one understands. Not my parents, not even me. And besides, it's not like it's an easy thing to tell a boyfriend. Can you picture it? We sit down to dinner and I causally say I see and talk to ghosts and might see his future while I'm asleep?" Willa shook her head, a mirthless smile on her lips.

Solace reached out a gauzy hand and put it over Willa's—who felt only a slight breeze on her skin.

"Dear, Willa. Listen to me, a girl who's already dead and probably knows more about these things than you, the living. The connection, the heat you felt, is not an everyday occurrence. This is more, much more. This is not a school fling, not just a boyfriend. You and Simon are soul mates. That is why your soul is so bright. It is alive in its completeness." Solace waited a beat until Willa looked up into her eyes. "Don't you dare turn away from it because you are scared of what he might think or because it doesn't make sense, isn't normal. You never know; if he's your soul mate, maybe he can do unusual things, too."

Willa hadn't considered that, but it sounded too good to be true. "Soul mates? I don't know if I believe in that."

Solace laughed. "Oh, yes you do, you're just being difficult." Solace dropped her eyes to the table. "I may not remember the details of my own life, but something tells me I'm right about this. There is something about you, and about how you felt with Simon. You *must* trust it."

Willa wanted to believe Solace, she wanted to jump right in and not worry about what came next. But the fear of rejection and of her secret being known pressed against her desire for happiness, pushing it aside. And there was her dream to consider—the one of her and Simon and the black cloud. All her dreams meant something—the hard part was figuring out what. So, was the dream a good sign or bad? Was it a prompt to be with Simon or to run the other way? Her instincts told her it was a good sign, but could she trust *that?*

She looked down at the table, following the curves of wood grain with her fingertip. The memory of Simon filled up all the empty space inside her, flooding her mind.

Solace dipped her head to try and find Willa's eyes. "Come on. You know I'm right. Don't you?"

Willa nodded, "Who am I to argue with a ghost?" She grinned, but it was fleeting. "I want to believe, but it scares me. A lot."

"Of course, it does! That's all right. A woman never hands over her heart without a bit of fear. Or a lot. That much I've learned from all these books." She smiled and waved a hand at a bookshelf behind them. "It's perfectly normal." Solace sat back and gazed blissfully out at the room. "Now, you must promise to come visit me more often and tell me *all* about it. I have to live vicariously through you. You can tell me all about being in love—and I mean details—and I can dream it's me."

Willa laughed weakly. "I promise, Solace." While Solace closed her eyes and daydreamed, Willa fought her fear. The night with Simon had been so blissful, felt so right. But now in the daylight, reality took over, doubt corrupted. *Soul mates?* Was it really possible to meet a stranger and fall in love in an instant? Was it truly possible to know someone before you met them? Was the fiery, electric connection between them more than a fierce attraction? *Is it fate? Does fate exist?*

Her phone in the pocket of her white shorts suddenly felt

as heavy as a rock. *I should call and cancel our date tonight. I don't know this guy! I can't trust this weird attraction. I can't!*

Solace started humming an old song, her voice drifting on the air around them.

Willa slipped her hand into her pocket, gripped the phone. Her stomach flopped, her face tingled where Simon had first touched it. Longing pulsed inside her. To be loved, to be known . . .

I can't.

With a sigh, she stood and resumed her dusting.

CHAPTER 4
WANING GIBBOUS

Present Day, June

After his early breakfast shift at the diner, Simon threw his hiking pack in the back of his black Jeep Wrangler and drove out of town. The mountains were the only place he could think clearly. A good long hike was just what he needed to logic out what had happened with Willa last night.

No amount of reason could push away the strong emotions he'd felt—and still felt—for her. From the moment he walked into the diner and the heat had boiled inside him, there'd been no way to deny it. The term *soul mates* wandered through his mind, tempting him to believe it, but could he?

Perhaps she was the reason he was drawn to this place.

Perhaps the need to leave his old apartment and rent one here in Twelve Acres was not the convenience to the University or the easy access to the canyons. Maybe, all along, he'd been pulled to her. It wasn't the kind of thing he normally believed in, but there were other elements of his life that had no rational explanation, so it wasn't impossible for him to stretch to unreasonable conclusions. It just didn't make him comfortable.

What do I do next? What do I think about this?

Simon parked the Jeep on the side of the canyon road, grabbed his pack and slung it onto his shoulders. He turned down the first trailhead he came to, only caring that it took him higher into the mountains.

He inhaled deeply, drinking in the pine-scented air and feeling of a clear mind. Here, there were fewer people, which meant fewer minds pushing in on his, fewer emotions to fend off. It was because of his ability to sense other people's emotions and intentions that he'd been so solitary all his life. His craving for human companionship was trumped by the need to keep out the noise that others put in his head.

Willa was different; all he wanted was to be near her again. They'd talked in her front yard until after midnight and still it'd taken all his self-control not to call her first thing in the morning. He'd held off until about ten o'clock. Just the sound of her voice on the other end of the phone had been enough to stir up that strange heat again. The thought of seeing her later tonight put a huge smile on his face. When he realized he was grinning from ear to ear, hiking alone, he laughed out loud, the sound bouncing off the trees around him.

What is happening? I've never felt this way.

Simon turned up the first switchback. He couldn't wait to see her, but he didn't have a clue as to what to do when they were together. Did he tell her about what he could do? It wasn't just the sensing of others' emotions. There was also his ability to heal, more strange and complex than the first.

The question of whether to tell her or not itched under his skin. He'd never told anyone—ever. The only reason his parents knew was because they had lived with him for seventeen years. And if they'd had their way, they would have him give up his awful abilities.

He wanted to be close to Willa, to tuck her into his life and never let go; he wanted that like the day wanted the sun. But his logical side, the part of him that demanded a reason for his actions, couldn't get past the part where he tried to hide his abilities. Because it was either hide them or tell her. And neither one sounded like a good way to start or keep a relationship.

For a moment, Simon listened to the sound of his breath and watched his boots kick up dirt. He waited for a clear answer to come to him, but the only thing that came was the image of Willa's face and the memory of her sweet, cool lips.

He pushed harder, quickened his pace, and soon he found himself at the summit, looking down on Twelve Acres, with its square city blocks and straight streets dotted with big trees. His heart pumped steadily and a few trickles of sweat moved down his neck. With a sigh, he sat on the nearest boulder and pulled out his water, taking several long pulls.

Willa.

There was only one thing he knew for sure: he wanted her, needed her. In his nineteen years, he'd never felt as at ease or as accepted as he did in those few short moments with Willa. His parents hated him and he returned the unpleasant sentiment. There was no love there, never had been. They didn't understand or accept his strangeness, and he refused to give it up. Friends were hard to come by—also because of his abilities—and he'd lived alone since he was seventeen. Long ago, he'd resigned himself to a solitary life. But Willa had awakened a desire in him he'd smothered in his childhood. The intensity of that desire rocked him, took his breath away. The thought of having someone, of not being alone, was a sweet, powerful temptation.

But his mind screamed caution. In his experience, getting close, opening his life to others, only ended in pain and rejection. Simon instantly thought of Stan, his best friend from kindergarten. Images of afternoons playing super heroes and sitting outside eating Cheetos until their hands were stained orange raced through his mind. Simon had never really had a friend before—his parents weren't ones to arrange play dates, and he hadn't gone to preschool, so the new thrill of a playmate had been intoxicating to his five-year-old self.

One afternoon, just as the weather was starting to turn cold, he and Stan played on Stan's backyard swing set, Stan as Batman and Simon as Captain America. Bad guys had no chance. With his homemade cape flapping behind him, Stan pumped his swing higher and higher, while Simon sat at the top of the slide. He'd watched Stan's cape flutter and flap, sharp pangs of jealousy moving through his gut. He wondered what would it be like to have a mother who made things for him. Then all of a sudden, Stan had dared to jump from his swing at its highest point, sailing through the air, flying for just a moment . . . before landing awkwardly on his right arm. At his first scream of pain, Simon ran to his friend's aid.

Stan rolled onto his back cradling his oddly bent, broken arm. Simon immediately reached out and put his hand on his friend's injured limb. At the same moment Stan's mother came running out of the house. She watched as Simon's touch moved the bones back into a straight line and pulled away the pain.

Simon had smiled at Stan's tear-wet face and then smiled up at his horrified mother.

That night Simon's parents locked him in his room without dinner. He'd never played with Stan again; Stan's mother transferred her son to another kindergarten class the next day. His young mind and heart knew exactly why: he was different, and different was bad. And that is when he knew his life would be lonely. He always saw himself separate from everyone else.

The hot sun poured down into the small valley and Simon brushed away the painful, sour memory. Now, as an adult, he still felt that sentiment; the basic principle the same, only now complicated by his more in-depth knowledge of life. Different was bad, and despite all his best efforts to explain his differences or ration them into normalcy, he remained exactly the same—a freak. He didn't want to change, desperately wanting to understand, although he was certain he never would. No one could explain to him why he was this way.

A rustle in the trees announced the arrival of a small rabbit, dragging a bloodied and injured foot behind, eyes watery with pain. Simon, out of habit and instinct, slid off the rock and bent down to the suffering creature. He placed his hand on the silky brown fur and a burst of hot energy moved from his palm into the rabbit. A few seconds later the creature bounced away, healed.

Simon stood, brushed off his hand and narrowed his eyes at the spot in the bush where the animal had disappeared.

Perhaps it was time for him to take a risk, to open his heart and his life. It may end in pain, but it may *not*. *It may not* . . .

Willa's face filled his mind again, her subtle lavender scent permeated his nose. For once, Simon would throw logic out the window and go with his heart. Consequences could be dealt with later. He snatched his pack and started off at a run down the trail. He'd call her on the drive home and see if he could pick her up earlier than they'd planned.

WILLA FUSSED IN FRONT OF the mirror in her room. On the bed behind her was a pile of discarded clothing. What did one wear on a date with the guy met in a swirl of electric heat the night before?

Frowning, she surveyed her latest outfit: a scoop neck, off-one-shoulder white top with short jean shorts, and her silver Toms. Her hair was down and she'd kept her make-up light and natural. She sighed. This had to be the outfit; Simon was probably on his way.

She hurried over to her dresser and quickly slid on a sheen of lip-gloss and then threw the tube in her small purse. Turning back to the mirror, she took one last look and found herself smiling, her stomach dancing with excitement.

"So, who's the guy?" her mom asked from the doorway, leaning against the doorframe, smiling at Willa with a knowing glint in her eye.

Willa tried not to let her smile grow. "Just a guy I met at the diner. He works there now. Goes to the University. Pre-med." Willa knew her mom would eat up that last detail.

"Really? Very nice." She took a step in the room. "Was this the same guy you were outside with last night, *in your pajamas?*"

Willa flinched and met her mom's knowing smile. "Yes," she admitted.

"Thought so. Don't worry, Dad was asleep." She stepped into the room. "Don't you want some earrings? Maybe those pretty, dangly silver ones?"

Willa nodded, crossed back to her dresser and dug through her small wooden jewelry box. She slid in the earrings and turned. "Approved?"

Her mom nodded. "Very nice." She stepped closer, looking as if she wanted to say something. "Sooo . . ."

"Yes, Mom?" Willa hooked her purse onto her shoulder.

"Well, it's just that I haven't ever seen you this excited about a guy. Come to think of it, there's never been a guy before."

Willa scoffed. "I went to most of the school dances and stuff."

Her mom sat on her bed, picked up a red scarf and ran it through her hands. "Oh, I know. But there's never been *a guy* before, just friends hanging out. But I can tell this one is different, and now that you're out of high school, about to start college . . . it just feels big. You know?"

Willa sat next to her, her stomach now tight, her hands clammy. "Yeah." They sat in silence for a moment and Willa let her nerves eat away at her previous excitement. "Mom?"

"Yeah, honey?" Sarah turned her compassionate eyes on her daughter and Willa wished she felt as confident as her mother always seemed. Even in her dad's old flannel shirt and paint spotted jeans, her mom looked so together and in control.

"Do you think it's . . . okay that I date?" Willa asked quietly, looking at her hands.

"What do you mean?"

"Well, with . . . you know . . . the things I can do?" Willa looked up to see the reaction on her mom's face. Her ghosts and dreams were something they rarely, if ever, spoke of out loud. Sarah's eyes widened and then narrowed with concern. She reached out and took Willa's hand.

"Of course. There's no reason those things would keep you from anything you want. Okay?"

Willa nodded, absorbed the words. "Yeah, okay."

Sarah looked like she wanted to say something more, but all she asked was, "Are you going to tell him?"

"I have no idea."

Sarah pressed her lips together, nodded. "Well, it's only your first date. Just have fun. I'm sure stuff like that will work itself out." Willa nodded, and then Sarah said, "So, what's his name?"

"Simon." She couldn't help the smile that followed.

"Simon. I like it." Sarah leaned over and kissed Willa's forehead. "Do you have time for me to paint your nails?"

Fifteen minutes later, with shiny black nails, Willa stood at the window in her living room. Heavy footsteps sounded behind her and she braced slightly, knowing who it was and what he was about to say.

"So, who is this guy?" her dad asked.

Willa turned to face him. Ethan Fairfield was tall, at least six-foot-five, and built like a sapling tree—thin, wiry, tough. His salt-and-pepper hair was always slightly mussed and his authoritative hazel eyes could intimidate the most arrogant of onlookers. He folded his arms.

Willa sighed inwardly. All her life she'd battled his over-protectiveness. "He works at the diner, Dad. His name is Simon Howard and he's a pre-med student at the University."

Ethan frowned. "And you met him last night?"

Willa folded her own arms, suddenly feeling a hot rush of defensiveness. "Yes."

Ethan stepped closer. "Willa, it's not safe to go out on a one-on-one date with a stranger."

"Dad, come on. Everyone is a stranger until you get to know them. But Simon is different. He's a good guy."

"How do you know that? He may seem like a good guy, but you don't know anything about him. I know he's not from Twelve Acres. So, where did he grow up? Who are his parents? Is he a good worker? Is he kind? Does he have a criminal record?"

"Good grief, Dad. You're way overreacting." Willa rubbed at her forehead. "You always overreact! And I don't want to do this. Simon will be here any second." She turned away and went back to the window.

For a moment, her dad was quiet. Then in his deep voice, he said, "I don't approve," then stalked out of the room.

Willa exhaled, closed her eyes and shook her head. Was he ever going to treat her like an adult and not like some stupid, naïve child? A pulse of anger rose in her throat, but she pushed it down. She didn't want to be angry; she wanted to be excited, giddy like other girls on a first date with a cute boy.

An electric hum started under her skin and, within seconds, Simon's Jeep pulled up in the driveway. Willa's stomach flipped and twisted as a tremor of energy moved through her.

Thankfully, her parents were nowhere to be seen—she could thank her mom for that.

The doorbell.

Willa took a deep breath and pulled open the door. At the first sight of his tall and broad stature nearly filling the doorframe, towering over her five-foot-six frame by nearly a foot, her heart squeezed shut and then leaped off at a pounding run.

He smiled and said, "Hi—again."

Willa smiled and laughed, suddenly at ease. "Hi." Tonight he wore a black button down shirt and tan-colored shorts. His curly hair was still damp from a shower and he smelled fresh, clean, and slightly like pine trees with a hint of peppermint . His eyes met hers and Willa felt her knees weaken. She had to resist the urge to throw her arms around his neck.

"You look gorgeous," he said quietly.

"Thanks," she said shyly.

"Ready to go?" he asked

"Yep." She stepped out onto the porch and closed the door behind her. To her surprise and delight, Simon immediately reached out and took her hand, his skin warm and dry. They walked in comfortable silence, exchanging smiles. Willa felt all the tension and worry leak out of her. There was something about being around Simon that felt natural, like home.

He opened the passenger door for her and she climbed into the Jeep. As Simon moved around to his side, she glanced up to her parents' bedroom window and found her mom waving enthusiastically at her. After a burst of embarrassed laughter, she offered a quick wave back.

Simon got in and started the engine. Then he turned to her. "So, since I'm the new kid in town, I was thinking that you could give me a bit of a tour. What's your favorite place in Twelve Acres?" As he spoke he reached out and touched her hair.

Tugs of heat pulled inside her and she found she wanted to touch him, too, and be close. She took his hand in hers. "The museum, of course."

"Then we start there." He put the car in drive with his free hand and pulled the car out into the road. "Town square, right? Main Street?"

Willa nodded, still smiling; she couldn't seem to stop smiling. She didn't really feel the need to make small talk, but she did want to hear him talk, to listen to his deep, soft voice. "Did you have to work today?"

"Yeah, breakfast shift."

"Ouch. I hate the breakfast shift."

"I know, but I guess everyone does, so that's why the new guy got stuck with it every Saturday for the next month."

Willa laughed, "Oh, no. That's so not fair."

Simon shrugged. "It's not that bad, I guess. I usually get up early to hike anyway."

"You're a hiker? Then you picked the right place to move. There are so many good trails around here."

"There are. I used to drive out here during high school

and explore the mountains. I've always liked this place." He caught her eyes and a ribbon of heat moved between them.

A few minutes later, still lost in their conversation, they pulled up at the museum. Simon met her as she got out of the Jeep and took her hand. Then he turned to the cream-colored stone building. "So *this* is your favorite place in town, huh?"

"Yes, it is," she laughed. "Kind of hard for a historian not to love the local museum."

Simon nodded and smiled. He waved his hand to the wooden double doors. "Well, I want to see everything."

They spent the next hour roaming the museum, Willa excitedly explaining each item and Simon asking questions, a captivated audience. Solace followed them around, ogling Simon and giving Willa a thumbs-up every time they made eye contact. Willa didn't really mind Solace tagging along, but her being there was a stinging reminder of what Simon didn't know about her. The tangle of nerves in her stomach returned and she had to fight the urge to turn to Simon and tell him *everything.*

As they exited the museum, Simon put his arm around her waist, pulled her close and asked, "So, what's your second favorite place?"

"Definitely Plate's Place, Ruby Plate's old house. It's just around the corner by the park. Wanna walk over?"

"Sounds good."

Simon kept his arm around her and they ambled slowly around the museum and down the road. Willa inwardly smiled at how he couldn't seem to let her go; they'd been touching in some form or another since they left her house. The heat between them remained, settling into a quiet simmer of contentment.

The night was warm and a sweet-smelling breeze ran through the streets. The sun lounged low in the sky, deepening the colors of the grass and trees. As they walked, Simon told her about his plans for medical school and how he hoped to work as an intensive care unit doctor.

"What about your parents and family?" she asked when he paused. "Where do they live?"

A shadow passed over Simon's face, fleeting and quick, but obviously there, and his jaw tensed. "They live by the University. They're both professors there. And it's just my parents. I'm an only child."

There was pain in his voice and Willa, though suddenly curious, decided it wasn't something he wanted to talk about. "I'm an only child, too. After I was born, my mom got really sick. She couldn't ever have any more kids."

"Are you close with your parents?"

"Yes, we're a pretty close family."

Simon nodded, looked away. "That would be nice."

Willa wasn't sure what to say next, but thankfully they had arrived at Ruby's house. "Here it is!"

Simon's eyebrows rose. "This? This old dump is the house of Ruby Plate—town founder and, as far as I can tell, sort-of your hero? What happened to it? It doesn't look like the picture you showed me in the museum."

Willa sighed and ran her eyes over the peeling green

paint, broken clapboards, sagging porch, and dead grass. For her whole life, she'd romanticized this place, looking past the neglect to picture what it must have looked like when Ruby built it. Simon was right—Ruby was a hero to her. She'd been a woman in the late 1880s who'd headed west and founded a town. She'd had a hand in every decision that shaped Twelve Acres. That was no small achievement.

Willa hated that her fabulous house was now a scar of neglect on the town landscape. More than once, she'd begged the town historical society to buy it back from the current owner—whom no one seemed to know—and restore it. She'd even volunteered to organize fundraisers, but each time she was told the owner refused to sell. There was nothing they could do.

Simon looked down at her, waiting for an answer. "Sometime in the 1930s the house fell out of Ruby's family. We're not sure how, but it's still owned by the family of the people who bought it then, and they refuse to sell it. But they do nothing to take care of it. It's terrible."

"You can tell it was amazing in its day," Simon said. "And look at that weeping willow in the back yard. I've never seen one that big. Good thing the house has some acreage around it to accommodate that tree."

"Ruby planted the tree herself. It's the only thing about the house that still thrives."

Simon shook his head. "It's too bad."

Willa half-smiled, pleased that he seemed to understand how important this house was to her and the town's history.

Most people refused to acknowledge it; some even wanted it torn down. "It really is too bad. Poor Ruby. If she saw it now, it would break her heart."

"So, no one lives here?"

"Nope. No one's ever lived here."

"Then how come a light just went on upstairs?"

Willa's head snapped up and she gasped. She blinked at the square of yellow light for a moment and then walked down the sidewalk and looked at the driveway. A gray beater truck squatted near the rear of the house. "Oh, my gosh! Someone is living here? I can't believe it."

Simon was at her side. "Maybe they'll start taking care of the place."

Willa nodded absently, "Maybe. It's just weird. Why now? No one has lived here in like eighty years."

Willa and Simon both jumped when the side door near the rear of the house opened and a figure stepped out into the shadows. With the setting sun behind the house, it was hard to see details, but Willa could just make out a bulky, solid figure, the shine of a bald head, and the darkness of a beard.

The man turned slowly, sensing their stares, and Willa instinctively took a step back. Goose bumps rose on her arms; a cold tickle of dread moved down her neck. Two penetrating eyes bore down on her with an icy stare. Simon took her hand and pulled her away, hurrying down the sidewalk, back toward the museum.

Willa shook her head trying to clear the haunting feeling of cold in her head and chest. *Who is that?*

When they were a good distance away, Simon stopped and pulled her into his arms. "Are you okay?"

Willa lifted her chin and looked up at his face. "You felt that, too?"

Simon's eyes narrowed. "Yes," he answered quietly. "There was something about that guy. Something . . . cold."

"Yeah, that's what I felt." She shivered and Simon hugged her tighter. "I don't think it's a good thing that he's living there."

"Me, either."

Willa had walked or driven past Ruby's house every day for most of her life. She'd spent many childhood hours tucked into the branches of the old oak trees in the park across the street, staring at the house and daydreaming. "I don't know why, but I feel like that man living there is worse than no one living there."

Simon nodded, and for a moment they were silent. "Okay, how do we forget about the creepy guy in the old house? You hungry?"

Willa put her hands on his chest and stepped back to look at his face. She reached up and tugged on one of his spiraled curls, something she'd wanted to do all night. "I'm starving. I'll eat anything but diner food."

Simon laughed. "Agreed. Come on, I'll take you to a little Italian place I know by the University." He took her hand and led the way back to his Jeep. Willa couldn't help glancing back over her shoulder at Ruby's house. The light in the second story window was now out.

CHAPTER 5
WAXING GIBBOUS

August 1923

The sun breathed fire across the late evening sky. Deep, rich red, pink, and orange washed the underbellies of the clouds, bathing the earth in decadent light. Thick, fresh summer air swirled down from the heavens and circled around the tall willow tree, tossing its lithe branches back and forth.

Amelia Plate put out her hand and let the slender leaves tickle her palm. She laughed and pulled her hand back to rub away the sensation. Tilting her head back, she looked up through the branches, watching them dance and play on the breeze. The motion made her pleasantly dizzy.

Standing there, under the umbrella of the old tree, she felt the magic moving, alive and vibrant. She often daydreamed of living in the willow, of climbing into its open branches, settling in and never leaving. A fun childhood fantasy. Willows are sacred trees, strong in the magic, and this one had whispered to her since she was an infant. As far as Amelia was concerned, the tree was as much a part of her family as anyone. Just another stalwart woman to look up to.

"Amelia? Come back to me, girl."

Amelia brought her chin down and smiled over at Grandma Ruby, who sat in a rocker on the back porch of her home—Amelia's home, too, since her father died in the Great War. She'd been only eight-years-old, and Ruby immediately became her whole world, the only source of comfort for her tiny broken heart—her poor mother was too lost in her own grief.

The familiar, rhythmic *creak creak* of the rocker brought a smile to Amelia's face. Noticing the wooden bowl of water and the blue candle, she didn't hesitate to answer her grandma's call. She skipped her way back to the porch, her auburn ponytail bouncing behind her.

"I'm back," she sang as she jumped up the steps.

Grandma Ruby smiled, her green eyes winking at her granddaughter, her pride and joy, her hope for the future. "Good girl. Sit with me and let's work on your powers."

Amelia sat, tucked her legs under her, and rested her chin in a propped-up hand, her full attention on her mentor.

"Beautiful sunset tonight," Ruby said.

With a contented sigh, Amelia agreed, "Yes, sunsets are my favorite."

"Mine, too." After a moment of gazing at the colorful display, Ruby nodded and said, "Now, you are thirteen on Saturday, a very important age. You're ready to begin the training you'll need to take your place in the Covenant one day. Very exciting, isn't it?"

Amelia beamed. "Very!" Even at her age she knew the rare importance of the Covenant; she knew the history. Her grandmother stood at the head, as Luminary, and Amelia hoped one day to be worthy to take her place. She smoothed her face and with due solemnity. "I am ready."

Grandma Ruby smiled. "I know you are. You are strong, my girl, very strong. I know you will do great things with your magic." She reached out a wrinkled hand and patted her granddaughter's cheek. "Let's try something new tonight."

Amelia's eyes widened and she sat up straight in her chair, eager and ready.

The older witch took a deep breath and then began her lesson. "Your gift, the Gift of Water, is very special. Water represents love and healing. You have a great capacity for love, and one day you will be a great healer. Water is also one of the most powerful tools for divination. It can open many worlds to you.

"Until now, you have learned only simple spells and charges. And you are extremely accomplished for your age,"—a proud-grandma smile—"but now it's time to start specializing in more complex things. Tonight I will show you how to tune into the Otherworld, to read the past, present, and future in the water."

Amelia's skin prickled with goose bumps in anticipation. It was a truly great moment in a witch's life to learn divination, the sight of things unseen. So much could be learned, although not everything was meant to be known. Divination was a double-edged sword: good and bad, profitable and dangerous.

She took a deep breath and steadied herself.

"Now," Ruby continued, her face also solemn, "first charge the candle with magic and then light it."

Amelia cupped the tall, wide, blue candle in her hands and closed her eyes. Breathing deeply, she projected the energy of the magic into the candle. Her hands grew warm and tingly with the effort, signaling the task was complete. She set the candle next to the wooden bowl and, with a sharp snap of her fingers, commanded fire to burst to life on the wick.

"Very good," Ruby said. "Push the candle a little closer to the bowl so that you can see the flame reflected in the water. Good. Now, charge the water as well."

Amelia leaned forward, her head dipping over the bowl. Her pale face and green eyes, framed by reddish-brown hair, stared back at her from the surface of the water. The reflection almost exactly matched that of her grandma at the same age.

Right hand stretched out over the water, hovering only an inch from the surface, Amelia closed her eyes and once again called to the magic. Hot energy flowed down her arm and into the water. The water in her body reacted to the magic, growing warm. She wanted to show off, to lift the water from its bowl, send it zooming around the porch and then back—something she had been able to do since she was two—but she resisted the urge, knowing Grandma would not tolerate silliness now.

She focused her mind and energy. The water bubbled for a moment and then stilled.

Amelia lifted her expectant eyes. "What now?"

Ruby tipped her body forward and quieted her voice. "Place your hands above the water and continue to send magic into it. Clear your mind, take deep breaths, and gaze into the water." Amelia complied, her heart pounding, the heat from the magic pushing a thin sheen of sweat onto her brow.

"Now think of a memory. Something from the past. The past is easy to divine because it has already happened. Picture the moment in your head, focus on it. Then repeat this spell: *Water so cool and clear, I hold no envy or fear. Open my mind, clear my sight. Reveal to me your mystic light.*"

Amelia inhaled the clean summer air and gazed into the water, willing her eyes to see the unseen. She pulled a memory from the recesses of her mind—a crisp fall day, picking apples with Grandpa Charles and her father, both gone now. "*Water so cool and clear, I hold no envy or fear. Open my mind, clear my sight. Reveal to me your mystic light.*"

After a moment she could smell the sickly sweet perfume of apples rotting into the earth and the tartness of fresh apples in her basket. The deep, resonant laughter of her two favorite men drifted to her ears.

Magic sparked along her skin.

The surface of the water rippled ever so slightly; an image formed in the bottom of the bowl and slowly floated to the surface: Amelia, six-years-old, with pig tails, grinning as her father lifted her up to reach an apple, and Grandpa watching with an equally happy smile. The sensation of the apple's warm skin against her palm, the heat of her father and grandpa's good magic filling her young heart, the weight of her dad's hand on her head as she lovingly looked up into his face—all became intensely real. The emotion of the moment grew so thick and tactile that a few tears pressed out of her eyes and dripped into the water.

She wanted to reach out and touch the men, to make them real, but then the water rippled and the image was lost. Amelia gasped and looked up to her grandma, slightly disoriented, the past still present in her mind and senses.

Ruby's eyes were wet and alive. She whispered, "Very good, my love. A sweet memory. And on your first try. I'm so impressed!" She stroked Amelia's forearm as it rested next to the bowl. "Now, let's try the present—a little more difficult." Ruby waited for Amelia to nod that she was ready. "Do the same thing, but this time focus on your mother, on her right now, in this moment."

Amelia nodded and extended her hands, focusing her gaze on the clear water. Repeating the words of the spell, she filled her mind with thoughts of her mother, on trying to see her right now. Nothing came. An owl hooted in the willow and she lost her focus. She looked up sheepishly at Grandma.

"That's okay. Try again. Focus harder."

Taking deep breaths, Amelia repeated the steps, saying the spell with more force and determination. This time the water rippled and an image floated to the top. It wasn't as clear as the last image, but she could still make out her mother, tall and skinny, her sunny blonde hair falling down her back as she reached for a book from a top shelf. It was her mother working at the library, where she currently was at that moment.

The water bounced and swallowed the picture.

Amelia raised her head and smiled triumphantly.

Ruby beamed back. "Excellent, Amélia! Now, we can either try to see the future or save it for another night. Seeing the future is extremely difficult and draining. Also, it takes most witches several attempts to see even the faintest of images."

Amelia's limbs were tired, her mind fatigued from the previous efforts, but she wanted to test her abilities. Seeing the future was too intriguing to pass up. "I want to try."

Ruby grinned, pleased. "Good. I knew you would, but don't be disappointed if it doesn't work these first few times. Many experienced witches can't divine the future. The future is very slippery, always changing, moving, morphing into something new as people make different decisions. Very few things are set in stone. Understand?"

Amelia nodded.

Ruby adjusted herself in her rocker, moving closer to the bowl and her young witch. "All right. Same routine but, this time, focus on *you*. On yourself in the future. Pick a specific time, an age or even a day, and then ask the magic to reveal it to you."

The younger witch nodded, eager to try, knowing she would likely see nothing. She wanted the experience anyway. Hands out, breath flowing and hot magic pulsing in her veins, she focused on her future self. A young woman of twenty-one. She imagined what she would look like, what she might wear and what she might be doing.

Water so cool and clear, I hold no envy or fear. Open my mind, clear my sight. Reveal to me your mystic light.

Several seconds passed and the water stayed clear and still. She didn't lose confidence. Instead, she steadied her mind and called for more magic. Her mind drained of everything but the image of her future self and the desire to see it. The words of the spell fell from her mouth with more authority and power, her hands trembling from the effort, the surfaces of her eyes grew hot and moist.

The air around her was electric, charged with magic. Everything but the surface of the water fell away; she was not even aware of Ruby anymore. Sweat poured down her face and neck, her blood rushed through her body like a mighty river.

The water sloshed in the bowl, splashing up onto her palms, and in an instant, grew eerily calm.

Very, *very* slowly, an image flickered to life and rose to the surface. Amelia gasped, a strangled cry of shock stuck in her throat. Cold fear moved through her, pushing aside the heat of the magic. Then, with unexpected, stunning power, the water exploded from its bowl. It hit her hard in the face and sent her toppling backwards, crashing onto the porch.

Ruby screamed in surprise and rushed to help her granddaughter.

Amelia, huddled on the ground, was hugging herself and sobbing. Ruby knelt down next to her. "Amelia! Amelia? What did you see? Tell me what you saw."

Between racking sobs the girl managed to say, "Me. I saw me!"

CHAPTER 6
WANING CRESCENT

Present Day, September

The first week of the semester had been busy. Between conflicting class schedules and shifts at the diner, Simon hadn't seen Willa in two days. They'd spent every day together since that first day in June and it surprised him how uncomfortable it made him feel to be separated from her. Thankfully, it was now Friday afternoon, which meant they had the whole weekend together.

His last class for the day over, Simon bolted to his Jeep and sped all the way back to Twelve Acres. Willa was just finishing a shift at the diner. He parked out front and sent her a quick text. *I'm in the parking lot. Hurry!*

Not thirty seconds later, Willa came running out. Simon

exited the Jeep and opened his arms. She jumped into them, her arms tight around his neck. "I officially hate being an adult," she said.

Simon laughed. "Why?"

"'Cause working and going to classes keeps us apart."

He laughed again and then nodded with a mock expression of seriousness. When she started laughing he bent and pressed his lips to hers, no longer able to resist. She answered his kiss with eager passion. He pushed her backward until her body was against the Jeep and then he brought his hands to her face, deepening the kiss even further.

A delicious sigh escaped her throat when he trailed his lips down her jaw line and to her neck. "What do you want to do tonight?" he mumbled against her velvety skin.

Willa laughed, the reverberations of her voice moving against his lips. He had to close his eyes, take a deep breath. With a slow exhale, Simon pulled back, but kept his hands on her arms. She smiled up at him, her blue eyes bright and sparkling like the ocean in the sun, her lips plump and red from his kisses. He was just leaning in for another kiss when the squealing sound of tires brought up both their heads.

In the road only ten feet away, a gray truck braked to avoid a small golden retriever running across the road. Simon braced; the truck wasn't going to stop in time. Willa gasped when the back tires rolled over the puppy. The truck didn't stop, didn't even slow down. Engine roaring, the driver pressed the gas and sped away.

"Oh, my gosh!" Willa said. "Was that the guy who lives in Ruby's house?"

"I think so."

Willa pulled away from Simon and ran to the poor broken dog lying in the middle of the road. Simon froze, every muscle tensed. For months he'd been able to avoid having to use his healing powers in front of Willa. On a few of their summer hikes, a bird or rabbit, even a coyote, had wandered out looking for his help. But he'd been able to carefully separate himself from Willa for the few seconds he needed to heal them.

But here . . . this . . . He couldn't let the dog die because he didn't want her to see. He'd never turned away from something or someone who needed healing.

"Simon! He's still breathing." Willa looked up at him from the road, her eyes pleading and confused.

Simon jogged over and knelt next to her. His palms itched to reach out. "Is there an animal hospital close?" he asked.

"It's on the other side of town. Do you think he'll last that long? He's so hurt!" Willa's eyes were wet with tears. The dog whimpered weakly as she put a gentle hand on its head.

Simon looked at her, then down at the dog.

"Simon? What's wrong?" Willa bent her head, trying to catch his eyes.

He didn't look up, but kept his eyes on the dog and its smashed broken body, its shallow, difficult breaths, its pleading black eyes. "Willa, please don't freak out," was all he said before he reached out his hand and laid it on the dog's head.

The heat rushed out quicker than normal, as if extra eager to do its work.

A moment later the dog barked, scrambled to its feet, licked Simon's hand and then ran off for home. Willa let out a sharp squeak of surprise and covered her mouth with her hand. Simon hesitated a moment before looking up at her. He wasn't sure what to expect, but he was certain it wouldn't be good. Suddenly, he was dizzy with regret. *Did I just ruin everything with Willa over a dog's life?*

He held his breath when her hand found his arm and finally forced himself to look up. What he saw took his breath away. Willa was crying, small tears dripping down her cheeks; she was *smiling.* A huge, beautiful smile.

WILLA'S HEART BEAT AGAINST HER ribs—it was hard to draw a full breath. She'd watched in awe as Simon reached out his hand and healed the dog. She'd felt a curious heat ripple from his body as he did it, similar to the heat that existed between them, but different, more calm. At first she'd been too stunned to fully grasp what he'd done.

He looked at her, eyes wide with apprehension. She said, "Simon, did you really . . . ?"

"I'm sorry," he whispered and looked away.

She reached out and put a hand on his cheek, pushing his face back to her. "Why are you sorry? That was amazing. Just . . . *amazing*, Simon."

He narrowed his eyes, suspicious. "But . . ."

"But what? Did you expect me to run away screaming?"

His brow furrowed. "Well, kind of. Yeah."

She laughed and took his hand, pulling them both up to their feet. "Come on." She led him into the park behind the diner. She sat on the first bench they came to; he sat stiffly next to her.

Willa held his hand tightly in hers. For the past three months, she'd wondered if she should tell him about the odd things she could do. Every day she asked herself the question, and every day she answered no, too afraid of the consequences. Things between them were so comfortable, even blissful. The last thing she wanted was to spoil it all with her strangeness. But Solace had been right! He was more like her than she realized and the revelation was intoxicating freedom.

"I see ghosts and have dreams about real events."

Simon's head jerked up, his eyes as wide as chocolate coins. "What?" he asked, doubtfully.

Willa nodded. "You heard me. And you can heal. Is that all? Is it only animals?"

"No," he whispered. "I can heal people, too. I also sense emotions, sometimes hear thoughts, but that's very rare. Or at least it was, until I met you." He paused to bite his lower lip. "Sometimes I can hear your thoughts."

Willa blinked, surprised, but thrilled. "Really?"

He nodded.

"Should I be embarrassed?" She offered him a playful smile.

He smiled back. "No, not at all." He put a hand on her thigh.

"Do you know why you can do those things? Have you always been able to?"

"No, I have no idea why. I was born this way and have fought with it all my life. I wanted to tell you before, but—"

"But you were afraid," She nodded. "Me too. People don't usually react so well, right?"

Simon scoffed. "No, not at all."

"Yeah, been there, done that."

Simon laughed. "So, ghosts, huh? And freaky dreams? Sounds like fun."

Willa shrugged. "Probably about as fun as always feeling what others are feeling."

"Yeah, that sounds right." He shook his head. "This is weird, right? You and I, what we can do, how we found each other? I knew we were alike, but this . . ."

Willa nodded, scooted closer to him, and dropped her head on his shoulder. "Very weird, but also very right. I've been alone all my life. My parents won't even talk about it."

"Me, too," Simon said in a tight voice. "Do *you* have any idea why we're like this?"

She sighed. "No. It's one of my mysteries. More than anything I'd like to know *why*." Knowing that Simon also had strange abilities wasn't exactly a clue in her search, but it was a comfort. The fact that she wasn't alone pointed to the existence of an answer.

They sat in silence for a moment. Simon shifted in his

seat, put his arm around her and pulled her close. "We are the same." He gave a short laugh. "I didn't think I'd ever say that to someone."

"Me neither," Willa said. "It makes me wonder if there are other people with strange abilities."

Simon nodded. "Maybe. At this point, it wouldn't surprise me." After a breath, he asked, "Have you ever had a dream about me?"

"The first night we met I dreamed we stood together in a white field. This creepy, scary black cloud of smoke barreled toward us. When I touched you, a bolt of lightning obliterated the cloud."

Simon laughed and Willa's head bounced on his shoulder. "So, is that going to happen to us? That doesn't sound like a real event."

"Well, it's complicated. My dreams are still like normal dreams, twisted and weird, but they always mean something. The hard part is realizing what. When I was eight I dreamed my dad was lying on the ground, a bird pecking out his stomach. I woke up screaming and had this overwhelming fear that something was wrong with him. I couldn't be consoled, so he agreed to go to the doctor for a check-up."

"And they found something?" Simon asked in wonder.

"Yes. A small tumor. Benign, but it could have been life threatening if it had been allowed to grow."

"That's incredible."

"So is healing a nearly-dead dog."

"The animals come a lot. Some came while we were hiking this summer. I always had to sneak away to heal them."

Willa laughed, lifted her head to look at him. "Really?"

"Yep. Kind of embarrassing, now. But hold on, let's go back to your dream about us. I want to try to interpret it." He cocked his head and pursed his lips. "I got it—our electric love can fight evil."

Willa laughed. "Oh, that's gotta be it." After a short pause, she added, "Our love, huh?" Simon's eyes flashed wide, realizing what he'd said. Willa wanted to laugh again at the sudden anxiety on his face. But then he smiled.

"I suppose while we are bearing our souls here, we might as well get it all out." He tightened his grip on her hand. "I love you, Willa. I've never been as happy as I am with you. And I will never, *ever* let you go." He lifted her hand and kissed the back of it, leaving behind a pulsing spot of warmth.

A pleasurable tingle moved down her spine, heat bursting to life in her chest. "I love you, Simon. Every day—especially today—I'm amazed at how perfect this is, you and I."

He leaned down and kissed her so softly goose bumps rose on her arms. With his face still close, he opened his eyes and she was lost in their darkness. She ran her fingertips over his cool lips and he closed his eyes at her touch. Willa studied the shape of his face, traced her fingertips along the laugh lines in the corners of his eyes, under the curls that fell across his forehead.

It seemed funny to her now how afraid she'd been to tell Simon about the ghosts and dreams. How she'd thought it would tear them apart. But now in the quiet of the afternoon, in the empty park, Willa had never felt closer to him. In a burst of bright understanding, she realized what she now had—a companion, a partner, an equal. Someone who could accept and understand every part of her, someone who shared in the strangeness.

A lump of emotion formed in her throat and her eyes grew hot with tears. Simon opened his eyes. "What's wrong?"

She shook her head, unable to speak at first. Then, in an emotion-strained voice, she said, "I never thought I would have this."

Simon smiled, complete and total understanding in his eyes; she didn't need to explain her emotions to him—he could sense them, he shared them. "I never thought it either. I never even let myself *dream* it."

Urgently, but tenderly, Willa kissed him. The warmth of their love swirled off their bodies, rustling the leaves in the tress overhead.

CHAPTER 7
NEW MOON

Present Day, September

Holmes could still hear the Light witch whimpering. The pathetic noise drifted up the basement stairs and somehow found its way into the kitchen while he was trying to have his evening meal. Grinding his teeth and glaring at the basement door, he considered going back down and binding her voice with a silencing spell.

He turned away and commenced eating his sandwich, but threw it down after a few bites. He rose to go down. Halfway to the door his phone rang. He growled and crossed back to the table to retrieve it. At the sight of Archard's name on the screen, he growled again.

"Yes?" he answered.

"Well? It's new moon. Did she agree?" Archard's smooth, perpetually angry voice barked at him.

Holmes pressed his teeth together and tried to calm his voice. "No."

"No? What is the problem, Holmes? It's been three months. Much longer than I *ever* expected to wait." There was a weighted pause. "I'm very disappointed."

With a sigh, Holmes said, "She is much stronger than we anticipated. Her magic is impressive."

Archard scoffed. "Your job is not to admire her magic, Holmes, it is to *break* her. Now, can you do it or not?"

"Yes, of course, but these things cannot be rushed. It takes time to break down a mind, especially a witch's mind."

"By next new moon—that's only a couple of weeks from blood moon—or I will have to fill two places in my new covens. Understood?"

Holmes barred his teeth. "Yes, Archard." The line went dead. Holmes threw the phone down on the table. It slid across the table and knocked over his beer bottle. For a few moments, he watched the liquid drip to the rotted wood floor, his anger boiling. Then he spun back to the basement door. He would take out his frustration on the whimpering witch chained to the wall.

CHAPTER 8
WANING CRESCENT

Present Day, October

Willa and Simon fell asleep before the movie was
half over. Lying together under a heavy blanket
on Simon's humble Ikea couch, Willa was too
comfortable to stay awake and quickly drifted off. But her
rest was soon interrupted.

The dream came on fast with unusual potency.

First it was only darkness and the musty smell of mold.
Crisp, cold air brushed against her skin and Willa wrapped
her arms around herself. Slowly, the small space around her
came into focus. Directly in front of her a woman sat on a dirt
floor, reclined against a stone wall, legs spread out, arms limp
at her sides, and head hanging down on her chest.

Willa inhaled sharply at the pathetic sight of the woman. The woman wore what was once a white, peasant-style dress, now filthy, crusty, and stained with large brown splashes. Her hair, a peculiar shade of bright strawberry-red, hung over her face in oily strands. Willa wasn't sure if the woman was asleep or dead.

When the woman moaned and shifted, Willa flinched and stepped back, bumping into a set of stone steps. Pulling her eyes from the person on the floor, she realized the space was some kind of basement, old, with sweaty stone walls and a packed dirt floor. A collection of forgotten junk was pushed up against the walls. A tiny window, slightly open and stuck at a crooked angle, let in grayish light and a small portion of fresh air.

The woman moaned again, followed by the ominous clanking sound of chains dragging against the stone. *Chains.* The poor woman was chained to the wall. Two heavy chains drilled into the stones snaked down to her ankles and clamped around her thin white legs with a thick band of metal. The chains had rubbed the skin on her legs raw and bloody.

A wave of hopelessness and despair descended on Willa, so strong her knees buckled, and she knew the dream was giving her a taste of what this prisoner felt. Willa dropped to the dirt next to the poor woman and caught her first glance of the prisoner's face. It was filthy, caked in dirt—the dirt tracked with lines from tears. At the same time this woman was also beautiful. Her radiant bottle-glass green eyes pierced the darkness, her slender cheekbones and nose curved as gracefully as a stone sculpture.

The woman lifted her delicate, graceful hands and pushed back her hair. The small amount of light in the basement caught the edges of a line of scars on her right hand and arm. Willa leaned closer. The small hash lines started on the back of her hand, tracking up her forearm nearly to the elbow. The ones on her hand were healed, lines of white, but the ones farther up her arm were pink and red, some scabbed, and a few festering and weeping infection. Willa recoiled, her stomach tight.

A crack of thunder startled them both and Willa turned her head to the small window as the first drops of rain tumbled down from the sky. The woman sighed and pushed herself to her feet, which seemed to take her a great deal of effort. Willa wished she could reach out and offer some support. Haltingly, cradling her right arm, the woman dragged herself forward, the chains clinking loudly as she went. She stopped under the window and stared up, mesmerized by the rhythm of the raindrops splashing onto the windowsill. She raised her right hand, palm lifted upward, and winced as her sores pulled with the movement. She closed her eyes and a stillness filled the basement, followed by the stirring of heat. The woman's hand trembled slightly, and then her eyes flashed opened.

Willa gasped when the droplets of water on the window lifted from the glass and sailed through the air, arcing over to the woman's outstretched palm. The water gathered there until she cupped a small puddle. Then, she brought the water to her mouth and drank, sighing heavily as the cold water trickled down her throat and chin.

The woman then took a few more hesitant steps toward the window, gazing out with a longing that brought tears to Willa's eyes. Slowly, cautiously, like prey emerging in the presence of the predator, the prisoner lifted her left hand and reached out through the crooked opening. As the rain hit her skin, making divots in the grime, the woman actually laughed, an aberrant sound in the dismal prison.

Fascinated, Willa watched her hand dip and undulate, dancing and weaving through the raindrops. Some of the despair and damage drained from the woman's face, replaced by a serene glow. Then, quick as a snake, the woman retracted her hand, startled by a small noise outside.

The woman gazed down at her hand, tracing the marks made by the raindrops.

A loud scraping noise came from the top of the stairs. Instantly, the woman cowered and hurried back to her wall. She stood, trembling, staring up at the door at the top of the stairs with wide, fearful eyes. Willa followed her and waited, her heart racing, her muscles tensed with anticipation.

Several bolts slid out of place before the door pulled open. Harsh light spilled down the stairs and a figure descended, hidden in the light. Willa squinted, trying to see who it was. She could tell it was a man, but his whole figure was blurred, as if she was seeing him through murky water.

The woman put a hand out to steady herself against the

wall, but she stood her ground, lifting her chin defiantly. Despite knowing this was a dream and she could do nothing, Willa placed herself next to the woman.

The man, the captor, stopped in front of his prisoner, his bulky, solid form looming over her. A dagger flashed in his right hand and Willa wanted to cry out a warning.

"Wynter?" he said in a hauntingly suave voice. There was some implied question in the woman's name that Willa didn't understand.

Wynter swallowed twice, kept her chin lifted and answered in a surprisingly steady voice, "No."

Even with his figure blurred, Willa saw the man's jaw set, the muscles in his right arm tense. With a startling swiftness, he threw himself at Wynter, pinning her to the wall and locking her right arm in a crushing grip. She tried to pull away, but his strength far outweighed hers. Willa, now panicking, stood next to the woman, close enough to hear the change in her breathing. Willa's own chest grew tight with fear and dread of what would come next. She wanted desperately to stop what she knew was coming, but she was helpless, only a static observer.

The man set the tip of his long, slender dagger to the skin of Wynter's forearm just above the last festering, red cut. He brought his face within a breath of Wynter's and she squirmed, trying to free herself. The air in the room shifted, turning colder, and once again Willa was able to feel what Wynter felt. Her captor was pushing into her thoughts, somehow forcing an image into her brain. Willa saw it clearly in her own head: Wynter standing in a circle with her captor and ten others, blackness all around them. He wanted her to accept the image, to want it, to agree to it.

"No!" Wynter affirmed, banishing the image from her and Willa's minds. Willa stood breathless as the man leaned his weight into Wynter, pressing her harder against the rough stone wall.

Wynter pushed her teeth together and met his cold stare.

Slowly—torturously slowly—he pressed the blade into her flesh and then pulled back, opening the skin, two white petals splitting back to reveal red. Fiery pain race up Willa's arm. Hot blood rushed out of Wynter's wound in a sickening gush; she cried out in pain.

Then she snapped her head to the side and met Willa's wide eyes. "Help me!"

SIMON LURCHED, AWAKENED BY WILLA screaming and thrashing beside him. Startled and disoriented he reached for her. She swung her arms, hitting him across the face and chest. He ducked and tried to dodge her next blow. More powerful than her thrashing were the emotions pouring out of her: despair, desperation, and thick, frantic fear.

What the hell?

When he finally managed to get a hold of her arms, she screamed louder and started kicking.

"Willa! Willa! It's me." He gripped her arms and brought his face close to hers. "Willa, what's wrong?"

She stopped thrashing, but her eyes remained wide and wild. The look on her face sent a chill down his spine. Her eyes pulled from him as she studied the small living room with its few framed nature photos, TV, and couch. Dull light from the streetlamps streamed in through the blinds on the two small windows behind the couch. "Simon?" she gasped.

"Yeah, it's me. What's going on?"

Willa collapsed against him, exhausted. "A dream."

He put his arms around her. "Must have been some dream."

"It was. It was the most powerful, terrible dream I've ever had." She turned her face into his chest. "It was awful." Tears rushed to her eyes, and soon, Simon's shirt was spotted and wet. He held her tight, kissed her hair.

"What was it?" he whispered.

For a moment, Willa didn't respond. Simon could feel her struggle to come out of the emotional after-shock of the dream. One image flashed in his mind, pulled from hers—the glint of light on a sharp blade. He shuddered.

After several deep breaths and being in the comfort of his arms, she told him everything. He listened quietly, his hold on her tightening with each terrible detail. "She needs my help, Simon. What am I going to do? I have no idea where she is."

Simon exhaled. "Oh my, Willa. I have no idea. There was no clue at all as to where that basement might be?" Her desperation to act became his and his mind whirled, searching for an answer, an action.

"None. I've never seen it before. The only thing I could see out the small window was grass and rain." Her face crumpled. "Oh, my gosh! He'll kill her unless I get there. I can feel it. She'll die. She'll *die*." Willa broke down into sobs and Simon tucked her into his chest again, stroking her hair.

He said the only thing he could say. "Okay, okay. We'll figure it out. We'll find a way to help her. I promise."

CHAPTER 9
New Moon

Present Day, October

R uby Plate's ghost stood under the giant canopy of the weeping willow's branches in her own backyard as October's first cold rain beat down on the earth. Ruby's soul was tethered here and had been since the day of her death so long ago. At first she'd been delighted to be around to watch over her granddaughter, Amelia, but now she was full of bitterness.

For years she'd watched her beautiful home fall to pieces, and now there was a Dark witch sleeping under her roof. The witch who infected her home, a virus that destroyed and devoured all that was once beautiful and strong, was talented and determined. All her attempts to stop him, get rid of him, had been met with strong resistance. Her own magic had mostly been lost with her death and there was little she could do. She couldn't even get to the poor Light witch in her basement. She could feel that the woman was fading quickly, the fight bleeding out of her.

To watch this Dark witch darken her doorstep and torture the life and magic out of a Light witch was like death repeated day after day. It was like her soul and heart were being constantly polluted. All her hard work to make this home and this town a haven for magic . . .

How did this happen? How do I fix it?

There *had* to be something she could do. Why else would her soul be stuck here? Ruby felt if she could right this wrong, then she'd finally be able to cross over to the Otherworld and find peace with Charles, her husband.

Oh, how she missed him!

Ruby shook the thoughts of his face and hands from her head and tried to focus on the task at hand. Ignoring the rain, she moved to the basement window and looked down at Wynter, who was asleep, sitting against the wall. Ruby sensed that some magic still clung to Wynter, enough to fight Holmes, but not defeat him. And not enough to free her from the basement. Ruby had tried all she was capable of doing and her creativity was now stretched thin, her ideas drying up like a puddle in the desert. This frustrated her beyond words. In life no one could match her power; she was not accustomed to weakness.

He would cut Wynter again soon. Ruby had forced herself

to watch every offense of his blade, fueling her determination to stop it. She could still remember the sensation of pain—she felt each and every cut of Holmes's knife she couldn't prevent.

Ruby suddenly felt like a prisoner herself, chained to the house, powerless to serve any great purpose other than annoying the Dark witch now inhabiting her haven.

She raised her eyes to the shadowy night. *Why? What do I do?*

Wynter moaned in her sleep. It was too much to stand. Ruby had to get away from the sight of the poor witch withering in her basement. She returned to the willow and sat against the trunk. She closed her eyes and tried to clear her mind, open her heart to the Powers of the Earth. There had to be a way to reach the magic, to beg for help.

SATURDAY NIGHT AFTER THE DREADFUL dream at Simon's apartment on Friday, Willa had the dinner shift at the diner. Simon was at a night class and her parents had the car for a date to the symphony in Denver. This meant she'd have to walk home.

Of course, ten minutes before the end of her shift it began to rain.

She stood at the back door of the diner, staring despondently at the icy October rain dripping off the small awning, puddling on the cement. The day had already gone badly. The dreadful dream lingered with her, an emotional hangover she couldn't shake. The woman's—Wynter's—damaged figure followed her every thought and haunted her every action. Her morning classes had been a waste of time and the diner had been extra busy. As if those weren't hard enough, now she had to walk home in the freezing rain.

I should really get my own car.

Willa pulled the hood of her inadequate jacket up over her head and sighed before dashing out into the rain. Within a minute the cold water had soaked through her jacket, shirt, skirt, and shoes. She hurried as fast as she could, but it made no difference. Head bent against the weather, she focused on the pavement, the familiar cracks and stains on the sidewalk enough to get her home. But as she neared Plate's Place, a coil of instinct moved up her spine. Willa slowed her steps.

Thunder rumbled in the distance and she shivered. All she wanted was to get home to a hot shower, but she couldn't ignore the urge to slow and look up at Ruby's house. Ever since the mysterious man—rumors around town said he was only known by the name Holmes—had moved in, Willa had avoided the house. He made her nervous, uneasy. Over the last few months, she'd only seen him a few times, mostly from a distance, but the sight of him always induced a ripple of cold fear in her stomach. He'd done nothing to improve the state of the house. In fact, it seemed to have aged another decade since his arrival, looking worse than ever. On top of all that, he'd hit that poor dog without bothering to stop.

Looking up at the derelict structure, Willa felt immensely sad. Her desire to rescue the house welled up in her throat and she found herself fighting tears. She shook her head. *I really need a shower and some solid, dream-free sleep.*

Willa took a step, ready to hurry on home, but was stopped by a ripple of movement on the side of the house. Stepping back, she peered down the side yard, trying to see through the curtain of rain and darkness.

At first, all she could make out was a white shape. Then there was movement. Automatically, Willa took a few more steps forward, moving off the sidewalk and onto the yellowed grass of the front yard, the neglected lawn protesting with a squashy crunch.

Finally, her mind was able to reconcile the image, the force of her realization rocked her back on her heels.

The hand. Wynter's hand!

Just like in her dream, Wynter's hand, wrist, and part of her forearm protruded from the open slit, a round peg in a square hole. Her fingers moved in small waves, undulating in the raindrops, weaving them over her skin like silk over a loom.

In the feeble light of the street lamps, Willa could see the spots where raindrops had penetrated the layers of dirt, almost like divots in the skin. She squinted harder, the jagged ridges of the scars now caught the light.

A stumbling step back.

Willa's eyes shot up to the house. All the lights were off. She tried to remember if Holmes's truck had been in the driveway and started to move toward the window, the weight of her steps producing a subtle squelching sound in the grass.

It was barely audible, but it was enough—Wynter's hand had disappeared. Willa almost lunged after it, wanting to dive to the ground and look in the window, call out to the trapped woman, scream that she was going to help, but the sound of a vehicle made her turn.

Oh, no. No!

Holmes pulled into the driveway.

Willa stumbled back to the sidewalk, her body tight with panic, her hair, neck, and face soaked with freezing rain. Torn between the need to help Wynter and the desire to get away from Holmes, she could only stand and gape at the vehicle and its occupant.

What do I do?

Holmes emerged from his truck.

Willa cringed and wished she could evaporate into the air. It only took him a second to find her and meet her eyes with a powerful stare. *Move!* She screamed to herself. She fumbled with her jacket, as if she had stopped to adjust it and not to discover the secret in this man's basement. He blinked several times and then stared, straightening up, cocking his head. His sharp-as-steel gaze assaulted her, dangerous and exposing.

Just walk. Walk past him.

Willa wanted to look back to the window, but she found her eyes locked with his. Cold moved through her body, sinking deep into the marrow of her bones. Something in his eyes . . . He wasn't just looking at her, he was looking *in* her. *Oh, no. No. Just a person walking home from work. No hand. No secret. I don't know.*

The cold inside her worsened. She wrapped her arms around herself and tried to force her weakening legs to move faster. Holmes's sharp eyes narrowed. He slammed his truck door shut. Willa jumped at the sound, her racing heart threatened to break out of her ribs. She gripped her purse and prepared to run, run as fast as she could, but Holmes turned and walked away from her, toward the house.

Willa almost cried out in relief. When she heard the side door slam shut, she broke into a run, her feet slapping hard against the wet sidewalk.

HOLMES STOOD IN THE LIVING room of the old house, peering out the window at the rain-drenched street. His phone was tucked between his shoulder and his ear.

"Any luck, Holmes?" Archard demanded.

"No, Archard. I just tried again and Wynter still refuses, but I can feel her increasing weakness. Her roots in the magic are almost dead. I'll push more assaults. It should only be a few more days."

"I hope you're right. Our window of opportunity has now shrunk to a pinhole. Time is short."

"I'm aware of that. I promise it will be done in the next few days." A car drove by and Holmes eyed it suspiciously, but it didn't slow.

"Don't fail me. Our circle must be complete for the blood moon."

"Yes, sir. I understand."

"Any other problems?"

Silence. Holmes checked the street again, uneasy.

"What's wrong?"

"I think I have a ghost."

Archard sighed irritably. "So what? It's just a ghost."

"Yes, well, this ghost doesn't seem to approve of what I'm doing in the basement."

"It doesn't matter."

Holmes frowned, biting back a rush of temper. "Yes, sir."

"Anything else, Holmes?" Archard now sounded bored and anxious to end the conversation.

"Well . . ."

"Well what?"

"A girl," Holmes said flatly.

"What girl? What about her?"

Holmes moved to another window and looked through the tattered curtains. "I'm not really sure. There was a girl walking past the house tonight and I sensed something from her."

"Like what?"

"Magic."

Archard scoffed. "That's not possible. We checked the whole town. There are no other witches left in Twelve Acres."

"I know that, Archard, but . . ."

"But nothing. If the girl is an undiscovered witch, then she is no threat to us. Forget about her."

"Yes, sir."

"Very good. Call me as soon as Wynter breaks."

Holmes ended the call and frowned down at the phone. He then went to check the yard from the kitchen window.

CHAPTER 10
NEW MOON

November 1930

A melia stood beneath the curtain of willow branches, hidden and safe within their embrace. A crisp autumn breeze caressed the branches, gently pulling a few slender, yellow leaves away with it. The sky above was velvety dark and dotted with stars, but the moon was nowhere in sight. Amelia looked down at the red pouch in her hand.

New moon. A time for healing and a time for beginnings.

She slipped the final ingredient, a red quartz crystal, into a pouch and cinched the purse strings. The accompanying puff of air smelled of the other ingredients: earthy allspice, sharp black peppercorns, and comforting thyme. Everything she needed for a courage spell. She thought briefly of doubling the contents of the pouch; she needed more courage than she thought existed in the whole world.

Sun and moon, help me!

For good measure she quickly plucked one of her long, red-brown hairs and tied it around the top of the pouch.

At her feet a circle of candles burned, all red except for one blue. Between the candles were placed small, round stones taken from the nearby stream. The stones and candles were charged with magic and a bowl of water sat in the center of the circle, awaiting her offering.

The amazing Ruby Plate was dead, her body at rest in the town cemetery. Somewhere in Amelia's heart, she hadn't believed it could actually happen, especially so soon; Ruby was only sixty years old. No one took it harder than Amelia. As a twenty-year-old woman, she thought she should have better control of her emotions, but she felt as helpless as when her father died. Maybe worse.

The cancer came on quickly, a devastating blow. During Ruby's last few weeks Amelia had stayed at her side night and day, working as many healing spells and rituals as she could. She was an excellent healer, extraordinary even, but nothing could be done. The earth had decided to claim one of its own.

Finally, Ruby had taken Amelia's hand in her own bony, withered one and said, with a smile, "My love, it's time to let go. Grandpa Charles is waiting for me, and I'm ready. No more magic now. Just lay with me."

Reluctantly, Amelia crawled into Ruby's bed and laid her

head near the witch's shoulder, listening as her grandmother took her final breaths. Tears flowing freely, blurring her vision and burning her cheeks, Amelia felt the old woman's spirit leave the room and some of Ruby's magic enter her own body. A last gift from Grandma.

Amelia knelt over the circle of candles, dangling the pouch over the water. She closed her eyes, summoned the magic. "*Help me, all powerful sun and moon. Bring me courage, swift and soon.*" She repeated the spell several times, the words merging together as she chanted faster and faster. The pouch began to sway back and forth, the magic accepting her offerings. Once more, Amelia chanted the spell, then dropped the pouch into the water. The water bubbled furiously and then calmed, the ritual now completed.

With a small silver snuffer, Amelia extinguished the candles one by one. She stood, hoping to feel fortified and ready to face what lay ahead. Instead, she only felt empty. And alone. She had lost so many people in her life: her father and Grandpa Charles to the war; her mother two years ago in a car accident; and now Ruby. Ruby had always been there after each death to catch her, to hold her, to help her. Amelia's new husband, Peter, did his best to console her, but even with their strong bond his help was not at all like Ruby's had been.

Her whole world was being pulled out from under her.

Not only was she forced to function without Ruby's help, the Covenant was now looking to her for leadership. *Leadership!* It was the last notation in her grandma's grimoire— *Amelia must take my place as Luminary.* Amelia had nearly fainted at the sight of the words in the spell book. Every other member of the Covenant, except young Solace, had more experience than her. Why on earth would Ruby want her to step into the role of leader? It was insane!

It just didn't make any sense. She attempted to convince the Covenant that Ruby must have been delusional with sickness when she wrote her final words, but everyone knew better—especially Amelia. And everyone also knew that the final words in a witch's grimoire were more binding than a legal will. Amelia had no choice but to find the courage to step into her grandmother's place.

The barn owl that made his home in the willow hooted down at Amelia a fond good evening. She glanced up at him, his yellow eyes and white face throwing the starlight back at her.

"What do I do?" she whispered. The owl remained silent.

She knew what she *must* do; she just didn't want to do it for fear of failure. The timing was terrible. Darkness was coming. She'd felt it since that night seven years ago when she saw the horrible image of herself in the water.

She was unprepared to face it, to fight it.

And worst of all, she was more than certain it would defeat her.

CHAPTER 11
NEW MOON

Present Day, October

Simon lounged in his chair, trying and failing to listen to the droning of his statistics professor. Half the class was already asleep and Simon was halfway joining them when Willa's voice cut into his head.

Simon! I need you. Now!

He sat forward, knocking his pen to the floor. Had he really heard that or was it the start of a dream?

Simon!

There it was again, clear and loud and intense with panic. Willa needed him. He didn't take time to figure out how he was hearing her; he snatched his bag off the floor and ran.

WILLA FOUGHT THE INTENSE URGE to turn back, each pounding stride a struggle. Wynter's haunting image floated in front of Willa as she ran, her thoughts fiercely battling each other. But she kept running, all the way home, adrenaline and fear pushing her legs. She didn't even dare stop to text Simon. Instead, she gambled on their ever deepening connection; she called out to Simon in her mind. *Simon! I need you. Now!* She didn't know if it would work; they'd been able to communicate with each other through their minds in silent conversations in the past couple of weeks. But those times were different—they'd been sitting on the couch, face to face. This time, Simon was miles away at the University.

Simon!

When her house came into view, she nearly cried with relief. Skidding to a stop at the backdoor, she dug out her keys and lunged into the kitchen. Oppressive silence met her, too quiet after the pounding of the rain and her feet. She dropped her purse and soaking wet jacket to the floor.

What do I do?

Staring into the gray of the room, she forced her mind to quiet and think. Conventional wisdom screamed at her to call the police—immediately. Willa bent and pulled her phone from her soggy purse. Her thumb hovered over the keypad and she hesitated, not sure why.

Antsy with indecision and panic, she began pacing the small kitchen.

What do I do? What do I do?

A forceful knock rocked the backdoor and Willa screamed, dropping her phone to the floor. "Willa!"

She sighed and opened the door to Simon. He immediately scooped her into his arms. "You're soaking wet." He kissed her hair. "I heard you in my head. What's wrong?"

Willa exhaled in relief, Simon's appearance a steadying force. "Wynter. The woman in the basement—I found her."

His eyes widened. "Seriously? How?"

"I was walking home from work and stopped at Ruby's house. Her hand—it was there, reaching out the basement window. But Holmes got home at the same time." She shook her head. "He scares me. I ran. I didn't know what else to do."

Simon nodded. "No, that's good. If you'd stayed he might have hurt you, too." He shuddered. "Did you call the police?"

Willa pulled back and ran her hands back through her wet hair. "I was just about to, but something is telling me not to. I don't know why. We *should* call the police, right?"

Simon narrowed his eyes at her, thinking and listening to her emotions. He reached out and took her hand. "What else would we do?"

Willa started to shake her head, but then doubled over in pain. A sharp flash erupted in her head and she fell to her knees. Simon was also on the ground, gripping the sides of his head. When the flash receded a picture came into focus.

The willow tree in Ruby's yard swayed in the breeze, its lithe branches rustling. The vision zoomed in closer and a woman appeared to stand near the trunk, her image flickering. She wore a long, red dress fashioned in a design worn during the turn of the century—long sleeves, tight bodice, and full skirt.

Willa gasped when she saw the woman's face. *Ruby.* The woman turned and fixed her vibrant green eyes on Willa. "You must come now. I can help you save Wynter. Hurry!"

Then, as quickly and as painfully as it had started, the vision ended.

Willa gasped for breath and realized she was now lying on the cold tile with Simon next to her. "What the hell was that?" he asked.

"That was Ruby. Her ghost at her own house." Willa scrambled to her feet. "We have to go. Now!"

"Whoa!" Simon jumped to his feet and grabbed her by the shoulders. "What are you doing?"

"Simon, we have to go. You saw it, right? And heard what she said? She's going to help us get Wynter out. Help us save her."

Simon shook his head. "How do we know what we just saw was real?"

"Why wouldn't it be?" Willa couldn't understand why Simon would hesitate. This was the answer.

Simon frowned and massaged her upper arms. "Willa, I don't know what any of this means and I'm not sure you do either."

"That doesn't mean we can't trust it. Put logic aside. When it comes to these weird things we can do, we have to go with instinct. And my instincts are *screaming* right now."

"But . . ." Simon paused, pressing his lips together.

Willa couldn't give him the time to rationalize it. If there was one thing she never ignored, it was a warning in a dream. Wynter needed her help and now Willa had a possible way to give it.

"I'm going." She pulled away from Simon and bolted for the door.

HOLMES COULDN'T FORGET ABOUT THE girl as Archard had suggested. Something about her unsettled him, scratched at his mind. The magic he'd sensed from her had been powerful, much more than the weak tremors of an undiscovered witch. And he couldn't shake the thought that she was a threat to him.

The basement was protected with a spell so no one looking in the window would see Wynter, but he felt that somehow the girl knew what was locked in the darkness. His gift had sensed a great fear and unease in her, but he'd been unable to look any further into her mind. She'd blocked him— another sign of power. What if she'd seen Wynter and gotten past the spells. The last thing he needed was the police or a mob of angry small-townies pounding on his door.

From his luggage, Holmes retrieved a softball-sized, black crystal ball and wrapped it in a kitchen towel. He ran out to his truck through the rain. Once in the truck, he uncovered the ball and held it in his hands. Closing his eyes, he called to the magic and soon felt the heat of its response. The crystal ball burst to life with a black flash of light. In his mind, he focused on the girl's image, asking the magic to lead him to her.

In the surface of the scrying tool he saw her young face, framed by a tumble of dark wavy hair, her eyes alive with untapped power. Then something he didn't expect appeared—the face of a young man. The boy's impressively sized body pulsed with great power and magic. Holmes frowned; the girl wasn't alone.

When the picture changed to the streets of Twelve Acres, a map to her location, he turned on the engine and followed.

Anger and anticipation roiled in his gut. He couldn't allow anyone to interfere with his progress with Wynter, not even accidentally. He was *so close!* And if anyone delayed the process any further . . . Holmes shuddered. He didn't want to think of Archard's fiery anger.

Soon, the ball showed him the correct house with its sharply pitched Tudor-style roof and thick ivy. He stopped his truck half a block away. He covered the ball with the towel, now flickering out, and got out of the car. Holmes ran down the sidewalk and wedged himself behind a large oak tree in the front yard of the house across the street.

The rain continued to beat down, the *drip drip drip* of water on leaves over his head loud, making its way through to fall on him. He ignored the rain's cold touch and peered at the windows of the house—all dark. Was she sleeping?

Holmes waved his hand over his body, effectively hiding himself with magic. He frowned and set to work, forming a plan in his mind.

WILLA WAS OUT THE DOOR before Simon could stop her, so he hurried out after her. He found her standing rigidly by the fence, face pressed to a space between the slats. It was still raining and she wasn't wearing a jacket, only her diner uniform—a thin polo shirt and short skirt. He pulled off his hoodie. "Here, put this on before you freeze to death." He held it out to her.

"Shhh!" she said, frantically flapping a hand at him, motioning for him to get down.

He dropped into a crouch beside her. "What is it?" he whispered.

Willa turned to him with wide, panicked eyes. "It's Holmes!"

"What?" Simon turned to the fence and squinted through the narrow opening. Holmes's gray truck was parked a short distance down the street. The driver seat was empty. Simon's gut tightened. "Did you see him?"

"No." Willa stiffened. "Simon . . . he knows."

"Knows what?"

"He knows I know about Wynter!" Willa wrung her hands, eyes skittering around the yard.

Simon took her hands and steadied them in his. "Hey, look at me. How would he know that? Did he see you looking in the window or something?"

"I don't know. Maybe. Why else would his truck be here?"

Simon couldn't argue with that. Why was it there? And more importantly *where* was he?

Willa stood and pulled on his hand. "We have to hurry."

He resisted, surprised. "You still plan on going there?"

"Yes, more now than before. If he's here then we have time to get Wynter out. Come on."

Simon opened his mouth to protest, but the look on her face and the feelings rushing out of her stopped him. Against all his logic, he followed her through the backyard into the neighbors', away from Holmes's truck.

CHAPTER 12
New Moon

Present Day, October

Willa and Simon slipped through backyards and dark streets, approaching Ruby's property from the back. Willa glanced over her shoulder every few minutes, a sickening sense of alarm and the jittery need for urgency pushing her on.

They trudged through the mud and deep weeds behind Ruby's house until they reached the willow. It loomed over them like a great, hairy beast, expanding outward, voluminously overtaking the yard. The grass and vegetation all around were dead or dying, brown and dusty, but the willow stood vibrant and alive, immune to the neglect given it.

No wind moved through the yard, yet the drippy branches swayed slightly.

Willa looked over at Simon, who looked back apprehensively, but took her hand. They walked around to the front of the massive tree where Willa saw Ruby's ghost. "She's right there by the tree, just like we saw," she whispered.

Simon nodded and they moved closer.

Ruby watched them approach and Willa's mind raced with thoughts. This was *Ruby Plate*. How many times had Willa imagined having a moment to talk with her, to ask her about Twelve Acres and her life? About the paper hidden in the candlestick. But there wasn't time now. Wynter's life was more important than answers to mysteries.

Ruby smiled. "I'm so pleased to see you. I wasn't sure if the vision would reach you, if the magic was strong enough. What are your names?"

Willa briefly wondered why she could talk to Ruby and Solace, but no other ghosts. *What makes them different?* Setting the question aside, she answered, "I'm Willa and this is Simon. He can't see you." Simon squinted at the tree, looking uncomfortable.

Ruby nodded. "I know, Willa. You are the one with the Power."

Power? "How did you find us? How did we see you in our heads?"

Ruby frowned. "I wish I had time to explain, but Wynter is very sick. He cut her again tonight. I think she may be dying. We must help her, and it will take all of us together to do it. Holmes is gone, but there is no way to know when he'll return. Are you willing to help?"

Willa looked at Simon, who looked back, questioning. Blood pounded in her head and ears; her stomach had never felt so twisted. Scenes from her dream raced across her mind. Ruby waited, her expression urgent. "What do we have to do?"

Two FOLDS OF RED FESTERING skin puffed open, thick with edema and oozing yellow-pink pus. Wynter stared in horror at the rippled, yellow fat layer and red striated muscle now exposed in the canal of the cut. Holmes's anger had pushed the knife much deeper than ever before. The wound needed stitches, a balm of sandalwood and calendula, and she could use a bee pollen tea. But of course, she didn't have those things.

Perhaps he had killed her after all, unintentionally. Perhaps this would be her end—chills, hallucinations, searing, spreading pain, her body cooked from the inside out by infectious fever, her organs shutting down one by one.

Mournful tears pushed their way out of her eyes, rolling down her cheeks, and over her trembling lips.

I give up.

Wynter gave into her sorrowful defeat, collapsing into a pitiful pile of dingy white cloth. There was no more strength left in her to keep fighting.

This is the end.

At least Holmes wouldn't be able to use her. At least she would never be forced to say yes and join their Dark covens. That would be one small triumph in her defeat.

With a shuddering sigh Wynter willed herself to sleep, opening her mind to places she had long kept locked tight. One face, the face of the person she loved most in the world, floated in front of her eyes before she succumbed to her exhaustion.

A few moments later she was startled awake by a strange sound. She opened one eye, finding the small movement a great effort. Gray light trickled in through the window. It was still raining, but she saw nothing else, heard nothing. She closed her eye, ready to go back to sleep, when the noise came again.

"Wynter!" Her name spoken by a female voice, the first voice she had heard besides Holmes's and her own in months.

An angelic chorus couldn't have sounded more beautiful.

Wynter pushed her weary, ailing body up into a standing position, a last-ditch jolt of hopeful adrenalin helping her to her feet. She leaned heavily on the wall, her chains creaked and groaned as she moved closer to the window. She blinked once, twice, three times to be sure her vision was clear and true.

A face in the window.

Clear, crisp, blue eyes, skin like amber honey, and wet, dark hair.

Wynter nearly collapsed in shock and joy, praying that

the girl was real and not an illusion of her weakened mind, or some wicked trick of Holmes's. He had forced so many images into her mind over the months that she was no longer sure of her own vision and what was real.

Be real, be real.

"Wynter?" the girl called again, shifting at the window, crouching lower.

Wynter hurried forward, hands clawing along the wall. "I'm here," she answered, her voice barely loud enough for her own ears to hear. She cleared her throat, found the strength to call louder, "I'm here!"

Relief fluttered briefly across the girl's lovely face and was quickly replaced with concern. "Wynter, we're going to get you out. Where are you? I can't see you."

Wynter pushed away from the wall and stumbled into the thin column of light streaming in through the window, a dismal spotlight. She didn't miss the look of distress on the girl's face, and didn't blame her for it; Wynter's appearance was certainly repugnant. One bucket of water a week could only do so much. Her dress was in tatters, stiff with dirt, her hair in clumps, her skin deathly pale where it was not caked in dirt. And she stood slumping forward, barely able to stand. A beaten, neglected animal.

The girl's eyes grew watery and pinched with concern. She swallowed several times before speaking again. "Don't worry, we're here. Ruby is going to help us get you out, but we have to hurry."

Out? Get out? But how? It would take great magic to break

through Holmes's spells and her chains. Of course, they had obviously already broken through the outer spells to see and talk to her. Hope trilled in Wynter's heart.

The girl turned her head and looked upwards, speaking. A pair of men's boots appeared in the window and then two large, strong hands reached down as if from the heavens to grip the bottom of the window. After considerable effort, the window gave and moved upwards, relenting its stuck position just enough for a body to pass through.

Wynter gasped in awe and relief, gripping her skirt in anticipation.

Next, assisted by the heavenly, strong hands, the girl was lowered into the basement. With her came the smell of freedom, fresh fall rain, and strong, but untapped magic. Without hesitation, and to Wynter's great surprise, the girl rushed over and threw her arms around her. Despite her filth and, no doubt, stench, the girl held her tightly with warm, genuine affection. Instantly, Wynter collapsed against the girl's young, stalwart body, floods of tears pulsing out of her. It was like being born again, coming out of the dark into the open, warm arms of love. The magic came off the young woman in waves and Wynter drank it in like ambrosia, feeling a bit of strength return to her.

A deep voice from the window broke their embrace. The girl pulled back and looked to the window, still firmly holding Wynter's arms. A handsome face with a set of dark eyes, framed by golden curls, spoke, "We need to hurry, Willa."

Willa.

Willa looked around the room, searching for something. Finally, her gaze locked on a spot near the stairs. "What now, Ruby?"

Wynter looked at the stairs and didn't see a soul. She looked at Willa and then back.

A ghost!

The only way this girl could see a ghost was if she had the Gift of Dreams with the Power of Spirits. A rare gift, and even rarer ability. A connection struggled to form in Wynter's mind. A ghost. Ruby. A ghost named Ruby. *Oh!* It could be only one woman, one witch: the great Ruby Plate, the luminary of the last Light Covenant. Wynter marveled, gaping at the empty spot near the bottom of the steps.

She had often sensed a spirit around the house. It had tried to communicate with her several times, but Holmes was always quick to interfere. Wynter would never have guessed it was Ruby Plate, but found she was not surprised.

Wynter looked at Willa. Ruby's spirit had a proxy, someone free from Dark spells, someone with the Power. Ruby could add her own magic to Willa's while also directing the girl's strength. That was how they'd broken the spell hiding Wynter from the outside world.

Willa nodded, listening to the ghost. Her face drained of color and she bit her lower lip. Finally, with worried eyes, she turned to Wynter. "Ruby says we must channel all of our powers to break the enchantments on your chains. They are very strong."

"I know," Wynter whispered. *This girl knows nothing of her powers, of who she really is. And this kind of magic could over-whelm her.* She said a quiet chant of strength—for all of them.

"Simon," Willa called and a second later the man slid down through the window. He was a tall, powerful creature with the bulk of well used muscles, the magic pulsing off him as strong as Willa's. He smiled hesitantly at Wynter and took Willa's outstretched hand.

"Ruby will help me guide my . . . umm . . . magic, she says," Willa explained uncomfortably. Simon's eyes grew wide in protest. Willa shook her head. "It's okay. It's the only way. Wynter's magic is so weak and you need to be strong to carry us out—if it comes to that. And besides, it wasn't *that* bad. I already feel back to normal, mostly." Willa half-smiled and Simon nodded, his brow furrowed, his reticent eyes scanning the room.

Willa turned her head and listened for final instructions from the ghost. With a deep sigh, she looked at Wynter, ap-prehension brimming out of her body. "I can't promise this will work. Simon and I have no idea what this is all about, but I promise we will do our best."

Wynter only nodded, a knot of emotion in her throat. It would work—it *would* work.

Simon touched Willa's shoulder. "Wait. Let me see if I can heal her first. If she's better, she can help more."

Willa blinked at him and then looked to Ruby for ap-proval, after which she nodded vigorously and kept her wide, blinking eyes on Simon. Wynter's jaw dropped in complete astonishment.

A healer! How is this possible?

The young man stepped in front of her, his kind face rimmed with nerves. "Give me your hands, Wynter."

Wynter raised her damaged, torn hands and placed them in his large, warm ones. He closed his eyes. The extraordinary magic inside him moved into her fingertips and palms; it felt like being dipped in a hot spring. A curious, delightful sensation traveled up her arms and spread through her whole body. Like a warm summer breeze, like a fleece blanket in winter.

Wynter watched with awe as the jagged edges of her most recent wound drained of redness, flattened out and knitted itself back together, leaving behind only a thin line. The fever left her body, her limbs and organs drank in the nourishment they had long lacked.

Within a few short minutes, her body was restored. The outside dirt remained, but now somehow looked less tragic.

Simon exhaled, released her hands and opened his eyes to Wynter's grateful smile and flowing tears. As Wynter gazed down at her arms, she vaguely heard Willa step next to Simon and quietly said, "I didn't realize you could heal so much damage. That's . . . incredible."

How did he do that? Wynter wondered as she flexed her hands. She raised her head and was about to give her copious thanks when the energy of magic suddenly surged back into her soul, a blast of voltage so strong she nearly toppled backwards. For a brief, wonderful moment she was aware of every tree, every blade of grass, every living creature close to the house. She sensed their life forces, their magic, each one rushing over her, a waterfall of nature's electricity.

Simon reached out a hand to steady her. She surprised everyone when she started laughing. "Oh, Simon. I can never thank you enough. Not only do I have my health back, I have my magic back. No words can truly describe how wonderful this feels."

The young couple beamed at her until Willa flinched and glanced sideways. "We've got to hurry. Holmes could be back any second. We are supposed to join hands."

The three clasped hands in a small, intimate circle. Wynter knew breaking the chains would be no problem now that she was healed. Willa looked to the side and then down at her arm. She hissed in pain as Ruby began channeling her power in and through the girl.

"Thank you, dear Ruby," Wynter said to the ghost she couldn't see, but knew was there. "I can guide us through the spell. The four of us should have more than enough magic to get the job done." She inhaled deeply, closed her eyes and called to the magic. "Focus your mind on the chains, on breaking them. Picture them crumbling, both the Dark magic and the metal. Make the image as strong and real as you can." A short breath. "Push all your energy to the task." Another breath.

Heat suddenly swirled around them, the air churning with magic, a feeling Wynter had sorely missed.

"Now, repeat this spell with me: *Heavy chains that lock and bind, keeping good where none can find. Mighty Earth, hear our plea. Break the Dark and set Light free.*" Wynter repeated the spell again, and on the third time Simon and Willa hesitantly joined in, their eyes squeezed shut. Their joined hands quivered and sweated.

On the fourth chant, the chains began to tremble and shake. "Again," Wynter whispered, her heart racing, her blood pulsing furiously. The dank basement air was now completely charged with heat and energy, unsettled, like a sea in a storm.

Heavy chains that lock and bind, keeping good where none can find. Mighty Earth, hear our plea. Break the Dark and set Light free.

A high-pitched screeching noise suddenly assaulted the air as the metal gave way and the Dark magic was defeated. For a moment, Wynter dared not look down, the muscle memory of the chains still feeding her a false signal. Slowly, she dropped her chin and opened her eyes. The metal lay in shards around her bare feet. A white line of less dirty skin winked up at her from both ankles.

Free. Sun and moon, I am free!

Testing her new freedom, Wynter took a few hesitant steps away, her legs as light as air. A quiet giggle bubbled up from her chest, turning into loud, unrestrained guffaws, verging on sobs. She trailed her fingers over both raw ankles, the skin wrinkled, calloused and cool.

I'm free!

In her blissful celebration, Wynter almost failed to notice the two young people on their knees, sucking air and shuddering. "Oh, my poor dears, I'm sorry. Are you all right? That was powerful magic, especially for ones unaccustomed to it. Your strength will return in a few—"

Bang.

Above them a door slammed shut, followed by the heavy thud of footsteps. All heads snapped upwards.

Wynter felt herself shrinking back, her new strength drowning in fear. To be caught now when she was so close to freedom . . . She couldn't survive it. Shivers of fear shook her limbs. Like a frightened animal, she searched frantically around the room for a place to hide from her predator.

A steady, warm hand.

Wynter looked over into Willa's shining eyes. "Wynter, come on. Out the window. *Fast!*" Willa pulled her toward the window where Simon was already scrambling up and out. Wynter's fear gave way; she was not alone. She was free and she was whole. She was no longer that man's cowering prisoner, her mind no longer his twisted playground.

Simon reached back in to pull Willa up, but she pushed Wynter forward. "Go first," she hissed. Wynter quickly muttered a spell to block Holmes's access to the basement. It wouldn't stop him for long, but it would buy them some time.

Wynter thrust up her hands. Simon pulled her out as easily as a scrap of paper. He set her on the grass and turned back for Willa. Wynter breathed in her first breath of fresh air, so much air. The wind found her first, dancing all around her, lifting her hair in a fond hello. The ground tried to rise up around her and wrap her in its arms. In response she bent and caressed the dead grass. In the backyard the willow tree shook its branches in celebration and the resident owl hooted loudly.

Hello, my friends!

"Wynter!" Simon yelled, his voice frantic. Lost in her reprieve once again, she had completely missed Holmes charging into the basement, bellowing angry spells. At her feet Simon was straining to hold on to Willa's arms while she screamed in fear and pain. Holmes held her with a spell, a strong one, trying to pull her back into the prison.

"No," Wynter whispered and surged into action. She lifted her right hand and thrust it forward, sending magic racing through the air. Holmes's spell cracked and Willa was free. Simon fell backward on the grass with Willa safely in his arms.

Wynter lifted her hand again, this time to the sky. The wind obeyed her call and came rushing down from the clouds in one long tunnel. It pummeled its way into the basement and knocked Holmes backward, slamming his body against the basement wall with easy vehemence. Wynter swept her hand in front of the window and thick, green vines broke out of the dirt, crawling outward, slithering inside the window, down the walls and across the floor to Holmes's unconscious body. In seconds he was wrapped, arms at his side, in a tight jacket of vines.

"That won't hold him for long. We must go," Wynter breathed and turned to leave, but then stopped. She squatted and cocked her head to the side to look at Holmes's slack face. Thrilling triumph moved through her. But next to her triumph stood her hatred for the man who had stolen the last five months of her life and tried to break her mind. That hatred boiled inside her.

She moved closer to the window.

"Wynter?" Willa breathed.

Wynter held all life sacred; it was against her nature to hurt or kill. To kill was to touch Darkness. But it was also against her nature not to do what was best for her covens and the magic. And how could she move on with life knowing Holmes was still alive?

Willa and Simon stood next to her, one on each side, their breaths short and labored, their energy scattered and confused. Wynter smiled at them both and then sent a simple command to the vines with a flick of her wrist. With comfortable pleasure she watched as they moved upward, creeping toward Holmes's mouth. His eyes flashed open the instant the plant moved down his throat, seeking his heart. His body flopped and fought, like a hooked fish, before going still and quiet.

Wynter raised one eyebrow and stood, turning away. Willa touched her arm hesitantly and asked, "Who are you?"

Wynter smiled. "Oh, sweetie, I'm the same as you. I'm a witch."

CHAPTER 13
NEW MOON

Present Day, October

R uby watched as Willa, Simon, and Wynter walked away with hurried steps. She had offered them a quick goodbye and sent Willa away with one last instruction. "Listen to Wynter, she will help you get your answers."

The ghost glanced down through the basement window at Holmes's lifeless, but still warm body wrapped in murderous vines. Ruby was proud of Wynter. It was never easy to take a life, but sometimes it was necessary. Wynter was obviously a great and wise witch; Ruby wished she could know her more.

Ruby prayed that Wynter, Willa, and Simon would be

safe. Holmes didn't work alone. Others would pursue his purposes with renewed vigor. There was still much danger in their future. The pieces of conversations that Ruby had overheard and the way Holmes acted pointed to the involvement of many Dark witches with one great purpose. She suspected and feared that Wynter's imprisonment was connected to a terrible sequence of events set in motion long ago. Something that had started with her poor, sweet Amelia. Something she had also been powerless to stop.

Poor Amelia. I'm sorry I left you so soon.

Ruby watched as Simon took Willa's hand just before they turned the corner. She smiled at the simple tenderness of the gesture and rubbed absently at her own empty, quiescent hands.

Charles.

How she missed the soft, gentle man beneath the rugged handsomeness. Her memories of days working by his side and nights in his arms, powerful passion flowing from his touch, were as vivid as if they had just happened. Such memories comforted and plagued her, a torturous reminder of her spirit's limbo.

Overwhelming weariness filled her. She'd finally helped Wynter, and Holmes was dead—there was nothing left to do. With a sorrowful glance at her house, Ruby retreated to the willow tree and curled up on the ground at the base of the trunk. She was tired from channeling her magic through Willa and only wanted to close her eyes.

"Hello, Ruby Plate."

Ruby jerked around.

Charles!

In front of her was the most amazing sight—her husband, tall, handsome and dressed in his favorite hand-made flannel shirt, work pants, and scuffed boots, smiling a devilish grin. His body pulsed with a brilliant, fiery light.

"Is that truly you, Charles Plate?"

He chuckled, the sound bouncing in the air around her. "Yes, my love. I've come for you at last. Your time here is done."

Ruby rushed forward into his open arms, tears soaking her shimmering face. His body was warm, as warm as the fire that once burned in their hearth. The smell of open fields and clean water drifted off his body. He kissed her hair and then her lips, warmth pouring into her long-cold soul.

"At last," she whispered.

In her flood of relief and joy Ruby barely noticed the odd tugging sensation that began in her belly, gained momentum, and then, in a flash of light, pulled the couple away, leaving the willow alone in its melancholy yard.

WILLA, SIMON, AND WYNTER HURRIED back to Willa's house, taking the fastest route directly through the main streets. Willa wondered how late it was. It felt like days since she left the diner, but she guessed it was probably only after midnight. Would her parents be home? She winced. What would she say to them?

When she saw their car in the driveway, Willa caught Simon's eyes, knowing he'd sense what she was worried about. He shrugged, shook his head. She inhaled and tried to prepare herself.

"This way," she said to Wynter and led the way to the backdoor.

When the three of them, wet, muddy and exhausted, stepped into the kitchen, her parents were waiting, sipping tea at the table.

"Willa!" her mom yelled leaping up and pulling Willa into a hard hug. "We've been so worried. We got home and found your stuff abandoned on the floor, including your phone. We thought something had happened. . . ." Sarah's voice trailed off when she noticed Wynter. Her jaw dropped and eyes flashed wide at the awful sight of the stranger now in her kitchen. Willa couldn't blame her for the reaction. What must her mom be thinking? Her dad, too, was now standing, blinking at Wynter.

"Willa, what's going on?" Ethan demanded. "Who's this?"

Willa opened her mouth to attempt an answer, but Wynter stepped in. "My name is Wynter Craig. Your daughter and Simon just helped me escape from the basement of Ruby Plate's old house where I was held captive for the last five months by a man named Holmes."

Willa's parents stared blankly as she held her breath for what they would say to Wynter's straightforward, but shocking, answer.

Her dad ignored Wynter and turned to Willa. "Okay, did I just hear that correctly?"

"Umm, yes," was all Willa could manage.

"You *rescued* this woman? Whom that creep Holmes had in his *basement?* No one in town trusts that guy, but kidnapping? Really?" Ethan's eyebrows climbed his forehead.

Willa nodded.

"Where are the police? How did you even know she was there? Why would you go alone? What—" Ethan's questions were stalled by his wife's hand on his arm.

"Let's all sit down and Willa can explain. Okay? Let me get you three some water; you look like you've been through a lot."

They all sat at the glass-top round table, on which Sarah set three tall glasses of water. Wynter immediately gulped down her entire glass, Willa's parents staring uneasily as she did so. Willa took Simon's hand under the table and turned to her parents.

"I know you guys don't like talking about it, but I saw Wynter in a dream. It was the most powerful dream I've ever had. I knew I needed to help her."

Ethan cut back in, looking more uncomfortable than before. "But if you saw her in a dream, why didn't you call the police? It's not your job to rescue kidnapped women."

"Dad, please," Willa tried to soothe. "It's more complicated than that. I don't know exactly how to explain it—"

"I do," Wynter stepped in again. She turned to Sarah and Ethan. "The police would have been unable to help. Only

Willa and Simon, with the assistance of the ghost of Ruby Plate, had the power to free me." Wynter paused, narrowed her eyes slightly. "Do you know what your daughter and Simon are?" Ethan furrowed his brow and Sarah looked down at the table. "They are witches, and so am I."

Ethan laughed mirthlessly. "You've got to be kidding me? Are you some kind of crazy person?"

Wynter's expression remained calm and in control. Willa's head was pounding, her palm sweating into Simon's. *There's that word again—witch, witches.* Images of black hats, bubbling cauldrons and green skin flitted through her mind, but none of them matched Wynter or what they'd just experienced. *So, what does it really mean?*

Wynter continued, "Willa dreamed about me because of her gift. She and Simon are both incredibly talented witches, but they've never been trained."

Simon said, "Wynter, are you serious?"

She turned to him. "Of course. Simon, you were part of the magic in that basement tonight. You've seen it with your own eyes, felt it with your soul, and you know what you can do. Haven't you always wondered why?"

Willa and Simon exchanged a weighted look.

Ethan shook his head and said, "Craziness aside, I still don't understand why *my eighteen-year-old daughter* saved you from a kidnapper."

"He wasn't a kidnapper. He was also a witch, a Dark witch. He captured me in hope of forcing me to join his Dark covens so that they could form a Covenant, which is the most powerful of witch circles."

Ethan threw up his hands. "I've had enough. I don't care why or how you got here, but I want you out. Now!" Willa's dad stood, knocking his chair back to the floor. Wynter rose calmly and Willa jumped up to defend her.

"Dad, calm down! You're totally freaking out. Can't you just *listen* for once? She's telling you the truth."

"The truth? Willa, this is nonsense. Sit down. I don't want to hear—"

"No! I will *not* sit down and you *will* hear what I have to say." Willa balled her hands into fists and her face felt hot as a sunburn. She'd never stood up to him before. "You guys have never listened to me about what I can do. You've always pretended like the dreams and the ghosts don't exist. Well, they do! And Simon is the same as me. He can sense emotions, hear my thoughts and *heal* people. He healed Wynter in the basement. She was almost dead!"

Her dad's eyes widened and his face flushed bright red. He jabbed at finger at Simon. "So this started with *him*? I knew he couldn't be trusted. I knew I should have put my foot down about you dating a boy I didn't know."

Simon tensed beside her, but held his tongue.

"Dad! This is not Simon's fault. Quit trying to blame this on someone else. This is me—this is *who I am!*" Willa was yelling now, all control lost. "Why can't you just see it and accept it?"

"Stop yelling at me, Willa. You may be eighteen, but I'm still your father."

"ENOUGH!" All eyes turned to Sarah, who was still sitting in her chair, hands folded in her lap. "Sit down, Ethan, and *shut up*." She looked at Willa with sad, weary eyes. "Sit down, honey. I have something to say."

Willa sat down, her blood still racing with anger. Simon put his hand on her thigh and it helped to calm her a bit. She kept her eyes locked on her mom.

After a deep breath, Sarah began, "Wynter is right. Willa is a witch. I've known it her whole life." Willa's jaw dropped and her breath caught in her chest. "My mother, your grandma, was a witch. She could do things with the air, but she kept her powers mostly hidden. I didn't inherit the magic, but she told me about it." Sarah slowly inhaled and then plowed forward.

"You never got to know her, Willa—she died when you were three—but we weren't close anyway. I hated that my mother was different than other mothers. I hated the rumors that flew around this town because of who she was and who her family was. Because she wasn't the only one. Many of the women in our family had magic." She blinked back tears. "Willa, I'm so sorry. I was only trying to protect you. I thought it would be better to ignore it, instead of embracing it. I thought you might outgrow your powers if we didn't do anything to encourage them. That was a mistake and I'm very truly sorry."

"You knew? All along? And never told me?"

Sarah nodded penitently. "I'm sorry."

Willa scoffed. "I was so confused, so lonely. *My whole life!* You let me be that way because you were bitter about your own mother, because you didn't want a witch for a daughter?"

Sarah broke into sobs and shook her head. "No, that's . . . I'm sorry, Willa."

"Stop saying that!" Willa's blood was on fire, her heart palpating irregularly. Part of her felt bad for yelling at her mother, the remorse on her face was genuine, but the hurt outweighed the guilt.

"Willa," Simon said quietly and she spun around to glare at him.

"No, this is so wrong. I can't believe she would do this to me." Willa turned to Wynter. "I want to know everything. I want to learn. If I'm a witch then I will be one the right way."

Wynter nodded. "Willa and Simon, I can help you both, but our first priority is to get us to safety. Holmes was not working alone. Others will come and they will know what happened." At Simon's questioning look, she added, "There are ways with magic to find out and they will use them."

"So, we're in danger?" Simon asked sharply.

"I'm afraid so. My home is not far from here. It's safe and protected, hidden away deep in the mountains. I suggest we all go there now. My husband, Rowan," her voice caught on his name slightly before she could go on, "and I will keep you safe and can help you learn, help train you to use your magic as it is meant to be."

Ethan dared to interrupt. "No! Absolutely not. Willa, you are not going with some stranger. . . ."

"Yes, Dad, I am, and Mom will let me go."

Ethan looked over at his wife, who was slouched in her chair still crying silent tears.

"We have to let her go, Ethan. If that's what she wants."

"But Sarah . . ."

She shook her head, the look on her face was enough to stop him. Willa nodded once and stood, an odd and slippery feeling of triumph at the defeated look on her dad's face.

"Wynter, would you like to shower and get some fresh clothes before we go?"

Wynter smiled briefly. "Thank you, Willa. I suggest you both pack for an extended trip. It may be a while before it's safe to return to Twelve Acres."

SIMON HATED THE EMOTIONS OF anger and hurt cascading out of Willa. He'd never seen her so mad and he wasn't sure how to help fix it. Her mother had betrayed her—he understood that better than anyone—but her parents weren't like his. Willa's parents were good, loving people. Overprotective perhaps, but there was nothing sinful in that. He didn't want to see their relationship destroyed over this.

Willa leaned over her bed, roughly shoving clothes into a duffle bag. She'd taken a fast shower before Wynter and was dressed in a fresh pair of jeans and a lime green hoodie. Her wet hair hung down around her face, swinging with her jerky movements. "Willa, are you sure you want to leave like this? Why don't you go talk to your mom? I'll get this stuff—"

"No," Willa said sharply, "I don't want to talk to her." She shoved a pair of jeans into her bag with unnecessary force. "There's nothing to say."

Simon bit his lower lip, wanting to say more, but also wanting to avoid turning her anger on him. "Okay," he mumbled.

Wynter emerged from the bathroom a completely different person. Her sculpted face was scrubbed clean and glowing. Her hair was washed and plaited. She wore one of Willa's mom's old white T-shirts and a long black maxi skirt, and although he guessed the two women were about the same age, something about Wynter made her appear younger. She grinned at them. "That's the best shower I've ever had."

Willa smiled, handed her a pair of flip-flops, and turned back to her bag. "I think I'm ready. We'll stop at Simon's apartment and . . ." She turned back, her face scrunched. "Then I need to stop at the museum. I can't leave without telling Solace. Is that okay?'

Wynter nodded, "Of course, as long as we hurry."

Simon took the bag from Willa, slung it over his shoulder, his arm placed around her shoulders. "Okay, let's go," he said.

Willa's mom was waiting at the bottom of the stairs, her dad nowhere in sight. Sarah's eyes were still watery, her face splotchy. She held her hands in front of her, gripping them so tight her knuckles were white. Simon frowned and Willa tensed beside him.

"Do you have everything you need?" Sarah asked quietly.

"Yes," Willa said, not looking at her.

"Umm . . . okay. Will you call or at least text me when you get there safely? Keep me updated, so I know everything is all right?"

Willa exhaled, still not looking at her mom. "Yeah, okay. We gotta go."

Sarah nodded. She looked like she had volumes more to say, but she just kept nodding. She moved to give Willa a hug, but Willa stepped away and opened the front door.

Wynter stepped in instead and said, "Thank you, Sarah. I know this is all very strange and upsetting, but I promise to keep Willa safe." She handed Sarah a piece of paper. "This is Rowan's phone number. Just in case."

Sarah nodded some more and new tears slipped down her cheeks. Simon tried to catch Willa's eyes and prompt her to say something more, make it better before she walked away, but she wouldn't look at him either. She took a few steps out onto the porch, looking toward his Jeep.

Simon put a hand on Sarah's shoulder. She looked up at him with pleading eyes and he offered her a small smile. She exhaled and turned away.

WILLA LOOKED AROUND THE *LIFE in Early Twelve Acres* room with a despondent sense of finality. She hadn't bothered to turn on any of the lights and the room was a collection of shadows, the darkness complimenting her mood.

What have I done?

In rescuing Wynter, she'd flipped her whole life upside down. Things would never be the same. Not only was she leaving the only home she'd ever known, a place she loved, but she'd left without giving her mom a hug. She couldn't see past the harsh glare of her anger, of the betrayal of being lied to her entire life. It wasn't fair and it wasn't right, no matter what reasons her mother claimed.

She looked down at her set of museum keys, shifting them in her hands. Who knew how long it would be before it was safe to come back? She didn't really even know what the danger was or how it would be resolved. She felt blind, fumbling out in the dark for a solid grip, unsure if she'd find it.

She slipped the keys into the pouch of her hoodie and took a deep breath. "Solace? I need to talk to you," she called out.

Almost immediately her ghost friend appeared, smiling. "Willa! I don't normally see you this time of day. Shouldn't you be sleeping?"

"Yeah, normally. Umm . . . something has happened and I have to leave town for a while. I'm not sure how long . . ."

"What?" Solace screeched. "You can't leave."

"I don't *want* to, but I *have* to. Simon and I helped rescue a woman from the basement of Ruby Plate's house. Now we're in danger. We have to go until it's safe to come back."

Solace's face was washed in shock, her eyes wide with hurt. "No! If you leave I'll be alone. I don't want to be alone again. No! *Please* don't go." The ghost's form shimmered and fluttered so much Willa could barely see her.

Willa's heart broke. "Solace, I'm so sorry. You know I wouldn't leave you if I didn't have to, and it's only for a little while."

"How long?" Solace held her hands twined together at her chest.

Willa blinked. "Actually, I'm not sure."

"So you might never come back!"

"Solace, please. Of course, I'll come back."

"But this stranger is more important to you than *your best friend?*"

Willa sighed. "Solace . . ."

"No, no. It's *fine*. Go off, leave me. I'm just the ghost of a dead girl, after all. Why would you stay here with me? Go!" With that Solace disappeared.

"Solace! Solace! Don't do that!" Willa yelled and then stood waiting, but Solace didn't come back. Willa wanted to sink to the floor and sob. First her mom, now Solace. She wasn't sure she could stand under the emotional onslaught. Her body ached with exhaustion and her mind felt smashed, deformed by all that had happened tonight.

What am I doing?

Was it really worth giving up her comfortable life to follow Wynter into a world she didn't know anything about? Should she turn around and tell Wynter they weren't coming with her? That they'd been happy to help her, but their life was here in Twelve Acres, as it always had been. What about school? Her job? Did she really need to know more about this whole witch thing? Had her mom been right to hide it from her?

The questions pulled at her heart, but her soul had one clear answer: Go! She'd wanted nothing more her whole life than answers, but these weren't the simple, written-in-the-pages-of-a-book kind of answers she was hoping for. These answers required sacrifice.

Am I strong enough?

Willa looked around the room one more time, then turned to leave. By the time she made it back to Simon's Jeep, her cheeks were wet with silent, determined tears.

CHAPTER 14
WANING HALF MOON

June 1931

"Amelia, you must push. Almost there. Come on, sweetie." Camille's head appeared in front of Amelia's half-open eyes. Her graying blond hair was mussed and damp with sweat, but she smiled. Amelia was so grateful that Camille was there. Just when she thought she'd lost all the strong women in her life, Camille Krance stepped in and had done so much to help.

Amelia blinked, rolled her head languidly to the side.

"Come on, now," Camille demanded sweetly.

Amelia took a painful breath and lifted her head. She groped for her legs, grabbed behind her knees and did as Camille instructed. Searing, burning pain split her world in two.

Flashes of silver spotted the blackness behind her eyelids. The pressure grew unbearable, the pain a coagulated mess so thick she couldn't even cry out.

Camille said something, but Amelia's ears were clogged with pain.

Then, all at once, the pressure was gone and something warm and wet was set on her chest. "She's beautiful," Camille whispered and kissed Amelia's sweaty forehead.

She opened her eyes, the fog of pain gone, the world suddenly bright and dazzling. Before her was a red face, round and perfect, two silver-blue eyes studying her. In an instant, Amelia loved her; it filled every space inside her. She laughed joyfully. "Sun and moon! Hello, little one." The baby watched her mother, her tiny hands folded under her chin, her tongue moving in and out between pink lips.

Amelia stroked the tuft of wet, dark hair on her baby's head, trailed a finger down her chubby cheeks and laughed again. "Hello, my Lilly. You are the prettiest flower ever created. Oh, I love you."

Solace stepped around the bed and laid a blanket over Lilly. She leaned down to look at the tiny face. "Oh, Amelia, she is the prettiest baby I've ever seen! I'm so happy for you."

Amelia looked up and smiled at her friend. "Thank you, Solace. I'm so grateful to you and your mom," Amelia smiled at Camille. "Thanks for being here with me while Peter is gone." She laughed. "He'll be so mad he missed his little girl's entrance into the world."

Solace stroked Amelia's hair. "Of course. It was an honor for us to be here."

The new mother turned back to her child, studying every curve of her baby's face. Touching her, nuzzling her, loving her. The potent magic in the room took on a Lightness and beauty that Amelia had never felt before. Holding her own creation, she felt closer to the earth than ever before. The music of it sang in her blood.

She lifted her hand and summoned water from a bowl on her nightstand. A trail of drops arced through the air and gathered in her hand. She then swirled her hand over the baby, moving the individual droplets on Lilly's skin, scrubbing her clean.

Dry and swaddled in a clean blanket scented with rose and lavender, the baby turned her head into Amelia's body, rooting for milk. Amelia tenderly brought the baby to her breast, cradling the small body in her arms, savoring the warmth of the baby's skin against her own.

A perfect moment in time, suspended in heavenly happiness.

Camille and Solace finished cleaning up the room. Camille set a small red candle on the nightstand, snapped it to life and then handed Amelia a cup of red raspberry leaf and willow bark tea. "Do you need anything else, my dear?" she asked.

"No, thank you so much. You are both so wonderful." Amelia sipped the sweet, soothing tea.

Camille smiled. "You did wonderfully." She stroked Lilly's head. "I'll check on you in a couple hours. Peter and the others should be back soon. He'll cry when he sees how beautiful his daughter is."

"He'll never forgive himself for missing her birth, but it couldn't be helped. I just hope they are all right," Amelia said, looking at Lilly's eyes, noticing they were the same round shape as Peter's.

"I can't believe these Dark covens," Solace said shaking her head. "Poisoning a whole town! What is the point of that?"

Camille nodded. "It's terrible. Peter's potion will save them though. He's good at fixing things." She leaned down and kissed Amelia's forehead. "Good night, dear. And don't hesitate to call if you need anything. You enjoy that little one."

"I will." Amelia smiled sleepily. As Camille and Solace left the room, she settled back into the pillows, the baby asleep at her breast. She didn't want to worry about Peter and the others, didn't want to dwell on what the Dark covens might be planning, but suddenly a shocking jolt of doubt clouded the room. She looked down at her child's peaceful face. "What have I done?" she whispered.

My poor little baby. How could I be so foolish, so selfish to bring a child into the world at this time?

Amelia had seen the future in the water, and although she held out hope that it would change, deep inside, she could feel time slipping away, like sand in an undertow. Her denial had been absolute when she allowed herself to become pregnant. All she wanted was happiness, a family with Peter, her partner in magic and in life. But she had been fooling herself, and Lilly was now the victim of her obstinacy. What did she have to offer this child but a shame-filled, motherless future?

"Holy moon! *What have I done?*"

Panicked tears formed in the corner of her eyes, and silent sobs hitched in her chest, disturbing the baby as she slept. A chill moved over Amelia's heart, so cold that she found it hard to draw breath. The flame of the red candle on the nightstand puffed out, and no smoke rose from the extinguished wick.

Suddenly, Solace burst back into the bedroom, her face flushed and eyes too-wide.

"Solace!" Amelia cried, sitting up so abruptly the baby Lilly began to cry.

"Oh, Amelia," Solace cried breathlessly, stumbling forward to the bed, collapsing to the floor next to Amelia. "Peter . . . and the others . . ." Solace up gazed at her friend with round, wet eyes and Amelia knew what she would say. She squeezed her eyes shut and shook her head.

Solace gasped out the terrible words. "They are all dead!"

CHAPTER 15
WAXING CRESCENT

Present Day, October

It didn't matter that they were all exhausted, Willa wanted some answers as soon as possible and the hour-long drive to Wynter's house was a perfect chance. She needed to know if what they were doing was the right thing. As soon as she could push back her tears, she turned in her seat to look at Wynter in the back.

"Wynter, can you tell us more about what's going on? Who we are? How we can do the things we do?"

Wynter smiled, her eyes half closed. "Of course, sweetie. I want to answer all your questions. I know you must be so confused and scared." She straightened up and exhaled. "Hmm. Where do I begin?" Wynter looked out the window at the night. Willa looked over at Simon and he took her hand.

"Let's start with the Six Gifts," Wynter said. "Every witch is born with a specific, dominant talent or ability. There are six in all. The four elemental gifts: Earth, Air, Water, and Fire. And the two gifts connected to the Otherworld, or the world beyond our own: Mind and Dreams."

"So, I have the Gift of Dreams?" Willa asked.

"Yes, but not just that. You also have an extra talent, a rare one that only a few Dreamers receive—the Power of Spirits. This, of course, means that you can see and communicate with the spirits of the dead who have not crossed over into the Otherworld."

Willa nodded. *Gift.* She had never thought to give that term to her abilities. If anything it had always felt more like a burden. "And what about Simon?"

Wynter looked at the back of Simon's head. "Simon is a bit of a mystery to me. You said you can sense emotions, hear thoughts. Is that right, Simon?"

"Yes," he said, quickly looking back. "I feel what people around me feel and can sense their intentions, the *kind* of people they are, I guess. It's rare that I hear actual thoughts, except with Willa. The longer we're together the easier it is to hear her."

Wynter nodded, "Yes. That is because you two are connected in the magic. The magic makes you closer, actually binds you to each other. Your souls are connected and always will be." Wynter smiled. "But what about the healing? Tell me about that."

"Well, I've always been able to do that, too. I've healed all kinds of animals with all kinds of injuries. And a few people, including you. Oh, and I guess myself. Any time I've had an injury, it heals almost immediately and I don't get sick."

Willa blinked in surprised; she hadn't realized that his healing power extended to his own body.

"Hmm," Wynter mused. "That is where the mystery comes in. You see, witches with a talent for healing are usually a Water witch, or have the Gift of Water. But you have the Gift of Mind. Have you ever been able to manipulate or control water?"

Simon shook his head, "No."

Wynter nodded and narrowed her eyes in thought. Willa studied Simon's face. A line of tension pulsed at his jawline. More mystery about his abilities was probably not what he wanted to hear. She tightened her grip on his hand and offered him a reassuring smile when he shifted his eyes to her.

Simon asked, "So, I have more than one gift?"

"Well, it certainly looks that way, but the thing is, that's not possible."

Simon looked from Willa to Wynter and then back at the road. His hands kneaded the steering wheel. "Not possible? But . . ."

"I know how that sounds, since you obviously *do*. That's the mystery. Witches are born with only one gift. I've never seen or heard of an exception to that rule. Of course, a True

Witch, or a well taught witch, can use the magic of all the elements, and many witches even become proficient at sensing others' emotions, but they remain the most proficient in their *one* gift." Wynter sighed. "But there's more."

Simon opened his mouth, but then shut it again.

Willa asked, "What is it?"

"Even the most talented Water witch cannot heal with the touch of his hand. Waters use potions and herbs infused with magic to heal, but Simon . . ." Wynter paused and looked out her window. "There are legends of a kind of witch—even rarer than a Dreamer with the Power of Spirits—known as True Healer. I think, Simon, that you are a True Healer, able to heal animals and humans with magic already inside you."

A significant silence followed Wynter's declaration. Willa watched Simon's face, his eyes narrowed and the muscles in his jaw flexing and releasing. Finally, he said, "Is that a bad thing?"

Wynter laughed, "Of course, not, sweetie. It's amazing. You don't need to be worried. In all my forty-two years, I've never come across a more talented, more magic-rich couple than the pair of you. You should feel . . . well, proud. Your gifts are incredible and you will be able to do great things with them once you are trained."

Willa and Simon held each other's eyes for a protracted moment, as long as Simon could manage to look away from the road. Willa rolled the information around in her head and found only more questions.

"Okay, but *how* did we become witches? Why were we born with these gifts?"

"It's usually through family lines, something in the genes. You have to be born with magic; it's not a learned talent. Willa, your mom said you had witches in your family. How about you, Simon? Any strange family history?"

Simon tensed. "Not any that I know of; I know very little about my family history. My parents are as far from magical as you can get." In five months together, Simon had only briefly mentioned his parents and always in such vague terms. Willa had never met them or even seen a picture. *How did they hurt you so much?*

Wynter nodded, seeming to sense the shaky ground that was Simon's parents. "Many witches don't know exactly where their gifts come from. Magic can skip many generations."

Willa nodded. "Okay, that all makes sense, I guess. Now, what about Holmes and what he did to you? What's going on there?"

Wynter frowned and looked away. "Witches choose a path, either Light or Dark. Basically, good or evil. Light witches use the magic to help, to improve. Dark witches bend the magic to hurt, to destroy. They use it selfishly. I'm a Light witch and Holmes was a Dark witch."

"You said he wasn't working alone?" Simon asked.

"Yes. Witches often come together to form covens, or groups. The magic is always stronger with more witches together. The strongest kind of coven is a True Coven, all male or all female, one of each of the Six Gifts. The Six Gifts together form a perfect magical circle. It's very powerful, but there is something even more powerful, and that is a Covenant. A Covenant is the binding together of two True Covens, one male and one female. It's a perfect balance of magic. As a Covenant the witches control a unique hold over the magic or the Powers of the Earth. All magic is rooted in the earth."

"Are you in a Covenant?" Willa asked.

Willa smiled wanly. "No. Covenants are extremely rare. It's difficult to find all the witches needed to form two complete True Covens. Some gifts are more common than others and there are fewer witches in the world than there used to be. Also, the secrets of how to bind a Covenant are well protected."

Simon asked, "Is Holmes in a Covenant?"

"No, but he and his coven-mates are trying to form one. They are led by a man named Archard, a particularly Dark witch." Wynter inhaled. "He will stop at nothing to form a Covenant." Wynter laid her head back on the seat. "This summer my husband and I, after nearly fifteen years of efforts, found the last witches we needed to form two True Covens. We were ready to bind the Covenant and needed only to wait for the October full moon, the blood moon, to do it. But Archard found us.

"He attacked late one night; we were completely unprepared." She paused, and when she spoke again her voice was strained. "We lost two dear friends that night before we were able to flee to safety. A few days later a letter came, addressed to me. From Archard. He declared that he had taken hostage another member of my covens, and that if I wanted her back, I must come to Twelve Acres and bargain for her life."

When Wynter paused for a long time, her eyes glazing over as she stared out the window, Willa gently prompted, "So you came?"

"Yes. I couldn't get in contact with my friend—the one Archard claimed to have; her home was empty. Foolishly, in an effort to protect the rest of my coven-mates, I came alone to Plate's Place. It was a trap. Archard is hellbent on binding his Covenant this blood moon, only a couple weeks away, but he's missing one witch to complete his covens. One Earth."

"You're an Earth," Simon said.

Wynter lifted her head and nodded. "Yes. Rowan and I are both Earth witches."

"So, Holmes tried to force you to join their covens?" Willa added.

"Yes. Holmes was a Mind witch, a powerful one, and he used his skills to break into my mind and try to break down my free will, my ability to clearly make the choice. He tried to manipulate me. Not even magic can force a person to do something against her will. So Holmes tried to change my will."

Willa shook her head. "I'm so sorry." She looked down at Wynter's right arm and the line of scars. A chill crept up her neck at the memory of watching Holmes cut her. "Why the knife then?"

Wynter also looked down at her many hash-mark scars. "He thought pain would hurry my change of mind." She ran a finger over the marks. "One for every time I said no." Wynter finally looked at Willa, her eyes bright with unshed tears.

A knot of emotion formed in Willa's throat. "I'm so sorry, Wynter."

"Willa, I owe you my life. That was something you did *not* have to do and I know what it has done to your lives. Please know how truly grateful I am and always will be. I'll do all I can to make things right."

Willa only nodded, wiping a tear from her cheek.

Wynter exhaled a long breath and looked out the window. "Take the next exit, Simon. We're almost there."

WYNTER PRESSED HER FACE AGAINST the window, smiling at the sight of her land, her trees, her home. The Jeep bounced down the narrow dirt road. Only minutes until she was home. Back at Willa's house she'd thought of calling Rowan to let him know she was coming, but what could she say, how did she explain? It would be better to do it in person.

Her heart pounded so fast she was dizzy. The hum of their connection flared under her skin and she had to stop herself from leaping from the car before it came to a complete stop. The sight of her cottage warmed her from head to toe. The yellow thatched roof, the cream colored stone walls hidden behind fall-red ivy, the large gardens, and the smiling paned windows. *Home.*

Sensing her arrival, Rowan came rushing out of the front door at the same time Simon parked the Jeep. Her chest tightened as sobs hitched in her throat at the sight of his handsome bearded face and radiant, creamy, blue eyes. She threw herself from the Jeep and ran to him, tripping into his waiting arms.

Together, arms tight around each other, sobs echoing in the night, Wynter and Rowan fell to their knees. "I can't believe it," he said into her ear, his rich Scottish accent so familiar. "Wynter. My sweet wife. You're alive. You're here. Oh, thank the earth!"

Wynter laughed and cried into his shoulder, then pulled back to look at his face. She touched his beard. "I'm so sorry!"

"No, no. I'm sorry I couldn't find you. I tried *everything*."

She shook her head. "I shouldn't have gone alone. I walked right into Archard's waiting teeth."

Rowan held her face and kissed her—hard, desperate kisses, pouring in all the love and pain of the past months. "It doesn't matter. You're here." His eyes scanned down her body and stopped at the scars. He lifted her arm gently to look closer. "Oh no!" A fresh wave of tears coursed down his face.

"Holmes," she explained and he nodded slowly. He lifted her arm higher and gently kissed the scars.

Wynter had almost forgotten about Willa and Simon. She looked over her shoulder and found them huddled together, watching, Willa smiling shyly. Wynter got to her feet and gestured to the young couple. "Come here and meet

Rowan." They came hesitantly, nervously. "Rowan, this is Willa and Simon. They saved me."

Rowan's eyes flashed wide as he stepped forward to wrap Willa in his arms. "Thank you so much!" He released a shocked Willa and held out a hand to Simon. "Thank you! I thought the worst. You've given me my life back."

"Let's go inside," Wynter interrupted. "It's cold out here and I'm sure you're hungry. I'm starving! We'll eat and talk some more before we all get a nice long sleep."

After showing Willa and Simon to the guest room and leaving them to put their stuff down and rest, Wynter hurried back to Rowan in the kitchen. He stood at the large stove, starting a batch of risotto. For a moment she stood in the doorway and drank in the wonderful sight of him, here in their kitchen, his shoulder length sandy brown hair falling over his face, the movement of his arms over the pot.

He looked up, caught her eyes, smiled and opened his arms. She stepped into them again, feeling safe and content for the first time in five months.

"Oh, Wynter," he whispered, his Scottish accent growing thick with his lowered voice. She'd missed the lilting sound of his accented words, the deepness of his voice as alluring as the Scottish moors from which he hailed.

"How did they save you? They are so young."

"Young *and* undiscovered. They didn't know they were witches, poor things. Imagine a whole life with your powers and not knowing what they mean, not having control."

Reluctantly, Wynter pulled away to set the table, but relished the normalcy of the task. "Willa is a Dreamer," she said quietly.

Rowan stopped stirring and turned to her. "A Dreamer! And the boy?"

Wynter smiled. "A Mind *and* somehow also a True Healer. The only reason I can stand here now is because of his powers."

Rowan's jaw dropped. "But that means . . ."

"I know. If they'll join us, we'll have two True Covens again and we can bind the Covenant."

CHAPTER 16
WAXING CRESCENT

Present Day, October

Bent at an odd angle, Holmes's mouth hung open, his jaw askew in a horrific final scream, the tail of a vine hanging from his sagging lips. The air was already heavy with the putrid scent of death and decay. Archard stood at the base of the stairs, a fine silk handkerchief held over his mouth and nose. With a bothered sigh he ran his other hand over his black, slick hair, making certain not a strand was out of place. He brushed absently at the thin lapels of his new Armani suit as if standing there could stain him.

He eyed Holmes's bloated, rotting corpse with a mixture of disappointment and disdain. After their conversation about Holmes seeing a girl with powers outside the house, Archard had worried. At first, it seemed insignificant, but then instinct kicked in. When Holmes didn't answer his follow-up call, Archard had hurried to Plate's Place.

He had always doubted the man's ability to get the job done—no one ever lived up to Archard's expectations—but he had expected more than this. Anger circulated under his skin like a poison, moving around inside him, threatening to break his control.

Archard clenched his teeth and narrowed his eyes, thinking of the person responsible for ruining his expertly crafted plan. He allowed himself the vision of kicking the corpse several times, an inward pout he wouldn't act on, if only to save his Prada loafers.

How did this happen?

Archard knew Wynter hadn't been strong enough to do this on her own, so how? Or more importantly, *who?* Stroking his perfectly shaped goatee, he considered the possibilities. He was certain no one knew of the plan, or of Wynter's incarceration. If only she had agreed, none of this would have happened. What a mess! Five months he had waited patiently while Holmes made his promises and assurances.

I indulged him for too long.

Archard had thought of finding another Earth witch, one that would be easier to break or was willing, but he wanted Wynter. She was the wife of Rowan, the Light Luminary, a man Archard despised on principal. And she and Rowan were trying to revive Ruby Plate's legacy. Breaking her, making her a part of his Dark Covenant was too tempting, too perfectly vengeful. If not for her misguided righteousness, his Covenant would be complete and the approaching full moon would have sealed their power. More importantly, *his power*. He would have been the leader of the first complete Dark Covenant since the Dark Ages. He would have succeeded where his ancestors had failed almost eighty years ago.

If only my grandfather had not failed at his spell. Archard frowned thinking of the mistake that had torn Ruby's Covenant to shreds, but failed to form a Dark one. His grandfather's spell had not been strong enough to force Ruby's granddaughter to join them. After the epic failure, the covens had broken apart, their faith in their Luminary lost. If it had worked, Archard would have *inherited* his position as Luminary of a Covenant, instead of having to scrape for it.

He wanted it so badly that he'd do anything—even scrape to the core of the earth. The prestige, the honor, the redemption tempted him more than any seductress ever could. The hunger for power often turned to physical pain, to an ache so powerful it threatened to break him. The pursuit consumed his every living moment.

I will have this.

He would get Wynter back and deal with her personally, as he should have in the first place. And to those responsible for her escape, he would deal with them, too.

With meticulous care, Archard folded his handkerchief, creased the edges, and placed it back in his pocket. Gritting his teeth, he moved to the corpse, stepping carefully. He squatted, wincing at the repellent smell and state of Holmes's face. He set his jaw and steeled himself for the task ahead. Flexing his right hand, he then touched the tips of his fingers to Holmes's forehead, doing his best to ignore the cold, slick sensation of decomposition. He closed his eyes and called to the magic, asking for the dead witch's final memories. The flesh of his hand grew hot, his arm tingled and then the scenes flashed across his mind, one after another, almost too fast to decipher. But it was enough.

He drew his hand away from the body, wiped it several times with an alcohol wipe before tossing it onto Holmes's body.

WITH THE WHISPER OF EXPENSIVE engineering, the sleek, black vehicle pulled up in front of a stark, modern-style home made of glass and steel in the foothills of Denver. Archard waited for the driver to open the door, and then he stepped out, straightened his suit, and headed for the front door. That, too, was opened for him by his dreary butler. The men exchanged no words, as was their way, but the butler handed Archard a black envelope, which he took with obvious annoyance.

What now?

His heeled shoes clacked loudly on the Venetian marble floor as golden-pink as the Caribbean sands polished to a high gloss. He traveled down a long hall, passing expensive pieces of art he never bothered to look at, and turned into his office. He sat behind the low-profile brushed metal desk and opened the letter. Drawn in the middle of a single page was one symbol: a thick black circle bisected by parallel lines.

Archard stared at the symbol for a moment, and then threw the paper over his shoulder, where it burst into flames and tumbled to the floor in ashes. The covens wished to meet, and although he was their Luminary, if the members called a circle, he had to comply. But he wasn't ready.

He wanted more time to think, to find a solution to the Holmes situation. He had to go before them with solutions, not just the two-fold unfortunate news. He had to prove he was in control, or things might fall apart. Too many of his fellow witches would be more than happy to take his place at the first hint of incompetence.

He had less than two weeks until the next full moon—and not just any full moon, the blood moon. It was the only moon powerful enough for the binding of a Covenant. If he didn't have things prepared soon, he'd have to wait a whole year. His covens needed two witches, an Earth and a Mind, both vacancies thanks to Holmes incompetency. How would he fill those spaces in such a short time?

Archard picked up an empty tumbler off his desk and threw it across the room, shattering it against the wall.

I don't want to wait a whole year!

Archard's emotions always ran hot, with an insatiable-ness that threatened to burn him from the inside out. If he didn't keep his Gift of Fire in check, it would control him, overwhelm him. For the most part, he had a handle on his passions. But often, beneath his cool, refined exterior, Archard raged out of control.

He took a few deep breaths and felt the rage settle. Then he stood, carefully removing his suit coat and draping it over the back of his chair with the reverence such fine material called for. With slender, manicured fingers, he removed his platinum cuff links and rolled up his sleeves.

He locked the office door.

At the far end of the room stood a magnificent fireplace. The hearth opened like the mouth of a deep, black cave, and the mantel—made entirely of white volcanic stone—rose six feet off the floor. Archard meticulously placed several logs in the grate and draped them with a few dried bougainvillea vines, portions of the crusty purple flowers flaking off at his feet.

Right hand extended, he projected magic into the wood and it burst into glorious flame, the last bits of moisture in the vines popping and hissing. He placed one red and two yellow pillar candles on the mantel, held his fingers over them, and snapped his fingers to call fire to the wicks.

On a tall pedestal, sitting on the flat marble hearth, rested a globe-sized, onyx crystal ball. The flickering yellow light of the fire bounced and refracted off the shiny blackness, illuminating Archard's face with a nefarious glow. He curved his upper body over the ball, a devious grin pulling at the edges of his lips. Next to the ball sat a long, thin, and wickedly sharp athame. He picked up the ritual knife, ran a finger lovingly over the smooth blade, and then from his pocket, produced one dark chestnut hair collected from the basement.

With precision he wrapped the long hair around the knife. Chanting under his breath, he held the knife in the roaring fire. "*Powerful fire, destroyer of all kind. Burn your way through the weak one's mind. Show me my heart's deepest desire, reveal it with the power of fire.*"

The hair turned to ash in seconds, which he took and sprinkled over the crystal ball. In the center of the orb, a pin-prick of red light sparked to life, growing steadily until the whole globe burned ruby-red. Archard held his spindly fingers over the ball, heat flowing back and forth between it and his hands, his skin quickly reddening. He repeated the spell three more times.

The girl who helped Wynter escape—she was his path to find them all. He simply had to break into her untrained, unprotected mind. Then, he could steal all the information he needed. Because she was untrained, she wouldn't know what was going on or who it was; she wouldn't warn Wynter he was coming. It was foolproof.

Laboriously, he pushed his way into the girl's mind, images popping up in the ball. Wynter and Rowan had protected their home, but the mind needed extra protection and they had failed to provide it for the girl.

Archard resisted the urge to brush away a bead of sweat making a path to his eye.

The girl's scream echoed through his head, sending waves of pleasure down his spine.

CHAPTER 17
WAXING CRESCENT

Present Day, October

S imon sat on the bed in the guest room. Willa had
clicked on a small lamp by the bedside, its weak light
pooled on the red comforter. He looked around the
small, simple room. There was a desk with several stacks of
books, the cozy double bed and a large window to his right.
Out the window, the dark forest slept. He stared at his reflection in the surface of the glass, his mind a jumble of thoughts.

I'm a witch. Willa is a witch.

It was hard for him to settle on that explanation, to move
past all the fictional characters and Halloween stories to make
being a witch a *real* thing. Something he was. It wasn't that
he couldn't believe it or didn't want to learn more about his

gifts—he wanted that more than ever, after what Wynter had said—it was just hard to step around his logic and create a new self-identity that involved magic. A term he had never used to define his abilities.

Magic.

Life had changed, but exactly how much? What about his classes on Monday? He couldn't miss more than a few classes or he'd have to repeat, and that would put him behind on his track to medical school.

And there was also his job at the diner. He had a shift in— he pulled out his phone and checked the time—three hours. *Man, it's three o'clock in the morning.* Feeling more tired than he had a minute before, he quickly texted the manager and lied about having food poisoning.

Wynter had said they were in danger, and, from what she'd said about Holmes and Archard, it sounded serious. But how long would they be in danger? How much was this going to screw up his and Willa's lives? He sighed and dropped his head into his hands.

When Willa returned from the bathroom, he sat up and opened his arms to her. She sat on his knee and he held her tight. "What are we doing, Willa?"

She shook her head. "I have no idea."

"We can't stay here long. We gotta get back to Twelve Acres."

"I know," she said, looking down and fidgeting with his shirt. "But I feel trapped. We can't just leave. I want to know more about this witch stuff. Also, it might not be safe in

Twelve Acres. What if this Archard comes after us for interfering? He sounds scary."

Simon nodded. "Yeah, I'm not sure what to do about that. But Archard is Wynter and Rowan's enemy, not ours. Maybe they can help us make a clean break. We can't get involved any more than we already are. Okay?"

"Okay."

Simon stretched his neck forward and kissed her. In an attempt to lighten the mood—he hated to sense her worry—he said, "But hey, at least I get to sleep next to you tonight, or this morning, whenever we actually get to go to sleep."

Willa laughed. "Good point. I think I will enjoy that very much." She kissed him slowly and he pulled her body firmly against his.

A knock at the door. "Willa, Simon? Food is ready," Wynter called through the door.

Willa smiled at Simon. "Coming!"

THE COZY KITCHEN WITH LIGHTLY stained knotty alder cabinets and white marble counter tops was tucked at the back of the house. A farmhouse table with benches sat parallel to a large picture window. A huge bouquet of white peonies and steaming bowls of delicious risotto with chicken and arugula waited on the table. Willa hadn't realized exactly how hungry she was until the smell of garlic and bread hit her nose. Salivating, she took a seat at one of the bowls and inhaled its fabulous smell.

Rowan smiled at her. He wore a pair of black fleece pants and a gray T-shirt; he'd obviously been sleeping when they'd arrived. Willa instantly liked him. There was something trustworthy about his soft, blue eyes and Scottish accent. "Dig in," he said. "There's warm bread there in the basket and I'll grab you both a cold soda." Willa took her first bite and closed her eyes, the flavors melting on her tongue.

Rowan set two sodas out for them and poured himself and Wynter a glass of white wine. Wynter had begun to eat. "Sun and moon, I've missed good food," she said between bites.

Willa smiled and dunked a chunk of bread into her bowl. For a moment she forgot about the looming, unknown future and felt content, at ease. Wynter and Rowan felt like old friends, despite the craziness of the situation.

Wynter pushed away her bowl and sat back. "Oh, I'm stuffed." She grinned and sipped at her wine. "So let's see— where were we?" She took another sip. "Rowan and I met about fifteen years ago in Scotland while studying the ways of the ancient shamans. One day, in a dark corner of an old library, we literally ran into each other, blinded by the stacks of books in our arms. In a dizzy pile of books and heated magic, we knew we belonged to each other."

"That's kind of what happened to Simon and me," Willa injected. "We met at the diner where we work and the first time there was all this heat. We were pulled to each other. Was that the magic?"

"Yes. All those things you felt were what it feels like to

find your soul mate, your partner in the magic. Wonderful, isn't it?" Willa smiled and Wynter went on. "When we had recovered from those first moments, we found a stray piece of paper in the rubble of all the books we'd been carrying. It'd obviously been ripped from a book and randomly tucked inside another.

"The page was old and tattered, and when I read it, I read for the first time about a Covenant. Of how it is formed and the magic involved. Magic practically dripped from that page and we knew it was our destiny to try to form a Covenant. But it turned out to be a very rocky path." Wynter looked to Rowan, passing on the story.

"That one small page was all we had, so first we had to discover more about the Covenant," Rowan took over. "It wasn't easy. The spells and information have been well protected over the years, only shared with a select few. After much research we were able to track down the only living witch who had been a part of a Covenant. She was in Italy and quite old and ailing, but agreed, after much persuasion, to talk with us." Rowan paused to sip his own wine. "She wasn't comfortable sharing many details, but after several visits, just before her death she gave us a grimoire. . . ."

"Sorry," Simon interrupted, "what's a grimoire?"

"Oh, of course," Rowan said with a smile. "It's a witch's spell book, a journal to record all magical activity, spells, and such things. They are extremely important, being passed down through generations. All magical knowledge is contained in grimoires."

Wynter cut in, "This particular grimoire changed our lives. Camille was very reluctant to hand it over, warning us many times about the risks of forming a Covenant, but I think she also understood the importance of trying."

Willa sat forward. *Camille? Could it be the same Camille?* It was a long shot. "What was Camille's last name?"

"Krance. Camille Krance," Wynter answered.

Willa gasped. "You've got to be kidding me? The same Camille Krance who was an original settler in Twelve Acres, one of the founders?"

"The exact same one."

Shaking her head in disbelief, Willa turned to Simon. "She's Solace's mother."

"Whoa," Simon said. "Small world."

Rowan said, "The witch world is very small. Who is Solace?"

"Solace is a ghost at the Twelve Acres Museum, where I volunteer. We are best friends, as weird as that may sound." An ache rose in her gut as she thought of her friend, alone now and hating her for leaving. Willa wished she could call or text her, try to smooth things over.

"Oh, that's right," Wynter said. "Solace's name is in some of Camille's personal grimoires. She gave us a few of those as well. But let me tell you about the most important grimoire." Wynter's eyes pierced Willa's. "The one that belonged to Ruby Plate."

Willa's jaw dropped and her pulse quickened. "Really?"

"Yes. Hold on, I'll go get it for you." Wynter jumped up from the table and hurried out of the room.

Rowan stood to clear the table. "Would you like anything else?"

"No, thank you, Rowan. It was delicious." Anxious to learn more, Willa asked, "If it's Ruby's grimoire, does that mean she formed a Covenant?"

Rowan sat back down and leaned his arms on the table. "Yes, that's right. Ruby Plate was the last Luminary, or leader, of a Light Covenant. She was a stellar woman, as you probably know. Her grimoire contains all the details of how to form a Covenant."

The thrill of discovery zinged in Willa's head. This was the secret of her town, the answer to the mystery of the note in the candlestick. Ruby and the town founders had formed a Covenant; they'd all been witches. Willa desperately wished she could tell Solace.

Simon touched her hand. "You okay?"

"Yeah, this is just so incredible. I knew there was something about Ruby and the town founders. I never thought it would be this."

Wynter came back into the room, carrying a large tome in her arms. She set it reverently in front of Willa. "Feel that?" she whispered.

"Oh, my gosh! Yes!" Willa inhaled deeply as a swell of warmth moved over her face. The book was large, like an old bible, and bound in rust colored leather, worn silky by time and the touch of hands. On the cover was a large gold embossment of a weeping willow. "The magic? Even this book has magic."

"Yes, powerful magic," Wynter said, now seated next to Rowan again. "Open it."

Simon scooted closer. Willa lifted her hand and trailed her fingers across the golden willow, her skin picking up the book's warmth. Then slowly she lifted the cover, which creaked, the binding giving with the movement. Another rush of heat hit Willa, and her body quickly absorbed it, pulling it into her blood. It sparked inside her, speeding her pulse.

The first page read, "Ruby Plate, Gift of Mind, Twelve Acres, Colorado." Willa pulled a fingertip over Ruby's name. "Simon, Ruby was a Mind, like you."

Simon nodded, his eyes fixed on the page. Under the words was a single symbol, a sun. "What's the sun for?"

"That's the symbol for a Luminary," Wynter said. "Rowan is our Luminary." She smiled at her husband.

Willa turned to the next page. More symbols stared back at her, these more familiar. "These symbols—I found them written on a note hidden inside a candlestick that Ruby owned. What do they mean?"

Rowan leaned forward to look at the page. "Those are the symbols that represent the Six Gifts. Each gift has a specific symbol. See the labels next to each one?"

"Oh, yes," Willa pointed to an upside down triangle with two interlocking circles inside it. "Here's mine—Dreams."

"The two circles represent this world and the Otherworld and how, for a Dreamer, those two worlds overlap," Wynter explained.

Willa nodded. The Otherworld, the place where her dreams

came from. "And here's yours, Simon." The Mind symbol was a triangle with a small dot just inside the apex.

Simon squinted at it. "Does the dot represent the mind?"

"That's right," Rowan said. "In this grimoire, Ruby documents the founding of Twelve Acres and the binding of her Covenant. The Binding spell is there. We think it may be the only grimoire left that contains this priceless information."

"Do you still want to form a Covenant?" Simon asked as Willa flipped a few more pages, each one increasing her awe.

She looked up in time to see Wynter and Rowan exchange a pregnant look. Wynter turned back. "Yes, we do." She scooted forward and placed her forearms on the table. "Willa and Simon, we'd like to ask you to join our covens."

Willa's hand stalled halfway through turning a page and Simon's jaw dropped open.

"What?" Willa asked breathlessly.

"The two coven-mates we lost to Archard—one was our female Dreams and the other our male Mind. I believe the magic sent you that dream of me, Willa, because you and Simon are meant to be a part of our Covenant. I think you are destined to be. Your gifts are so powerful and unique. You're tailor-made for this."

Willa dropped the page and blinked at Wynter, her mind numb, not quite registering the full weight of what the witch had just asked them. All she could think of was what Simon had said. *We can't get more involved in this.*

Willa turned slowly to Simon who was also staring in

shock at Wynter. She opened her mouth to say something, but was stalled by blinding, searing pain in her head.

SUDDENLY AND VIOLENTLY, WILLA'S WHOLE body convulsed. She screamed, shrill and chilling, clutching her head. Her body jerked backwards, falling hard to the wood floor.

"Willa!" Simon yelled, reaching for her. She only continued to scream, her body arching and flailing on the floor as she clawed at her head. He crouched next to her, hands quaking above her, trying to grab her, but not wanting to hurt her as she thrashed.

Simon spun to face Rowan and Wynter who had risen from the table and were standing over Willa, faces frozen in terror.

"What's happening?" Simon demanded. "What did you do?" Willa's scream intensified, pitching and peaking, filling the room with fear.

"It's not us, Simon," Wynter said loudly. "This is Dark magic. Someone is trying to break into her mind." She and Rowan both dropped to the floor beside Willa and held out their hands.

"What are you doing?" Simon said.

"Trying to stop it!" Rowan said, his eyes closed tight in concentration.

When Willa only screamed louder, Simon yelled, "Then do it! I can feel her terror. Stop it, now!" He'd never felt anything like this before, such pure, black terror. His whole body ached with the need to stop it, get it away from Willa. He looked from Wynter to Rowan and back at Willa. Whatever they were doing didn't seem to be helping. He reached out a quivering hand and placed it on Willa's head. Instantly, her screaming stopped.

Wynter and Rowan looked over at him, shocked.

Willa whimpered and rolled onto her side. Simon pulled her gently into his lap, cradling her. She was muttering, unclear and jumbled.

"What is it, sweetie?" Wynter urged.

"He knows," she mumbled into Simon's chest. "He's coming."

"Who?" Rowan pushed. "Did you see a face?"

Willa whimpered again, began to cry in earnest. "Long, thin face. Black hair, goatee. Empty gray eyes."

Rowan stood up slowly, his face pale. His hands clenched into fists. "Archard."

CHAPTER 18
WAXING CRESCENT

Present Day, October

Willa was still tucked protectively in Simon's arm as he sat on the floor. The conversation drifted over her aching head and only half registered in her violated mind.

"Archard?" Simon asked. "It was Archard hurting her! But why and how?"

Rowan was at the windows, his eyes searching the yard. "He used her mind to find where we are, to gather information. I protected the house, but failed to think about protecting your untrained minds."

"So this is your fault?" Simon yelled.

Wynter knelt down next to him. "Simon, this is not

Rowan's fault. It's Archard's. He obviously found Holmes and has used magic to discover what happened. He knows you and Willa helped me escape." She paused. "He *knows who you are.*" Uneasiness moved through the room and Simon shifted, his heart thumping faster under Willa's ear.

"I'm so sorry Willa was hurt." Wynter put a hand on Willa's arm. "The last thing I want is for her or you to be hurt, but by saving me you've become a part of this, whether you want it or not."

Simon looked down at Willa and she blinked up at him, trying to focus on what was being said. Simon kissed her forehead. "So what now?"

Rowan crossed to another window. "It's not safe. We have to leave. Now."

Willa shifted and turned to Wynter. "We have to leave again? We just got here." All she wanted was to sleep. Her head was pounding, her body useless. How could they run—again?

Wynter frowned, her eyes sympathetic. "Yes, sweetie. I'm sorry."

"Where will we go?" Willa asked.

Rowan answered. "Jackson, Wyoming. A couple in our covens own a ranch there. It'll be safe while we plan what to do about Archard. I'll call everyone." Rowan fled the room, already in action.

Wynter turned back to the couple. "Before we do anything else, we need to protect your minds. Simon, you'll want to remember this spell. It can help block out all the noise from other minds, others' emotions, and it also protects the mind from invasion."

A spell? Willa looked up at Simon, his face scrunched in disbelief.

"In your minds picture a strong, solid door, and imagine placing behind it all your thoughts, memories, everything. Picture that door with a nice sturdy lock. Got it?" Wynter explained. Willa looked from Wynter to Simon and back to Wynter, unsure of what to do. Simon also looked confused.

"Wynter, I'm not sure . . ." Willa began.

"Just close your eyes and picture the door. Focus on it. Magic starts in the mind. You have to first visualize what you want it to do," Wynter urged patiently. Willa closed her eyes and did as Wynter instructed. Soon, she could clearly see a big, black door with a solid deadbolt lock.

"Good," Wynter said. "Now, hold on to the image and repeat these words: *Powerful Earth, accept this mind-lock. A magical door, make it solid as rock.*"

Feeling a little awkward Willa repeated the words and on the second time Simon joined in. On the third chant the door in Willa's mind began to glow and a wave of heat moved over her. "Is that it? Did we do it?" She asked, carefully opening her eyes.

"The door is glowing," Simon said in wonder.

Wynter nodded. "Yes, good. Now get your stuff," she said gently. "We leave in fifteen minutes." Then she was gone, off to help Rowan.

Simon didn't move. He looked down at Willa. "Willa, I don't know what to do."

"We have to go with them. I felt him . . ." she winced at the pain in her head, "in my mind. He's . . . evil. The kind of evil I didn't know really existed. If we go back alone, he'll be able to find us and he'll come for us. Our only chance is to stay with Rowan and Wynter. They can protect us."

"But they already failed at that. Your mind—*your mind*—was broken into, violated. I can't let you get hurt anymore. It was bad enough watching Ruby use you to channel her magic. Now this."

Willa smiled weakly. "Simon, do you really think we can protect ourselves? We don't know anything about magic. Wynter just helped us protect our minds, so that can't happen again. But who knows what other crazy stuff Archard can do."

Simon frowned and looked away. "What have we gotten ourselves into?" he whispered.

"Witchcraft," Willa said matter-of-factly. Simon looked back at her, his eyes flickering with emotions. "We better go get ready." She moved to get up, but the pain in her head flared and she fell back, dizzy.

Simon caught her. "I'll heal you, okay? Take the pain away." He stared down at her.

Willa blinked, her pulse quickened. "You've never healed me before."

He nodded slowly. "I know. Do you want me to? I won't if you don't want me to."

She inhaled. "No, of course I do. Please do. I can't even stand up. I need your help."

After a slight hesitation as he studied her face, Simon took her hand in his. "Ready?" he asked.

She nodded, swallowed. "Okay." Immediately, Simon's palm grew warm against hers and a rush of hot magic, like a wind blowing into her, moved up her arm and swept through her whole body. It tingled pleasantly, working to take away the pain, which quickly disappeared. Her head cleared, her strength returned. She sighed in sweet relief.

Simon's face was edged in apprehension. "Okay?"

"Yes. Wow, Simon. That is amazing. I feel better than I did *before* Archard broke into my mind." She touched his face, rubbing at his beard stubble. "Was it you who stopped Archard?"

Simon blinked in surprise. "I . . . I don't know."

"Because when you touched my head, it stopped." Willa wondered if Simon's healing powers had stopped the attack. It made sense, in a way. Archard was hurting her and Simon stopped the hurt.

Simon scoffed, shook his head. "I have no idea."

"Well, thank you. For stopping it, if you did, and for healing me."

He nodded shyly and hugged her tighter. "All right, let's get our stuff."

THE EARLY MORNING MISTS GATHERED around the feet of the old

white church, its roof sagging toward the earth, bowed under the weight of time and apostasy. The stained glass windows, now caked with layers of dust and grime, mourned their once great brilliance. The steeple still reached for the heavens, but its spire was cracked, its brick crumbling, its faith faltering. The front door, a tall, spectacular piece of carved dark walnut, leaned on its frame, gapping open like the mouth of someone who died of shock, empty, sad, and wanting. The only remaining parishioners, a collection of ancient trees, bowed their limbs forward in futile prayer.

Archard enjoyed the sacrilege of it, the mockery—his Dark covens meeting in this place of goodness and worship to plan and perform their evil deeds. Each time he stepped onto the sacred ground and felt the earth cringe, he smiled.

They gathered now, ten witches trickling into the church, beads of water into one murky puddle. As a ruse to curious outsiders, the church façade remained derelict, but the inside had been fully restored to Archard's particular taste. The walls were draped in black velvet and twelve throne-like chairs formed a circle in the center of the room, their backs towered five feet high, each carved with a triangular symbol at the top representing the Gifts. Archard's chair held an extra symbol: a sun, symbolizing his role as Luminary. In the center of the circle was an iron fire pit, its blazing, crackling fire throwing shadows around the room and puffing its smoke up into the rafters.

The permanently frigid air always smelled of burned things.

Archard sat on his throne, leaning his right elbow on the armrest, observing his coven members with his metallic eyes. Occasionally he stroked his goatee. The seats filled, only two vacant. His eyes lingered on the empty seats for a moment, pondering his plan to fill them. Scorching desire rose in his throat.

Two chairs. Two witches. One solution.

A sheen of sweat threatened to leak out onto his brow. He rolled his neck, breathed deeply and pushed his desires aside with practiced composure. His hard, scrutinizing eyes returned to the gathering witches.

None of the witches looked him fully in the eyes as they sat.

He wasted no time with welcomes or pleasantries. "Why did you call this circle?" he asked with accusation and annoyance.

Eyes shifted around before someone finally answered. A stout, muscular, Native American man, built like a battleship, shifted forward in his chair. He sat beneath the Dreams symbol. "The full moon approaches and we hadn't heard from you in almost a month. I had a dream that Holmes was killed. We want an update."

Archard heaved a petulant sigh. "Leon, I have everything under control, as always."

"Then the Earth witch agreed?" asked the female Air, a slender woman with pale features, a sharp chin, and wicked black eyes. She wore a yellow dress.

Archard raised an eyebrow. "No, Dora, she has not." A

ripple of murmurs moved around the circle and he raised his hand to silence it. "She hasn't agreed because she escaped with the assistance of two undiscovered witches and Ruby Plate's ghost." An uproar of murmurs. "And," Archard yelled, "Holmes was, in fact, killed during the escape."

The murmurs erupted into hisses and shouts. Gavin, the male Air, shot out of his seat, pulling at his tweed sport coat and pushing his glasses up his nose. "How could you let this happen? I knew this was an ill-fated endeavor. We should never have trusted you or Holmes to get the Earth witch to join us. We should have been working on the spell our predecessors attempted and gotten it right. But we trusted you; and now look at us. The blood moon approaches and we have two empty chairs." He exhaled some of his frustration and pushed at his glasses again. "We will never bind a Covenant."

Archard listened to the rant with a slack, expressionless face. When Gavin was finished, Archard casually flicked his hand and the man's shoe spat out fire. Gavin jumped and screamed, dancing around until he could compose himself enough to put forth his own hand and extinguish the flames with a burst of air. Bent in half, hands on knees, huffing and puffing, he scowled at his Luminary.

Archard stood, cool and reserved—almost bored—and brushed at his steel gray lapels. He then turned eyes as hard as flint upon his subordinate. "You forget your place, Gavin." The witch slumped back to his chair.

The other witches watched Archard with trepidation, gripping the arms of their chairs. Angst drifted down from the rafters and hung limply around their heads like wilting halos. They each flinched when Archard's voice boomed out.

"Now, I understand you are concerned, but as Luminary, you must trust in my ability to make things right. Trust in the process. We *will* make this Covenant happen by *this* blood moon. It is our destiny, our duty, our right. If you doubt that, you are welcome to leave." He glared at every witch in the room, challenging those who even thought of defying him.

"Good," he growled when no one moved. "Now, I have broken into the mind of one of the witches who helped Wynter escape, a girl Dreamer. I know exactly where they are." Archard cocked his head and let the extent of his skills sink in for a moment. "We will go and get Wynter, and then I will deal with her myself."

"And what of the empty Mind chair?" Rachel asked, the female Fire, a blond beauty. She gestured a delicate hand at Holmes's empty seat.

"While perusing the girl's mind, I also discovered that the other undiscovered witch is a male Mind."

Rachel scoffed. "A female Dream *and* a male Mind. And with Wynter returned. They have all the members of their covens. A full Covenant!"

The circle erupted, people popping out of chairs and yelling again. Archard allowed their tantrum. He sat in his chair, crossed his legs. "Are you done yet?" he finally said, projecting his voice across the room with an air of authority and power. The words brought an instant hush to the room. The witches took their seats and leaned forward, eager to hear the Luminary's plan.

"Yes, they do have two complete True Covens, but it means nothing unless they can perform the Binding. We have plenty of time. This is our gain, not theirs. You see, they have every-one *we* need." He allowed the moment to stretch, savoring their anticipation. He brushed a piece of lint from his thigh and folded his hands on his lap. "We simply take them both."

AFTER SLEEPING FOR A FEW hours, Willa woke with a stiff neck from leaning against the vibrating Jeep window. She blinked at the early morning light and watched the unfamiliar coun-try along the highway roll by. Rubbing at her neck, she turned to Simon. "Do you need a break?"

He shook his head. "I'm fine. Did you sleep?"

"Yeah, a little." She turned to the backseat. Wynter and Rowan were both awake.

Wynter smiled and leaned forward. "Did you get some rest?"

"Yeah, you?"

"Some." Wynter shrugged. "But now that you're awake, I have something for you." She reached down into a bag on the floor and pulled out three yellow cloth bound books. She held them out. "These are Camille's grimoires. I thought you might like to read them to pass the rest of the drive. She talks about her daughter, Solace, your friend."

Willa took the books. "Thank you. Yes, I'd love to read

them. Solace can't remember her life and she'd be thrilled to learn anything." She frowned, remembering the hurt on Solace's face when she'd told her she was leaving. Maybe these grimoires could be a sort of peace offering for when they got back. Willa blinked back a sudden worry. *If we get back.*

Although Simon had taken away the pain, he couldn't take away the lingering fear of Archard. He'd left behind a film of darkness that she struggled to shake, but wanted desperately to be rid of. She hoped that placing time and distance behind her would help ease her anxiety. She set the books on her lap and opened the first one.

Wynter said, leaning forward, "Camille was an Air. You'll see several of her spells written to music and notes about traveling, finding things for people. Airs are very good at all that. Anyway, most of it is pretty boring, day-to-day stuff, but some of it I know you'll enjoy."

Willa smiled. "Thanks again."

Wynter nodded and then sat back. Willa settled in her seat and started to read. The first several pages detailed Camille's fervent desire to have a child. There were recipes for herbs and potions to help fertility and spells for health. But nothing seemed to be working for her. She wrote:

March 10, 1910

Ronald and I have been married for over ten years now and still no children. I despair that we will never be parents, that the magic will never see fit to send us a healthy, living child. After the sorrow of five miscarriages and the morbid, endless pain of one lost baby, our sweet Connor who lived only an hour, I don't believe I can try anymore. My heart has been broken too many times.

Willa put a hand on her own heart and eagerly read on. Several pages later, Camille wrote:

February 2, 1912

I'm forty years old today. I try to hold on to hope, but I fear I have missed the window of motherhood. I'm too old to carry a child now. I spent most of the day sitting in the rocker by the fire, holding Connor's blanket on my lap.

I didn't know it was possible to ache so much inside, to want for something until it carves out a jagged hole in your heart.

Ruby and Amelia visited today, brought me a chocolate birthday cake. Ruby has been so blessed—a daughter, and now a beautiful granddaughter. I love when they visit, but today it only reminded me of what I will never have. My envy is shameful. I would give all that I have, even my magic, to have a little girl of my own. Someone sweet and beautiful to love, to visit friends with, to make chocolate cake with.

The final entry in the grimoire made Willa cry.

June 2, 1916

Sun and moon be praised! I have a daughter! She is the most beautiful and perfect thing I have ever seen. Her hair is thick and soft, the color of midday sunshine. Her eyes are so round and bright that my first look at them softened all the jagged edges inside me. I knew when Ruby placed her in my arms that she was my savior,

my solace. That will be her name: Solace. Nothing else would fit.
I never thought I would survive the pregnancy, but all that bad is
now forgotten.

She sighs in her sleep next to me and nothing has ever sounded
so sweet.

"That is beautiful," Simon whispered. "Solace will love
to read that."

Willa's head jerked up. "What?"

"I could hear you reading. That last part about Solace is
beautiful." He nodded to the book in her lap.

"Wait, you could *hear* me reading. *In my head?*" Willa
laughed, amazed and also a little uncomfortable.

"Yeah. As soon as you started reading, I could hear the
words in my head. Like you were reading them out loud. I was
gonna say something sooner, but it got interesting." Simon
looked over and frowned. "I'm sorry. I didn't mean to—it just
happened. Are you okay?"

"Yeah, of course. It's fine. It's just a little weird. Right?"

"Yeah."

Willa looked down at the book and pressed her hand to
the page, trying not to feel awkward about Simon being able
to hear her thoughts so easily. She closed the first book and
opened the second. The first page was dated October 16, 1931,
fifteen years later. Confused at the time gap, Willa opened the
third book, but the first date was December 10, 1965.

She turned to Wynter. "There are big gaps in time between these books."

Wynter nodded. "Yes, I know. But Camille only gave us those three books. I have no idea what happened to her others."

Willa looked back at the second book. 1931. Something twitched in her mind, a thought trying to form. *Something is missing. What am I missing?* Then it hit her. That was the year Ruby's house was sold to the mysterious owners. "Wynter, what happened to Ruby and her Covenant?"

Wynter inhaled and exhaled. "Well, we aren't entirely sure. Ruby died young; she was only sixty. So, that is when her grimoire ends, and at that time the Covenant was thriving. The last note in it was to make her granddaughter, Amelia, Luminary of the Covenant. So, we know the Covenant stayed together, at least for a time. There are rumors of some Dark covens coming to Twelve Acres in the early 1930s, but we don't know exactly what happened."

"It's not in Camille's grimoires?"

"No, and she wouldn't tell us when we spoke in Italy."

"Hmm. That's strange."

Wynter nodded and Willa went back to the books. The first entry, under October 16, 1931 simply read:

I planted Lilly in a safe place.

A note on gardening? In mid-October? Confused and intrigued, Willa flipped through the rest of the book. Camille had stopped writing about magic. There were only notes on gardening, her daily routine, a few mentions of neighbors and recipes for dinner meals. Not a spell, not a potion. Nothing.

What happened, Camille? Willa silently asked the pages.

The last entry read:

July 14, 1932

> *Checked on the Lilly today. Safe, healthy, and thriving.*

Something was odd about these notations about a Lilly. Why would Camille capitalize the name of a simple flower, and why did she check on it so often? Willa flipped through the third and last grimoire. It was filled with more boring, magic-free entries, several of which mentioned the Lilly, always in vague, quick notes.

An idea hit her. "Wynter, who's Lilly? Did Camille have another daughter?"

Wynter furrowed her brows. "Lilly? No, I've never heard of a Lilly connected to Camille. Is that in the grimoires?"

"Yes, look." Willa pointed to the first entry in the third book.

December 10, 1965

> *The Lilly has reproduced. So strong, so beautiful. If only she could see her.*

Wynter read the entry and frowned. "Maybe lilies were Camille's favorite flower?"

Willa shook her head. "No, look. She always writes Lilly capitalized and spells it like a *name*, not a flower. And here she says, 'her'—'If only she could see *her*.' I think Lilly was or is a person. Camille was checking up on her, watching her, but trying to keep it secret or at least not obvious."

Wynter's eyes widened. "Wow, you really are a good

historian. I totally missed that when I read those." She shrugged. "You may be right, but I've never heard of any Lilly. Sorry."

Willa sighed and turned back to the front. A tickle of instinct told her that she was right and that Lilly was important. If Camille was trying to protect her then there was a reason. But how could Willa find out more?

She turned to her window. The sun was high in the sky now and more cars spilled onto the roads, carrying people off to busy, normal Saturdays. Willa rubbed absently at the cloth on the books and wondered. *Another mystery.* Maybe Solace would want to help with this one, too. Maybe she could remember who Lilly was. If Camille knew her, there was a good chance Solace did too.

Who are you, Lilly?

Sweet, glorious destruction! The catharsis of it was almost enough to quell Archard's blistering fury. The heat of the fire reached out to him, caressing his face. It tripped happily from fuel to fuel, consuming eagerly, feeding itself. Furniture, books, clothing, wood, metal. It wasn't picky; it would eat everything, its flames growing fat in the gluttony. Destroy and create.

Lustrous orange light radiated from the structure of Rowan and Wynter's cottage, painting itself on the trees, the ground, and the afternoon. The heat of the fire glimmered and moved, like walking vertigo. Bizarre, broken shadows burst to life and danced in a circle around the dying cottage. Sparks sashayed upwards, giving up their light to the cold air. The accustomed quiet of the forest was tainted by the crackle and hiss of the fire.

Archard clenched his jaw, pushed his tongue against his teeth, a statue of black in the orange light. He blinked quickly, the surface of his eyes hot and moist.

Twice! Twice these witches have eluded me. How?

A section of the cottage roof gave way, crumbling into the flames with a satisfying, crunchy *whoosh* of air.

The girl couldn't have recognized him, or suspected what he was up to—he was sure of it. The invasion of her mind should have only brought pain, not understanding of any kind. But the cottage was empty. No Wynter. No boy Mind. No one to channel his anger toward.

He could smell their magic on the air, the thick, gagging smell of Light. It hadn't been long since they left, but their trail was cold, and a magical wall blocked his attempts to find it. A dead end. Anger trembled inside him, as potent and hot as the flames destroying the house. His control was slipping, which made him want to throw more fire at the house, throw it from his hands like punches and to yell, scream and kick. Rachel and Leon stood twenty feet behind him, arms folded, eyes accusing him as if this was his fault.

The handful of days until the blood moon rose up before him in his mind. The days stood shoulder-to-shoulder, legs apart, weapons cocked and aimed. Ready to shoot him down, poke holes in his body, each one a failure. He *had* to bind the

Covenant this year, or the covens would surely turn on him, and everything would be lost.

The fire jumped to a cluster of trees near the front porch and the branches lit like matches, puttering for a brief moment before flaring to life. Archard craned his head upward, his eyes instantly cooling as they moved away from the flames. *Where are they?*

More and more trees caught fire.

Time to go.

He wished he could stand there until everything around him turned to smoldering ash, then breathe in the completed destruction. But time was cocking its gun. One deep breath and he turned and walked away, his head bowed toward the ground in concentration. Rachel and Leon watched Archard approach with wary expressions

Rachel boldly opened her mouth, "What now, Luminary?"

Archard raised his eyes to her, his chin still tucked to his chest. The whites of his eyes sneered at her beneath his hollow irises. She stood her ground and met his stare with equal power.

"We find them," was the cryptic reply. He meant it, but he was at a loss as to *how* to do it. It irritated him like an itch he couldn't scratch, that his cleverness had been trumped— twice. Now, no clues, no plan.

The Dark witch stepped past Rachel and Leon and slid into the car, his fine suit whispering over the leather seat. The door's slam echoed in the forest.

CHAPTER 19
BLOOD MOON

October 1931

Amelia's eyes and forehead itched terribly, covered by a heavy wool cloth. She wanted to drag it off her face, hurl it away, but her hands were also bound behind her back. The air around her smelled fresh, like forest-breath, but also enclosed, like a cave. She shivered, her skin too exposed for the cold October night. She swiveled her head from side to side, following the sounds of feet moving around her and whispers drifting over her head.

Next to her, Solace whimpered.

It's happening. Holy mother moon, it's happening!

Amelia's pulse fluttered, skipping viciously. Her brain seemed to pound within the confines of her skull. Ever since the moment the dark figures had burst into her house, dragged her out into the night, all she could think about was her sweet, tiny Lilly. *Please, dear earth, help Camille keep her safe. And one day, help her to forgive me.*

Solace's whimpers were rising to hysterical sobs. Amelia leaned her face down closer to the sounds. "Solace, I'm here. Take some deep breaths. Stay with me."

Solace hiccupped, whimpered. "What's going on, Amelia? What is going to happen to us? I can sense Dark thoughts. I can feel it all. Holy moon!"

Amelia knew what would happen to herself, but she couldn't tell her poor young friend the truth; she was frightened enough as it was. It was her duty as Solace's friend, and as her Luminary, to keep the situation under control as much as she could. She had to give Solace some kind of hope, some thread of strength, even if it was a lie.

"Solace, listen to me. I need you to calm down. Can you do that please? I'm here. Lock your mind as tight as you can. You don't need to hear any of that." Amelia scooted closer, lowered her voice. "These are the Dark covens. They took us as some part of their plan to break up our Covenant and bind their own. Just like when they lured Peter and the others to that town."

"But they were killed!" she interrupted, her chest heaving with more sobs. "The Covenant is already broken!"

Amelia took a deep breath. "I know, I know, but if we work together, maybe we can find a way to escape, or at least survive long enough for our coven-mates to rescue us. Okay?

I'm here. Just stay with me and lock your mind." She bit her bottom lip and held her breath, wishing she could look her friend in the eyes.

Solace hiccupped again, but then her breathing steadied. "Okay, okay. What do we do?"

"We wait until they leave us alone. Then—"

"No one is going to leave you alone, pretty Amelia," a silky, male voice whispered in her ear. She flinched away from its warmth and evil, and flinched again when a cold finger trailed across her collar bone where her nightgown left the skin exposed.

"Don't touch me!" she spat.

The voice chuckled darkly. His body, so close to hers, smelled of coffee and jasper, his icy fingers lingered at her neck. "I'm going to make you mine, Amelia. I'm going to make you a part of my Dark Covenant. I need one more, and you, my dear, are the lucky one."

Amelia's skin crawled. "You can't force me to join you, not even with magic."

Another laugh, smooth and warm next to her ear. "Oh yes, I can. I found a way. A way to *possess* you." His finger moved over her lips. She snapped her teeth at him, barely missing flesh, shocked at her own ferocity. He laughed, loud this time. "It will be my pleasure to break such a willful spirit." His body shifted away. "And this sweet Mind . . ."

Solace whimpered and Amelia lashed out her feet, kicking toward the sound of his voice. "Stay away from her!"

Two surprisingly strong arms grabbed Amelia's shoulders,

pushed her backwards and pinned her to the ground. Her head hit the rock ground with a sickening *thud*. The man's voice hissed right in her face, his breath moving into her mouth as he spoke. "Control yourself, Amelia. I do not tolerate tantrums." With that he pushed roughly against her and was gone.

Amelia rolled onto her side, curling into herself. Hot tears collected on the wool mask, the soggy fabric now sticking to her skin. Solace whispered her name. Amelia wanted to ignore the girl, to withdraw into herself and wait for what was to come, but she couldn't abandon her terrified friend.

Amelia half-crawled, half-rolled back to Solace. "I'm okay. I'm right here."

Solace began to cry in earnest again. Amelia sat up and leaned her body against Solace's in an effort to give them both some comfort. Several quiet and agonizing hours passed. Solace and Amelia drifted in and out of hazy sleep, propped against each other and resting back on the cold stone of the cave. Then, all at once, as if materializing next to her, the voice was in her ear again.

"It's time, Amelia."

Those same cold, rough hands lifted her up to her feet and ripped the wool blindfold from her face. The light was dim, but she still had to blink her eyes into focus.

No!

There it was.

The landscape she had seen in the water when she was thirteen—the cramped interior of a cave, a stone altar with thick chains, and the two nearly complete Dark covens gathered like wraiths around it, watching her with hollow eyes.

She shook her head. "No." Panic gripped her body and she screamed it, "NO!"

"Oh, yes, my dear." The voice had a face. It was thin and oval, rimmed by neatly trimmed black hair and a beard, dominated by frigid silver eyes. He pushed her toward the altar. She fought, but his strength was too much for her. She tried, for the thousandth time, to summon the magic, but nothing happened. They had put some kind of block on her powers.

She was alone.

Helpless.

Facing her horrible, set-in-stone future.

Another grim figure had dragged Solace to her feet. The girl was whimpering and collapsing in his grip. Amelia turned to her captor. "Let her go. You don't need her. Just let her go. Please."

Her desperate plea had no effect on the madman beside her.

"Actually, we *do* need her," he said, sounding perversely amused.

He jerked his head, signaling to the witch holding Solace, who then dragged the girl closer, placing her in front of Amelia. The Dark Luminary ripped away the trembling girl's blindfold, and Amelia stared directly into her friend's wide, terrified eyes. She groaned with the emotion of watching Solace suffer, so innocent, so scared. *Why Solace? Camille must be going out of her mind.*

Solace's face was an abyss of terror, swallowing Amelia whole. "Please," Amelia begged again, "please let her go. I will stay, do whatever you want."

The silver-eyed man brought his lips to her ear. "So sorry, Amelia, but she is the key to our little spell. Her blood will bind your possession." His hand shot forward to grip Solace's head, his fingers a claw around her crown. She squirmed, her cropped blond hair shifting and tangling across her eyes. Thick rain-drop tears drowned her face, and her whimpers climbed into a high-pitched scream.

Amelia's arms were passed to another witch, his grip painfully strong. The bearded man then brought his other hand to her head, exactly how Solace was treated. The cold of his fingers seeped into her scalp, chilling her whole body. The man whispered under his breath, mumbling words Amelia couldn't hear. She bucked and pushed against the hands that held her and thrashed her head, but it was useless.

As the Dark man whispered his spell, Amelia felt her body grow colder and colder. She stopped thrashing and looked into Solace's weepy eyes, holding her gaze.

"Amelia?" Solace whispered.

"I'm so sorry, Solace," was all Amelia could whisper back. A quiet resolve fogged over Solace's face which made Amelia's heart die a hundred deaths.

Amelia cried out as a flash of electric pain shot through her body to complete the spell. Solace screamed, too, even louder and more agonizing. Breathless and freezing, Amelia watched in horror as the man holding Solace brought his arm around, hooking it forward, a knife flashing in his grip. He drew the knife over Solace's pale, exposed throat. Solace's eyes flashed in total horror as crimson blood spilled out onto her favorite purple dress, and Amelia's nightgown and bare feet.

The scream that ripped from Amelia's body reverberated off the cave walls and startled the trees in the forest outside.

Solace's body crumpled to the ground. Nothing could stop it now.

The magic churned and swelled above Amelia, a thick, dark cloud, a hurricane thirsty for a path of destruction. She shrank away, pulling her body down against the stone altar. The eleven shadowy figures, their faces lost in the fog of the spell, loomed over her frail body, like vultures sniffing out a meal.

Nothing could free her.

The possession spell would soon be completed and she'd be a part of their covens, a puppet forced to fill whatever role the nefarious Luminary desired. He would possess her mind, body, and magic.

She would rather die.

Please let me die. Please let me not survive this spell.

Amelia's wrists and ankles were raw and slick with blood under the thick metal chains that had been screwed into the stone floor of the cave. Spell after spell, whispered under her breath, failed to break the shackles, and her strength was nearly gone from tugging and pulling at them. Her wounds throbbed with every breath and flared with pain at the slightest movement.

The black cloud above her continued to roil and crackle with building energy. Amelia tried to pull her attention from it, to coax her mind into another place, another time. A mist of desperate tears clouded her vision, but she locked her eyes on one small patch of her white nightgown that was still clean, still untouched by the events of the night. A small white circle, white as snow.

A memory came, sudden and shocking in its beauty. The cave, the darkness, and the pain all fell away.

The winter solstice, many years ago.

Snow fell outside the windows of her childhood home, wrapping the world in white, spreading cozy silence through the streets of Twelve Acres. Her mother woke her just before dawn, as was their custom on winter solstice. With her tiny five-year-old hand held tightly in her mother's, and sleep a happy memory on her heavy eyes, Amelia followed her mother into the living room.

Grandma Ruby, crouched at the hearth, was building a fire, the scrape and shuffle of the wood breaking the morning silence. Her mother left her with Ruby and went to the kitchen. Amelia stood next to her grandma and watched as she snapped her fingers to bring the flames to life, the deep yellow light reaching out to bathe the room in heat. The wood crackled sleepily and the snow whispered on the windowsill.

Amelia studied the strong, beautiful profile of her

grandmother—her auburn hair woven with silver, her green eyes as bright as ever. Her child heart swelled with love and admiration for Ruby—grandma, friend, witch, and mentor.

The scent of cinnamon and chocolate floated in from the kitchen, a special breakfast prepared for after their ritual.

Ruby moved to the armchair near the fireplace and beckoned Amelia to sit in her lap. "Why do we build the fire, my love?"

Amelia climbed into Ruby's soft lap and said dutifully, "To welcome the sun's returning light and to celebrate the longer days ahead."

Ruby smiled, the wrinkles around her eyes warming with the growing firelight. "That's right. And why do we wake just before dawn?"

"To ring the bells and watch the sunrise." Eager to please and prove her knowledge, she added, "The bells call to the earth, asking for protection and good magic."

Ruby kissed her cheek and hugged her close. "So smart, my little witch."

Mother came back into the room, a black box in her hands, followed by Grandpa Charles and Amelia's dad. Amelia scrambled down and ran over to pull her own special bell from the box. It was small, silver, and hung from a black, silk ribbon. It also had her name engraved on it in swirly letters. This special bell was saved only for winter solstice. Amelia had never heard anything produce as pure a sound as her winter bell. Her tiny fingers tingled to hold it.

Mother handed her the bell with a smile. "The solstice is

a time to remember that death is not an end, but a rebirth. The future is nothing to fear. The sun always comes up in the morning no matter how dark the night."

Dawn's first joyful sunbeam burst into the room. Amelia ran to the window and lifted her bell. The snow paused in its descent, bowing reverently to the sunrise. Together, the family rang their bells.

The tinkling sound of the bells echoed in Amelia's head as reality pulled her back, a stinging slap to the face. The pain rushed back, assaulting every nerve, and she cried out in agony. This was her endless night and there would be no rising sun, no redemption, no salvation. And death—this awful kind of death—was not something good, not something that would bring rebirth.

It would only bring more pain.

Lasting, lingering long after her neurons stopped firing.

Endless pain.

One ghostly figure stepped toward her—the Luminary, his tall, thin, lethal body more intimidating than before. The stench of evil, of Dark, oozed from his skin and turned her stomach. He lifted his hand and a whimper escaped her lips despite her best efforts to remain strong. Dangling in the air, dripping down from his fingers, was a long silver chain and pendant. A crude piece, soldered by an unskilled hand, but plain in its purpose. The pendant was formed into the shape of a fat diamond with two stick legs—the symbol for possession. Amelia shook her head, tried to move away, fiery pain erupting as her body protested the movement.

The witch dropped the silver chain over her head and pulled it into place around her neck. Where the pendant touched her bare chest, the skin froze and died in an instant. Terror moved through her in thick waves and she knew her mind and body could not take much more.

Her chest ached as the necrosis from the necklace spread outward. She shivered and sweated all at once. Ruby's face flashed before her eyes. "I'm sorry, Grandma," she cried. "So sorry!"

The Luminary stepped back into the circle and raised his hands to the swirling spell cloud. She knew this was the moment; she'd seen it in the water years ago. But what she didn't know was the outcome. She would either be fully possessed or die.

Please let me die. Sun and moon, I beg you. Let me die!

The hurricane of magic was given a path.

A terrible scream ripped from her body, so shrill and awful that her own ears didn't recognize the sound.

Then, there was only blackness.

CHAPTER 20
WAXING CRESCENT

Present Day, October

It was nearly five in the afternoon before Simon pulled up in front of the gate to the ranch. The black gate had straight, narrow posts, and at the top, where the two halves met, the iron had been formed into a picture of a roaring fire. The gate was attached to a tall, gray stone wall that extended out in both directions, marking the boundaries of the property.

He looked around for a keypad or lock. "So, how do we get in?" He looked at Wynter and Rowan in the rearview mirror. Rowan smiled and lifted his hand. With a wave of his fingers the gate opened. Simon raised his eyebrows and looked over at Willa, who was blinking at the gate. Simon drove through.

The narrow dirt drive was lined with huge maple trees, their leaves a brilliant ruby for fall. He had never seen such vibrant foliage; he leaned over the steering wheel for a better look. Soon the house came into view beyond the red trees.

Positioned on a slight rise in the ground, the impressive lodge-style log home boasted large windows and a steeply pitched roof supported by cedar character posts. The lower half of the façade was decorated with pristine stonework. Above, round handcrafted logs glowed yellow in the afternoon light, the white chinking visible between them. Behind the home, the Teton Mountains rose, jagged, angular, touched by the pink of the sun that was beginning to set.

Simon parked his Jeep and they all hurried out of the car, their bodies stiff and humming from the road. Willa moved to him and took his hand. "Look at his place," she whispered. He nodded, staring at the impressive, luxury home.

The front door opened and a woman came bounding out, whooping in excitement. She was middle-aged, probably Wynter and Rowan's age, with lovely curves and pleasant features. She wore a pink pearly-snap shirt and a pair of dark-wash skinny jeans tucked into turquoise cowboy boots. Her long blond hair trailed out behind her as she ran to Wynter, nearly knocking her over as she threw her arms around her friend.

"Holy mother moon! I never thought I'd see ya again." She pulled back, looking at Wynter from head to toe, tears running down her cheeks. "Poor thing! You are so skinny and . . ." she gasped and reached for Wynter's scarred arm. "Oh, honey!" She threw her arms back around Wynter's neck.

Finally, Wynter was able to pull away and give introductions. "Simon and Willa, this is Darby. She's our female Fire."

Darby turned her bright hazel eyes on the couple. She gasped and put her hands to her mouth. "Sun and moon, aren't you two the cutest things ever!" Then she rushed forward and Simon winced as she pulled them both into a crushing hug. Willa laughed. Darby drew back. "I can't thank y'all enough for bringing our Wynter back and now you're joining our little covens and helping us form the Covenant." She heaved a dramatic sigh. "I just can't believe how things have worked out."

Simon opened his mouth to protest. The Covenant? They hadn't agreed to that yet and he didn't think they could. He'd been planning to bring it up on the drive, but he and Willa hadn't had a chance to talk about it alone, to discuss and decide. He'd only agreed to come to Jackson to keep Willa safe. He didn't think that was implied consent. They'd only just found out they were witches. How could they join a coven and be part of something as huge as a Covenant? Things were already getting too out of control for his comfort; he wasn't about to join up with a group of witches who were battling other witches, one of whom had broken into Willa's mind.

Before he had a chance to say anything, Darby grabbed one of his hands and one of Willa's. "Come on ya poor things. In the house. Come meet everyone, have some supper and then I bet ya'd like a nice hot shower and some sleep, right?" She didn't wait for a response and proceeded to drag them behind her into the house.

The inside of the house was even more grand and impressive than the outside, all exposed wood, stone work and fine leather furniture. Conversation and laughter floated in the air, growing louder as they moved through the house. Darby pulled them into the massive kitchen where several more people were gathered around a long wooden table. All noise ceased the moment Simon and Willa entered the room.

Simon frowned at the large antler chandelier above the table, swallowed and felt his cheeks grow hot. All eyes turned on them; he could see the expectations written on every face and feel the emotions in the air. He glanced over at Willa. She looked as apprehensive as he did.

Darby charged immediately into introductions. "Look y'all! I want you to meet our new babies." She swept them into her arms and pulled them closer to the table. "This little lovely is Willa, our new Dreamer, and this handsome young stud is Simon, our Mind. Aren't they adorable?"

A swarm of people advanced on him and Willa, offering hellos, nice-to-meet-yous, and glad-you're-heres. Simon wanted to push away from them and run. But he gritted his teeth against the onslaught of their greetings and their emotions, more uncomfortable with each passing moment at the thought that they'd already assumed he and Willa had agreed to join them.

Finally, Darby shooed them all back to the table. "Okay,

kids, now let me give you the tour of all these crazies." She pointed to two younger people. "Those two there are Charlotte and Elliot. They are your gift counterparts. Charlotte is a Mind and Elliot a Dreamer. You'll want to be best-friends with them 'cause they can help you the most with your gifts."

Willa lifted a hesitant hand and waved. Charlotte was petite with the look of a porcelain doll—white skin, red lips, and dark blond hair tied back in one long braid. She wore a red sweater and jeans. Elliot was also short, but broad and muscular, like a wrestler. His black hair was cut close to his head, and his skin and eyes were the color of milk chocolate. He wore a white polo shirt and faded jeans. Simon guessed they were both about his and Willa's age. Elliot's arm was around Charlotte's shoulders, so he also assumed they were a couple.

Darby moved on. "That big cowboy right there is my husband, Cal, and our other Fire." She pointed to a large man, even taller than Simon, with a weathered, tanned face and big, light brown eyes. He nodded and smiled. "Those two over there," Darby pointed to an elderly woman with dusty gray hair and another middle-aged man wearing geeky, horn-rimmed glasses, "are Hazel and Toby, our Airs." Simon nodded stiffly.

Next, Darby's finger moved to an Asian girl, mid-twenties, with spiky black-blue hair and tattoo-sleeved arms, and another cowboy, early thirties, dressed in a carefully ironed denim shirt and sporting a large black Stetson. He tipped his hat as Darby said, "And finally these are our Waters.

Rain—yes, that's her real name; her parents went for the obvious there—and Corbin." Rain rolled her eyes, but smiled.

Exhaling, Darby turned back to Simon and Willa. "And, of course, our Earths, Wynter and Rowan round out the two covens." She pointed to them as they came into the room and sat at the table. "So, have a seat and we'll start dinner."

Simon didn't move and neither did Willa. He wasn't about to sit down with all these people and pretend everything was fine and that they were a part of the covens. He looked over at Willa and she moved around Darby, taking his arm.

"Actually, Darby, I really don't feel good. You know, after what happened . . ." Willa touched her head.

Darby brought her hands to her chest, "Oh, yes, you poor thing. Wynter told me all about it when she called. Here, I'll take you to your room and send up some food in a bit. Will that be okay?"

Willa nodded. "Thank you," she said weakly. Simon looked down at her, confused; he hadn't sensed any pain from her. She flicked her eyes up to him and gave him a just-go-with-it look. So, he put his arm around her and supported her while they followed Darby to one of the many guest rooms.

DARBY FUSSED FOR A MINUTE before finally leaving Willa and Simon alone. Willa exhaled and threw herself on the big four-poster bed dressed in a patchwork quilt. Darby had lit a fire in the large stone fireplace with a snap of her fingers and pulled the cream-colored curtains over the large windows.

Willa lay on her back, looking up at the wooden beams, hands on her stomach. Simon sat down next to her. "Are you okay?"

"Yes, I'm fine, but I couldn't stay down there and I could tell you didn't want to either." She smiled when Simon sighed in relief.

"Good! What's going on? We never agreed to join the Covenant."

Willa shook her head, sharing Simon's frustration. "I know. I'm as surprised as you are. Did Wynter and Rowan tell them we agreed, or is everyone just assuming since we're here?"

He scoffed. "Wish I knew."

She sat up and crossed her legs, sitting beside him. She rested her chin on his shoulder. "What do we do?" Simon was so careful about all his decisions. She knew he had already made a list of concerns and possible actions in his head. She was too confused to know which way to go. Part of her wanted to join, to be with other people like her, other witches. Her instincts were pushing her in that direction, but she had no idea what the reality of joining the covens would be. Her experiences since meeting Wynter hadn't exactly been encouraging.

"Well, first, we need to talk to Wynter and Rowan and tell them we have *not* agreed to join," Simon said. "I think we need to train with them, learn about witchcraft and magic for a while before we can even come close to making that decision. Don't you think?"

Willa nodded. "Yes, I do."

There was a knock on the door. Simon got up and answered it, pulling the door wide open when he found Wynter and Rowan there with a tray of food. Wynter came over to the bed and sat by Willa while Rowan set the tray down on a table by the window. Wynter put her hand on Willa's knee. "I'm so sorry about that. Darby jumped to conclusions. She's a bit . . . enthusiastic about things, as I'm sure you gathered." She smiled. "We know you haven't agreed yet and we'd never assume to speak for you."

Willa exhaled in relief. "That is good to hear. We got a little nervous down there. It's not that we necessarily *don't* want to join. It's just that . . . well . . ."

Simon handed Willa a plate of roasted chicken, mashed potatoes, and green beans and then sat on the bed with his own. "We need to know more," he finished for her.

"Of course, you do," Rowan said. "This is absolutely your decision. We are not here to pressure you. We are here to talk, to help."

"Do you have more questions we can answer?" Wynter asked.

"Will we have to leave Twelve Acres, school and all that?" Willa asked, scooping potatoes onto her fork.

"No, not necessarily," Wynter answered. "You've come to us at an unusual time. There aren't always Dark witches determined to destroy us." She put a hand on her scars, a shadow moving over her face. "Most of the time we live fairly normal lives, coming together as witches and covens on a regular basis. Everyone lives their own lives and has their own homes. We're not asking you to give that up. We'd really just like to add to your lives by giving you knowledge about and control over your gifts and powers. And also offer the support and strength that the covens provide."

"However," Rowan said, "if you did join the covens and we bound a Covenant, life would not be risk free. Even if we are able to defeat Archard, which we plan to, that doesn't mean there won't be other Dark threats in the future. Witch-craft at this level is a high stakes game. We command great magic and power, but with that comes greater danger."

"What is going to happen with Archard?" Willa asked, a shiver of fear running down her neck.

"We'll have to fight him," Rowan said, crossing his arms over his chest. "Oh, don't worry; we're safe for now. The ranch is very well protected, but Archard is a powerful witch. Either he'll track us down or we will go to him. There are less than two weeks until the blood moon. He's desperate to bind his Dark Covenant, and he can't do that with us in the way. He'll know from looking in your mind Willa that we have all the witches we need to form a Covenant and he will want to stop that. You see, if we bind the Powers, he can't. Only one Covenant can exist at a time, whether Light or Dark."

Another shiver of fear moved through Willa as she looked over at Simon who frowned down at his food. Without looking up, he said, "What's the blood moon and why is it so important?"

"It's the full moon in October," Rowan explained. "Witches have a name for every full moon. The blood moon is a time of change, or death as the earth prepares for winter, but it is also a time of great power. On this one night, the veil between our world and the Otherworld thins and the magic is powerful enough to bind a Covenant. It cannot be done any other time."

"So, it's a race to the blood moon and we are the best answer to defeating Archard?" Simon said tersely. "That doesn't sound like giving us much of a choice."

Rowan and Wynter looked at each other. Wynter said, "The last time a Dark witch formed a Covenant the world was thrown into the Dark Ages. If Archard is allowed to rule the Powers of the Earth, *everyone* will suffer. I know that sounds very doomsday-ish, but it's true. With a Dark witch at the helm, the whole balance of the earth and everything in it will be thrown off. Yes, the best defense against Archard or any dark threat is to Bind a Covenant."

"If *we* bind a Light Covenant," Rowan added, "then we maintain the balance, even improve it, offering the earth a time of great magic. As well as preventing any witch from forming a Dark Covenant."

Willa set down her plate, her stomach now too tight with anxiety to eat. She looked at Simon and hoped he would hear her thoughts. *What do we say to that?*

Simon's eyes widened as he heard. He answered back,

mind to mind, *Yesterday we didn't even know we were witches, now they want us to save the freaking world? There's nothing to say to that.*

Watching them closely, Wynter said, "I know that makes it sound like you don't actually have a choice, but you still do. We can fight Archard, and defeat him before the blood moon. We don't *have* to form a Covenant just because we can. Besides, his covens are now missing two witches. He's already crippled. It would be a miracle if he found two witches to join him in the next week."

"But you've been working to form a Covenant for almost fifteen years. Isn't that what you said, Wynter?" Willa asked.

Wynter looked down at the quilt, tracing her fingers along the pattern. "Yes. It's our dream, but we don't want that dream to be fulfilled at the risk of *your* wants and dreams."

Willa's shoulders sagged forward, heavy under the burden of the decision before them.

A moment of silence stretched out between them. "Why don't you get some sleep?" Wynter said. "Tomorrow we will do a crash course in magic and start your training. After you have a little better feel for the magic and for everyone in the covens, you can make a decision. Sound good?"

"Okay," Willa said quietly.

Wynter gave her a small smile and then she and Rowan moved to the door. Before they left, Simon looked up and asked, "How long would we have to be a part of the Covenant? Could we join just long enough to help stop Archard?"

"The Covenant is *for life*," Rowan said, his head hung low. "It is only broken when a coven-mate dies."

LATER THAT NIGHT, WILLA LAY awake, staring at the darkness, listening to Simon breathe. Despite her aching exhaustion, she could not turn off her mind, couldn't stop thinking about joining the Covenant and worrying about what Archard might be planning. Mostly, she couldn't stop remembering what it felt like to have him push into her mind and rob her of her thoughts. That sense of violation would never leave her.

Her phone buzzed from the nightstand and she closed her eyes in annoyance. She didn't want to worry about her mom, about her attempts to apologize. There were too many more important things to worry about—contemplating forgiveness for a lifetime of betrayal was not one of them.

With a sigh, Willa lifted the phone and squinted at the bright screen. The text, one of nearly twenty piled in her inbox, read: *Please let me know you're okay! You can be mad, but I need to know you are safe. So does Dad. We love you!*

Willa had sent exactly one text since leaving Twelve Acres. She sent it as soon as they arrived at Wynter's cottage and all it said was: *We are there.* As mad as she was, she didn't want her parents wondering if she was alive or dead. So, she entered a reply: *I'm fine. I'm safe.*

Her thumb hovered over the send button. She thought of telling her mom they had moved on from Wynter's to the ranch, but knew it would take far more explanation than she had energy for, and would also just increase her parents' panic.

She pushed send, put the phone back and rolled over.

CHAPTER 21
Waxing Crescent

Present Day, October

Wynter and Rowan stood off to the side near the edge of the yard while Simon and Willa attempted to learn how to lift and move an object with magic. Wynter smiled when Simon succeeded after the second try.

"I feel awful," she said to Rowan.

"Why?" he asked. His beard had a bit of dust in it and his ponytail was slightly askew from an earlier attempt to help Willa blow away a pile of leaves by controlling the air. There were scraps of leaves on his black tunic shirt and linen pants.

Wynter brushed at the leaves on his shirt. "Because we've placed them in an impossible position. By helping me, they are now in grave danger, and their lives will never be the same."

"Yes, but they have also discovered who they really are. That's priceless, and I think they understand that. Sometimes sacrifices have to be made of an old life to live a better one."

"But is it really better? Being the target of Archard's anger? I know that hasn't been very good for us." Wynter pulled at the long sleeve of her green jersey dress.

Rowan reached out, took her arm and kissed the back of her hand where the oldest scars were. "We knew there would be sacrifices. And the rewards may still prove to be very sweet. Look at those two. Have you ever seen an undiscovered witch, especially one already into adulthood, pick up the magic so quickly? And Simon—he's incredibly powerful."

Wynter watched Willa levitate several pieces of firewood and move them across the yard, her face red with concentration. When she set them down on the target spot, the group erupted in cheers.

Wynter smiled. "No, I haven't."

"They are meant to be with us. The magic knows that, and soon they will, too."

WILLA ACCEPTED THE HIGH FIVES and congratulations from the other witches. All morning, she and Simon had been testing out the magic, forming basic skills. At first she'd been so nervous, but soon, with the help of the others, she'd grown comfortable, even started to enjoy it. Simon on the other hand, though doing incredibly well, had been quiet and withdrawn all morning. Lost inside his head, thinking things out.

After talking with Wynter and Rowan last night, she and Simon had crawled into bed and said little about what they'd learned. They were exhausted, having only slept a few hours in the last two days. Simon said they could talk about what to do after some good sleep and training. But while she was feeling much better about things, Simon didn't appear to be.

Charlotte, the other Mind, came running over, her long braid bouncing behind her. "Willa! That was awesome. You are doing so well."

Willa smiled shyly. Charlotte was being especially attentive and helpful, and Willa liked her. She reminded her of Solace. "Thanks, Charlotte."

"How many times do I have to tell you, call me Char. Everyone does and it's much easier to say than Char-o-let-te," she said, dragging out the syllables of her name.

"Okay. Thanks, Char."

"Much better. Now, how about a drink break? You and Simon come with me and Elliot back in the kitchen for some water. Elliot wants to talk to you about dreams and I can ask Simon about his mind." On cue, Elliot arrived with Simon at his side, after which Char proceeded to lead them into the kitchen.

Darby was there, pouring them all tall glasses of water. She set a plate of chocolate chip cookies on the table. "Cookies are health food around here, so eat up." Then, she slipped outside, leaving the two couples in peace.

Willa gulped down half her water and began nibbling a cookie. Simon pulled two cookies from the plate.

"Okay," Char said. She and Elliot sat across the table. "Go ahead, Elliot."

Elliot smiled, his teeth extra white against his dark skin. "Willa, from what Wynter has told me, it sounds like you are a very proficient Dreamer, so I don't think there is much I can help you with except for a Dream Cradle." He reached into his pocket and pulled out a small blue pouch, which he placed on the table in front of her.

The pouch was made of a soft velvety material and on it was inked the symbol of a single eye looking to the side. Willa ran her finger over the symbol, the fabric warm to the touch. "What does it do?" she asked.

"It records all your dreams."

She looked up, surprised. "Records them?"

"Yep. Open it," Elliot instructed.

Willa tugged open the purse strings and carefully tipped the contents out on the table. A milky white, oval shaped stone slid toward her, followed by two sprigs of fresh lavender.

Pointing at the stone, Elliot said, "That's a moonstone. It will record and hold your dreams. It's powered by the herbs and a spell. Keep the Cradle by your bed, and before you go to sleep say this spell: *Dream Cradle, take this dream of mine. Moonstone, hold it until the right time.*" Elliot took a cookie. "Sometimes the hardest part about dreams is remembering all the details, all the little things that could mean something big. Right?"

Willa nodded. "Yes, definitely."

"That's where the Dream Cradle comes in. It keeps everything safe, and when you need to remember something, you can view the whole dream by using another spell: *Dream Cradle, reveal your nighttime keep. Moonstone, reveal what you hold deep.*" Elliot reached into his other pocket. "Here, I wrote them down for you." He handed her a folded and slightly smashed piece of paper.

"Thanks, Elliot." Willa tucked the stone, herbs, and spells back in the pouch, imagining what might happen when she wanted to look at one of her dreams.

Charlotte turned her attention to Simon. "So do you have any questions about being a Mind? Wynter said she already gave you the mind-lock spell."

"Right, and I can tell it's working. I don't feel nearly as many emotions and feelings as I normally do."

"That's good. The best thing to do is practice opening and closing that door. Sometimes you *do* want to know what others are feeling and thinking. Like in a fight against a Dark witch. It's pretty handy to open that door just enough to get a feel for what he might do. But you don't want him pushing in on your mind, so you have to be good at quickly closing it or only leaving it open a little. Does that make any sense?"

Simon nodded, "I think so."

"Try it now. Close your eyes and picture your door." Char waited while Simon complied. "Now, I want you to crack the door open just a little and see if you can sense how many people are still outside."

Willa watched Simon's face harden in concentration. This morning he'd been reluctant to try different things with the magic, but now he was more willing. After a few seconds he said, "There are . . . five people."

"Good. Can you tell who? That's a lot harder, especially since you don't know us that well yet," Char said.

Simon squeezed his eyes tighter. "It's . . . Wynter, Rowan . . . Darby . . . Hazel and . . . Rain, I think."

"Whoa! Very nice, Simon. Okay, let's try this. Can you tell me where the others are?" Char leaned forward, watching Simon closely.

The air around Simon stirred and grew slightly warmer. Willa waited, wondering if he could do it. "Umm . . . Cal is somewhere with horses. Toby and Corbin are in the front of the house. And . . . we are all right here." Simon exhaled and opened his eyes. "Is that right?"

Char raised her hand. "High five! That's incredible. You shouldn't be able to do that for like a year."

Simon returned her high five and blushed. "I didn't realize I could do that. I mean, I can always sense Willa, but I'd never tried to find anyone else."

Willa smiled. "Pretty cool. Good job."

Darby burst back into the room. "Okay, kids, time to play with fire. First one to get burned loses." She grinned and wagged her eyebrows.

Willa turned to Simon. "Fire? Really?"

He shrugged. "I guess we'll give it a try." He leaned closer, "And if you get burned, I can always heal you." He smiled and Willa laughed, happy to see him letting go of some of the seriousness that had plagued him earlier.

"Well, that's very lucky 'cause I have a bad feeling about playing with fire. I was afraid of fireworks until I was like fifteen," Willa said.

Simon laughed, kissed her quickly and pulled her to her feet.

LATE THAT NIGHT SIMON CRAWLED in bed next to Willa. Her shower-wet hair smelled like lavender and citrus, her skin glowed pink. He couldn't resist reaching down to run his hand over the soft skin on her legs. She smiled sleepily up at him. "What are you thinking?" she asked.

"All kinds of things," he raised his eyebrows at her playfully.

She laughed loudly and he drank in the happy sound. "That's not what I meant!"

He leaned down to kiss a sliver of bare skin at her waist, where her tank-top had lifted slightly. He closed his eyes when she sighed. "Suddenly, I'm not very tired," he said into her skin.

She laughed again and tugged on his arm. He reluctantly relented and lay down next to her, pulling her close, nuzzling his face into her divinely scented neck. "But you smell so good."

"I want to hear how you feel about *today*. What you're thinking about the magic and everything," she said.

Simon sighed and pulled his face out of her neck. "How I feel about today, huh? Well, I feel . . . tired. They worked us really hard."

She gently slapped his arm. "You know that's not what I mean."

Simon smiled. "Yeah, sorry." He narrowed his eyes in thought, trying to decide exactly how he felt. "I've never felt like that before."

"What do you mean?" Willa shifted her head and concentrated on his face.

"I guess, like I *belonged*. You know? I didn't expect that."

She nodded. "Yeah."

"And I liked that feeling."

"Me, too."

"Does that mean I think we should up and join their Covenant?" He pushed a hand back through his hair. "I don't know."

"I don't know either. I go back and forth in my mind. It's hard to get past that *for life* thing Rowan said last night." Willa's hand found his face and ran her fingers over the two-day stubble he'd been too lazy to shave off. He closed his eyes at her warm touch.

"That is definitely hard to swallow," he said. "I like these people and I find myself trusting them. And I love how it feels to control the magic. I think I've been looking for that feeling my whole life."

"Me, too. We are witches, Simon. Have you said it out loud yet? It's a strange sensation."

He smiled. "We are witches. We are witches." A curl of heat moved over their heads. "Okay, that *is* a weird sensation."

"And we can do magic."

"And we can do magic." Simon exhaled. "Very surreal."

"Very."

"I suppose we still have a couple of days before we need to decide."

"Yeah, a little more time with the magic might help make things clearer." Willa dropped her hand to his chest. "I hope, anyway."

"Yeah, but I don't know if I can get past the thing with Archard. He already hurt you once. I don't really want to willingly step into a fight with him." Simon pulled her closer.

Willa shivered. "I agree. Having him in my head was bad enough. I can't imagine meeting that awful man in person."

Simon kissed her hair. "Let's get some sleep and see what tomorrow brings. There's nothing we can do but take this one small step at a time."

They lay in silence for a few minutes before Simon felt himself drift off to sleep.

A FEW HOURS LATER WILLA was lost inside the mystical world of a dream.

She ran. Hard and fast. Even faster. Her feet ached each time they hit the cold, hard earth. Her lungs burned, screaming for more air, her heart pounded, pleading for a rest.

No. Faster!

The thick crescent moon grinned, its milky-silver light lengthening the shadows, giving the night an ethereal creepiness. Willa felt Archard's Dark magic pursuing her, its long-reaching fingers clawing at her back. It urged her to stop, to relent and give up, but she couldn't. Simon was in trouble and their deep-rooted love, their incorruptible connection pushed her past her limits.

Faster! Simon, I'm coming!

Tall, spindly trees flashed past her line of sight, blending together in one unending scene of forest. She dodged branches as best she could, but they reached out and clawed at her face, arms and legs. In her haste, she hardly noticed the pain.

The *huff huff* of her breath reverberated off the trees and circled back to her ears, labored and loud. The trees finally gave way to a clearing. On the other side of the clearing was the yawning, black mouth of a cave. Willa hurled herself toward it, but when she tried to enter she met a solid, invisible wall.

She pressed her hands to the cold barrier and then began pounding, yelling. *Simon! Simon!* In the cave there was only thick darkness as she strained her eyes to see through it. Then suddenly, Simon appeared, standing far back in the chamber, his eyes closed, skin deathly pale, face spotted with blood.

Simon! I'm here! Simon!

But he didn't open his eyes. Willa continued to pound and kick the wall until her hands and feet were bloody pulp. She collapsed to the ground, sobbing. A deafening series of cracks louder than thunder split the night in two. She flinched, clapping her hand protectively over her ears. Rolling to her back, she looked up at the sky through the canopy of trees.

White lines spread across the sky like cracks in dried mud, as bright and terrifying as lightning, and moving alarmingly fast. Then, like a million mirrors dropping onto a stone floor, the sky shattered, snapped, and fell apart. Sharp shards, as bright and silvery as glass, tumbled down toward the earth. All around her the shards struck the ground, slicing and stabbing. Some were as big as a house while others as small as raindrops.

She spun around and peered into the cave. Simon was gone; her chest tightened with fear and pain.

Thud thud thud.

The shards fell faster. As Willa struggled to her feet, scrambling to get out of the way, one of the pieces of sky tore a deep gash in her forearm. The pain pushed her onward, her need for shelter overwhelming her horrified fascination. She searched frantically for a place to hide and found a small opening in an outcropping of rock coming off the cave.

She put her head down and ran, the shards slicing and bruising her. The dark area between two large boulders winked at her. She skidded to a stop, slamming into the rocks, before dropping to the ground to try and squeeze her battered body into the space. She managed to push her head, torso, and hips inside, almost safe, when a large dagger-shaped shard pierced her calf, slicing all the way through the muscle, pinning her to the ground.

Willa woke up with a jolt, pain radiating from her calf. She tossed the blankets back and inspected her leg—normal, safe. *Just a dream. Just a dream.*

When she turned to look at Simon, all she found was cold, empty bed.

CHAPTER 22
WAXING CRESCENT

Present Day, October

Archard's pristine appearance had slipped into disrepair over the course of a day. His hair was mussed, shooting out in chaotic, crusty threads. He hadn't shaved and his goatee was morphing into a beard. The white dress shirt he wore was wrinkled and sweat-stained, and he had rolled the sleeves up to his elbows. He'd eaten only scraps and emptied too many bottles of Scotch.

The air in his office was stale and tired, trapped behind the thick door and heavy drapes. A fire blazed in the magnificent fireplace, sucking more clean oxygen out of the space. The walls watched nervously, cringing each time empty bottles were hurled at them; several black rings in the carpet still smoked from angry punches of fire.

Archard stood with his forehead to the smooth surface of the mantel, mumbling incoherently, tapping a finger nervously on his thigh. *Nothing is working. Where the hell are they? There has to be a way to find them!*

Behind him, the desk was half buried under at least a dozen different books. He'd emptied his shelves, dragging each and every grimoire from his extensive collection to the desk. It was an impressive display of magical records, some as ancient as the written word. Some were stolen, some paid for, some killed for. After all, knowledge was power, and the more he had available to him, the more power he had to build upon. But none of it was helping him now, the fire-hot emotion of his want threatening to cook his sanity.

A quiet knock came at the door.

"What?' Archard roared, his voice cracking in his desert-dry throat.

The door creaked open a few inches and the white, drawn face of his dreary butler appeared. "A package, sir." The edge of a brown box passed the boundary of the door and hovered in the air.

Archard leaped across the room and pounced on the box without a word. He pushed the door shut and hurried over to his desk. With a wave of his hand he sent the stacks of books flying in every direction, an avalanche of pages. He ripped into the rectangular package.

The packing paper tossed aside, Archard stared down at

his last resort with hungry, blood-shot eyes. A grimoire, the most important one ever. He'd heard rumors about it years ago, but now he hoped they were true; he *needed* them to be true. It'd taken his man nearly a year to track this book down.

Now, here it was, in his hands, and it couldn't have come at a more dire moment. Archard took it as a sign.

He fumbled for his chair and sat down. He lifted the large, black leather book with due reverence. The ancient pages and worn binding creaked under his touch. He ran a hand over the metal adornments on the cover and thick metal clasps that kept the book closed. The cover held no title except for the symbols of the Six Gifts arrayed around the Luminary sun symbol engraved on a metal medallion in the center. The symbols were almost worn away and hard to identify. One symbol, below the sun, was impossible to decipher. But he knew, without a doubt that this was *the* grimoire he'd been searching for.

Goose bumps rose on his forearms. *Holy mother moon!* Archard held the book to his nose and breathed in its power.

Many had claimed it lost, burned, destroyed, buried— anything but intact. At first he had scoffed at the rumors of its discovery, but then the possibility of using the magic inside had kindled in his mind like wildfire; the urge to possess such a tome had become far too tempting to ignore. If it did exist, he *had* to have it. In his mind it was rightfully his. The grimoire of Bartholomew the Dark, Luminary of the last Dark Covenant, could only belong to him

Little was known about Bartholomew. His magic and

power were the stuff of both legend and nightmare. He and his Covenant were solely responsible for keeping the world in the Dark Ages, and every Dark witch since that time dreamed of knowing the secrets of his power. Some even said he found a way to take away free will, the one thing everyone knew the magic would not do. Archard knew that if Bartholomew had been able to do *that,* then he had been able to do *anything.*

With a delicate touch, Archard removed the clasps and lifted the cover, nearly giddy with anticipation. As the book sucked in its first breath, a wave of Darkness washed over him, chilling even his black heart. The corners of his lips twitched.

Page after page revealed Dark magic like Archard had never seen. Some were simple, but remarkably ingenious spells, others twisted rituals he couldn't wait to try; and some pages were blank, concealed by spells he wondered if he'd ever be able to break.

The power of it all rippled over his skin, seeping in, intoxicating him. The fire of his desire sparked on his fingertips, leaving scorch marks on the pages as he flipped through the book, now certain of his success.

Three hours into his exploration, he found what he needed: a scrying spell that could find anyone, anywhere, no matter the protective magic and without a personal item to link the spell. Clutching the massive book against his chest with one hand, Archard flew around the room gathering the items he needed for the spell.

Soon, he was outside, beneath the waxing moon, his

supplies laid out on the ground. The trees turned their faces away from the Dark that trailed after him as he moved around, preparing things.

On the ground he placed an iron bowl, into which he poured holy water. The first step was to taint the water with blood, his own. With his athame he sliced the flesh of his forearm and let the hot, red blood drip into the water, the drops suspended in the liquid, slowly spreading out into tendrils of red. Then, to staunch the blood flow he pressed his palm to the cut and sent a wave of concentrated fire, cauterizing the skin. He hissed through clenched teeth, but hurried to continue with the spell, ignoring the pain.

He added the ashes of seaweed and three fire-blackened amethysts, their pleasant lavender color hidden, marred. The final ingredients were the key to Batholomew's spell: the eyes and heart of an owl.

Even in Archard's abundance of evil he had never sacrificed another creature for the magic. Certainly, he'd been responsible for the deaths of others, but this was much different.

All witches, even Dark, maintained a level of respect for the creatures of the earth. There were rules that must be followed to control the magic—they can be bent, and twisted, but never broken. To purposely kill in the name of the magic, to rip the very fabric from which it is made, to sacrifice to draw power—that was breaking the rules. And it was crossing a line, or more appropriately, it was climbing over a wall and jumping down the other side into the kind of Darkness from which there was no return or redemption.

Archard did not hesitate to jump.

He stood, his gaze piercing the night as he searched the several acres of woodland behind his house, home to many owls. He watched the trees for several moments, his sleek athame dangling in his right hand. His mind came to a grinding halt, stopped in one place, focused on his task until he was oblivious to all else. He felt nothing but desire to find his prey.

Finally, he saw it—the silver, shadowy form of a common barn owl, drifting soundlessly on the air.

He stepped over the iron bowl and walked forward, his stride long and determined, eyes trained on his victim. He rubbed his thumb against the cold blade of his knife in anticipation. As he walked, he raised his left hand, waved it over his body, cloaking his movements with magic. The crunch of his feet through the brush instantly muted.

The bird landed comfortably in the high branches of a thin tree, spread its golden-white wings to straighten the feathers, blinking out at the night. Its white facial disk, like the face of the bright moon, framed two coal eyes and a long, sharp finger beak. The owl scanned the ground for its own prey, oblivious to the hunter drawing near.

The knife sliced through the air and found its target. With a sickly thud, it plunged into the bird's breast. The owl fell out of the tree, its dying screech fouling the air.

Archard didn't flinch.

A tear-drop stain of blood spread over the white feathers, seeping into the fibers, a badge of Darkness. Archard scanned left to right, half expecting some instant punishment for his actions, but the woods were silent, eerily still. He walked over to the bird and stared down at its black-hole eyes looking up at him accusingly. A curious thread of pleasure wormed its way into his blood, stitching a cold sense of power through his veins. Something in his soul shifted, a down-step toward power yet untapped. With sinister eagerness he scooped the body of the owl up from the ground and hurried back toward the house.

Archard placed the bird next to the iron bowl and knelt in front of it. Tightly gripping the knife's handle, he pulled upward and the blade came free with a slick sucking sound. The owl's blood bubbled out of the wound and ran down both sides of the small ribcage. He placed the sharp tip of the knife on the bird's breast just below its round face, while securing the delicate body with his other hand, the silky smoothness of the feathers caressing his palm. With sure strength he pressed downward and pulled back.

The owl's chest opened up.

The earth shook beneath him.

The blood was thick and warm as it bathed his hands and wrists. The hollow bones snapped easily, sending a spray of speckled blood over his face. Soon, the slick heart was in his hand. The fouled water sizzled when he dropped it in. Next, he held back the owl's eyelids and with an almost culinary detachment, slid the knife around the eyes, disconnecting them from the sockets. He tossed them into the water with a sizzle; the two eyes then bobbed to the surface.

The job was done.

Archard tossed the mutilated carcass away, carrion for some opportunistic scavenger. Then he knelt back down, the hard ground biting at his knees. He curled his body over the water and began the chant, glancing only once at the grimoire for reference. The words slithered out of his mouth, slinking down into the charged water. The ground shuddered, bucked against his will, but he persisted, perspiration soaking his shirt, dripping from his nose into the water. The contents of the bowl bounced and sloshed. Ice-cold wind slapped Archard in the face, several crows dived out of the sky to snap at his flesh; still, he persisted.

And then there it was, the image he needed, forming on the surface of the red-black water like a film of oil.

He collapsed to the ground, a hideous smile on his dry, cracked lips.

ARCHARD'S COMPOSED COUTURE HAD RETURNED. He stood on the sagging steps of the white church, perfect in an espresso-brown pinstripe suit and cobalt blue shirt. Tilting his head to the sky, he studied the afternoon sun, bright and triumphant, just as he felt. The giddiness of his discovery tingled inside him, bubbles of delight that wouldn't subside. In his hands, now scrubbed white and washed of the blood he'd spilled, he held Bartholomew's grimoire. His great treasure, his key to dominance.

Remorse was not something Archard knew or understood. The owl's life had simply been what was necessary. He didn't care that the earth was furious with him, or that it often shook dangerously beneath his feet in a scolding reproach. In fact, it pleased him that he could anger it so, but still command the magic—it was the ultimate dominance! He now understood why Bartholomew had reigned so long and with such potent Darkness. This kind of power was irresistible and unstoppable.

The cars began to arrive with the rolling crunch of dried leaves. Archard wanted to reveal his plan, to brag of his newfound power, but he didn't want his fellow witches to see it. He carefully smoothed his features into an expression of haughty indifference.

Very soon, his coven-mates were gathered at the bottom of the steps, looking up at him eagerly. "Come inside. I have news," he said.

Archard stood in front of his regal chair and watched them all file to their seats, cross their legs or fold their hands. Each kept an eye on the book in his hands. When they were ready, he lifted it up in front of him and said loudly, "This is the grimoire of Bartholomew the Dark."

Eyes flashed open, jaws dropped, and the whispers ran around the circle. Archard grinned.

Gavin cleared his throat, fingered his glasses. "No

disrespect intended, but are you *sure*? General belief is that it doesn't exist."

Archard rolled his eyes and cocked his head in Gavin's direction. "Yes, I am *sure*. Do you think I would say it if it weren't true?" He scoffed. "This is Bartholomew's book, without a doubt. I've already put its magic to work, and I've never felt anything like it. This," he raised the book higher, "is the answer to everything." He lowered it and pursed his lips together briefly. "I know where the Light witches are—all of them. We leave immediately. Not only can we take the two witches we need, we can kill the rest for good measure. All problems solved."

He expected awed whispers, looks of disbelief, even applause—anything but the heavy silence that filled the inside of the church that stank of fear. He looked from face to face, all downcast except for Rachel, who met his glare with steady ice-blue eyes. She nodded her approval.

Archard flicked his eyes back to the rest of the group. "Why do I smell fear?" he roared, throwing down the grimoire onto the seat of his throne with a satisfying slap.

Dora bravely raised her eyes. "Forgive us, Luminary. Perhaps it's the rumors that surround Bartholomew. We've all heard the stories—too horrible for even our tastes. It feels dangerous to toy with his magic." She folded her arms primly and moved her eyes to her fellow witches, begging for support.

They all nodded and mumbled in agreement. Archard folded his arms. "To this day, Bartholomew is the only witch *ever* to form a Dark Covenant. That tells me something, and it *should* tell you something. We can't do this without his magic. It is the key. Are you all really that naïve, that *cowardly*, that you won't take this road with me?" He spit the words at them, red sparks falling from his mouth, hissing out in the cold air. He took a deep breath and pushed down the fire of his anger. Then he said, "I am offering you a way to form a Covenant, to grant us power we can't even imagine. But perhaps I chose my coven-mates too rashly."

The room now smelled of shame and wounded pride. None of them wanted to admit cowardice. They might not have had Archard's deep-rooted inclination for evil, but they were all extremely powerful Dark witches, ravenous for power and prestige. Even if they feared Bartholomew, they still wanted their names tacked into witch history next to his.

Slowly, each face rose and met Archard's challenging stare.

Jaws tightened.

"Then we go," Archard whispered.

CHAPTER 23
Blood Moon

October 1931

A melia woke in a panic, darkness all around her. In a rush of pain and sorrow, the memories of the night's events swooped down on her. She spun around, flinched away, expecting to see the Dark witches emerge from the blackness to finish the job, but there was only silence.

She was alone.

Where are they? What happened?

With a groan, she shifted her battered body off the stone altar, the chains broken on the ground, and took a few hesitant steps forward, straining her ears for any sound indicating the covens were still there. *Am I dreaming? Am I dead?*

At the cave's entrance, she peered out into the cold night,

listening, waiting, but the only sounds to answer were the wind in the dry leaves and an owl hooting far off in the distance. She stepped out into the night, her heart thumping loudly, her hands gripping the ragged skirt of her filthy nightgown.

Run!

Amelia didn't wait to figure out what had happened. If the covens had left her alone, she wasn't about to sit around and wait for them to return. She bolted off into the trees, but before long fell to the ground, a bizarre pain firing to life in her chest.

She reached to her chest and found the chain and possession pendant. She tugged, pulled, lifted, tore, gnashed but it would not leave her body—a slowly working noose, a wicked leash.

Images of illuminated faces, green with power, orange with fire, burned on the surface of her eyes. They floated up from the ground, taunting her, bringing with them echoes of terror, pain, and wrongness. She flinched and shivered.

This is not real. This is not real.

The words thundered along the front of Amelia's mind, a storm of disbelief, as she lay on the cold ground in a layer of chiffon darkness. October cold snapped at her skin leaving bitter blue and white bite marks. In the sky above, the brilliant blood moon hid its shamed face behind a mask of thick clouds. Uneasiness rippled on the air.

What happened? What's wrong with me?

Crawling through the fallen, rotting leaves, Amelia tried

to put as much distance as she could between herself and the cave, but the effort was monumental. She collapsed in front of a cluster of aspens, their white trunks like towering skeletons in the night. She gathered her tattered nightgown around her as much possible, but it was an inadequate barrier against the frigid night.

Left to die.

That part she hadn't seen in the water when she was thirteen. She'd always assumed the Dark coven's spell would end in her death, but here she was, alive and alone. Their spell to make her a part of their Covenant must have failed and they'd abandoned her, probably assuming she was dead. Amelia dug her fingers into the dirt, reaching into the earth for some hint of magic, just an ounce of power to break the necklace and undo what had been done to her. Empty, cold silence. The earth no longer heard her. She began to truly panic.

Not only was she alive and alone, but changed. The spell may have failed in its ultimate goal, but it had done something else to her. She didn't recognize herself. She felt displaced and forsaken. The heat of the magic no longer pulsed inside her. Instead, there was a gaping, aching hole the size of the world, where her gift should be. Her body was wrong, her heartbeat, her breath. And without her magic, how would she survive?

Gone. Extracted. Changed.

What am I?

SEPTEMBER 1991
Harvest Moon

She was the walking dead, a crone with no soul, no purpose. Trapped and waiting only to die. Amelia had never left the cave; it became her prison. For sixty years she'd wandered the woods, only able to go about half a mile before collapsing and crawling back to the cave in defeat. Her broken, deformed body required little sustenance and she survived on what nature provided.

And waited to die. *Always waiting.*

The morning dawned cool and gray. Amelia huddled in the cave, tucked into the black shadows, staring out at yet another morning. Her white night gown had long ago disintegrated to dust and she now wore a filthy black flannel shirt and baggy hiking pants she'd stolen from a backpacker who'd passed by and left his pack unattended for a time. The clothes hung from her bony frame. Her skin had soured to a sickly gray, her hair thinned and grayed into wisps, feathering off her head like Medusa's snakes.

Her mind was a hollow shell, scooped clean of all that she loved. She'd tossed it all aside many years ago, throwing it away to avoid the hurt that was wondering. Wondering why no one came to save her? Wondering what had happened to her little, precious Lilly? Wondering what they did with Solace's body? Wondering if Camille, her husband Ronald, and the few remaining others had escaped? And most of all, wondering what had gone wrong to curse her with such a life?

A robin landed near the entrance of the cave, picking the dirt for bugs. Amelia, head resting back against the stone, watched the intrepid creature with a vacant, vague stare. Then, a warm breeze rushed into the clearing and the bird spread its wings and flew off. The air swirled into the cave and moved over her sunken, skull-like face. Amelia sat up.

Is that magic?

With the breeze came a tickle of energy that stirred in the space behind her heart. She gasped and strained to feel, to hold onto the sensation. It grew, pulsing now and prompting her to stand. *Walk, walk, walk,* it whispered to her and she was compelled to listen.

She stood and stumbled out of the cave, blinking at the sunshine. The air grew hot, stirred by magic. Tripping over her eager feet, Amelia followed.

For hours, she walked, led by the whispering wind. When night fell, and the large harvest moon, September's full moon, rose into the sky, she walked on. Miles and miles from the cave, her broken heart beating oddly in her chest, her feet now bloody from so many miles, but her body did not fail her as it had so many times before.

When the full moon reached its zenith, she saw in her mind the face of a baby, a fetus, unborn, but pulsing with power. She must find this unborn child; he could save her— that was what the wind whispered as it pushed her on.

Soon, she stopped in front of a quiet, Colonial-style house, the white clapboards glowing in the moonlight, the many windows dark and sleeping. The wind spiraled around her. *Here, he's here!*

Stumbling up the stone steps to the front porch, Amelia held her breath, ignoring the trail of blood her feet left and the nagging call of her body to stop. The baby's face, plump and pink, grew bright in her mind.

She fell on the door, scratching her yellowed and blackened fingernails down the mess of the screen, the *screech* echoing ominously in the still night. She scratched and pounded, desperate sobs building in her throat. *Please. Please. I need his help!*

After several minutes the front door pulled back and the wild, angry face of a woman with bluntly chopped blond hair and a swelling pregnant belly, appeared. At the horrific sight of Amelia, she stumbled and then fell backwards, crab walking away from the door. Amelia summoned an ounce of strength and pulled open the screen door, falling into the foyer. She pulled her mouth open and, in a voice like crackling paper, said, "Please. I need his help." She lifted her skeletal hand and pointed at the woman's belly. The mother-to-be put a protective hand over her womb and continued to back away.

"Get out!" she spat at Amelia.

Amelia pulled her body forward, digging her fingernails into the polished wood floor. "Please," she wheezed. "I only need to die. Your baby . . . he can break the curse."

The woman froze, petrified. She lowered her wide, terrified eyes to her stomach where the baby rolled and kicked.

A strange look of understanding and defeat moved over her face. Amelia, now close enough to touch her, lifted her arm, hand trembling and touched the firm swell of the woman's belly. The baby quieted. Amelia felt a small pressure under her hand, an outward push, and then there was a massive rush of heat from him to her, and then from her to him.

A blissful peace filled her body and she dropped her hand to the floor and sighed in long awaited relief. The Dark necklace around her neck burst into flames, turning to ash. Amelia's heart beat correctly just once before it stopped. The poor woman beside her screamed, gripping her belly as a contraction seized her body.

Amelia closed her eyes and died.

CHAPTER 24
WAXING CRESCENT

Present Day, October

"Simon?" Willa whispered, moving her eyes around the dark room and straining to hear a response. Then louder, "Simon?" She jumped out of bed and ran to the bathroom. Empty. She couldn't breathe right. Suddenly, her heart and lungs were gripped with panic and her body cold with trepidation. *My dream. No, no, no!* "Simon!" she yelled.

She ran out into the hall, slipping on the smooth, polished wood floor. The house was dark, quiet. She froze to listen. The ticking of a clock. The hum of the heater. Hurrying down the stairs, she kept her senses tuned outward. "Simon?" she called, her voice echoing loudly. She went to the kitchen first. Empty. She looked out the back door and found the yard also empty.

Her panic was now acid in her throat, chills raised the hair on her neck. "Simon?" she said louder. Running again, she went to the front of the house and skidded to a stop in the foyer. The front door was thrown open and Simon stood on the porch in only his boxers. Cold, snow-scented air blew into the house, hitting Willa in the face. She gasped and then exhaled in immense relief. She tipped her head and stepped slowly forward.

What are you doing?

Simon's hands were at his sides, balled into fists, his head lifted to the sky. Willa stepped next to him. His eyes were squeezed closed, his face a stone of concentration. "Simon?" she whispered and put a hesitant hand on his cold arm; the muscles were ridged, coiled tight like he was ready to spring.

"Do you feel that, Willa?" he whispered, not opening his eyes.

Willa looked out at the night, the massive maple trees and the pines surrounding the house. "All I feel is the freezing cold," she said hugging her arms over her chest, her tank-top and shorts doing little to keep her warm.

Simon shook his head, a small jerky movement. "No, there is . . . something."

The hairs rose on her neck again, a cold sense of dread wormed into her heart. "What?"

Simon finally opened his eyes and looked down at her, his irises black in the night. "Someone is here."

SIMON GRABBED WILLA'S ARM AND pulled her back inside. The feeling had woken him, an odd itch in his mind, but now he was sure there was something or someone close. And he was even more certain that the icy presence meant they were in danger.

"Simon, what—"

"We have to wake everyone, *right now!*" He looked down at her confused eyes.

She stared back for a few tense moments and then said, "Okay, let's go."

He nodded, grateful for her understanding. They ran back to their room and threw on jeans, hoodies and shoes before running first to Wynter and Rowan's room. Simon pounded on the door. A moment later, Rowan answered, eyes bleary, his hair a mess around his face. "Simon? What's—"

"Someone is here," Simon cut in. "I can feel it." He pushed meaning into the words, hoping Rowan could understand.

Rowan narrowed his eyes and then they flashed wide. "Wake everyone. Meet in the kitchen. Go!"

Simon went one way and Willa the other, knocking on doors and pulling people from their beds. Within two minutes, the witches were all gathered in the kitchen, one dim light turned on over the sink. Grumbles of questions moved around the room, but Simon waited for Rowan before he said anything. Rowan crossed the room and stood in front of him. "What do you feel?"

The room instantly quieted as all eyes locked on Simon. "It woke me up. Some cold feeling. Sorry, it's hard to describe."

"No, it's fine. Go on," Rowan prompted.

"I went out front and it got stronger. It feels like a presence. I can't quite tell if it's one person or a group, but it feels dangerous." Willa, standing at his side, took his hand and he looked down at her wide eyes.

Rowan whipped around. "Charlotte?"

Charlotte already had her eyes closed. "He's right. It's there, beyond the walls of the ranch. I don't know what it is either."

"It's Archard," Wynter said quietly. Everyone turned to look at her. "Who else would it be?"

Rowan nodded. "Agreed."

Simon's stomach tightened as he pulled Willa closer. "But you said the ranch was protected and that it would take him a while to find us?"

"I know, and he *shouldn't* have been able to find us so quickly. I don't know how he did, but there isn't time to discuss it. We have to fight, here and now."

"Fight?" Simon gasped. "Willa and I just started training yesterday."

Rowan put a hand on Simon's shoulder. "I know, Simon," he said gently. "You two stay here in the kitchen with Charlotte and Elliot. Help them cast some protection spells. The rest of us will go out to meet Archard. If he somehow gets past us, don't try to fight—run. You run out the back and down to the barn at the base of the hill. There's a truck there with keys in the glove box. Get away as fast as you can. Understood?"

Simon nodded. Charlotte and Elliot moved to stand with him and Willa. They nodded, too. "Yes, Rowan" Charlotte said.

"Good." He tried to smile reassuringly and then turned away. "The rest of you, follow me."

ARCHARD STOOD AT THE GATE of the ranch. Behind him loomed a row of black shadows—his covens, standing shoulder to shoulder. Their feet and hands shuffled restlessly, nervously, but Archard was like stone, looking at the shadowy path beyond the gate

Once more he went over the magic in his head; he couldn't afford a last-minute fumble. The new spells and incantations from Bartholomew's book were etched onto the slate of his mind. He would make no mistakes.

Everything has to be perfect.

He motioned with his hand and two shadows broke off from the line, moving toward the gate. Leon and Gavin each held a small bottle of fresh cat blood. Archard observed how they held the bottles far from their bodies, heads tilted away. He rolled his eyes at their revulsion.

Pathetic!

They looked at him.

"Do it," he hissed.

Carefully the two men poured the stolen blood on the earth all along the front of the gate; the thick liquid hit the powdery dust and congealed. When the task was finished, the two witches retreated, and Archard stepped forward. He raised his hand and muttered the required spell. A blast of icy wind rushed from behind, blowing past the witches, and racing up the lane, smashing the protective spells around the house as easy as snapping a twig.

Archard chuckled under his breath.

With a quick sweep of his hand, the gate ripped from its hinges with a loud creak, exploding backwards onto the ground. Archard advanced, his covens following. The enormous trees withdrew their branches, cowering as far back from the stench of evil as they could.

Archard drank in his own power, each step forward a jolt of wicked anticipation.

The house was quiet, the windows dark. No one was expecting him this time. Archard stopped at the edge of the trees, ran his eyes over the grand wooden posts and log walls, briefly wondering how they would look ablaze with fire.

Not yet—patience!

He rotated his head to the side. "Do you feel them, Ellen? Where are they?"

A curvy woman with skin the color of fine espresso closed her eyes. Her hands trembled with the effort. "In a room at the back of the house, Luminary."

"All of them?"

"Yes, all of them."

A grin spread across Archard's face as he spun on his heel. "Follow me. And be ready."

WILLA'S BODY WENT NUMB WITH fear. *Archard? No, not here. Not now!* She turned her face into Simon's shoulder and he put his arms around her. She looked up at him as he spoke to her mind, understanding her fear. *I will not let him hurt you again.*

She nodded, trying to even the rhythm of her breath. Char put a hand on her shoulder. "Help us do the spell, okay? Rowan and the others are all extremely powerful. They can beat Archard and his covens."

Willa nodded. "What do we do?"

Char half-smiled and nodded. "Simon. In the fridge, get some basil. Willa, from that cupboard there," she pointed, "get the salt." Willa nodded and did as she was told. Charlotte raced into the large pantry, where hundreds of jars lined the shelves filled with herbs and stones. Willa grabbed the box of kosher salt and set it on the table. Elliott had already drawn a large five-pointed star on the wood with a small piece of chalk. He took the salt and started to pour it over the chalk lines.

"What is all this?" Willa asked when Char came back to the table with a jar of pine needles, another of sage, and a few fat white pillar candles.

"All herbs, stones and minerals—everything that comes from the earth—have magical properties. We use them to help channel the magic and also to help tell it what we need it to do. These all represent protection." She unscrewed the lid and handed the jar of dried sage to Willa. "Throw it onto the star, and Simon, do the same with the basil."

Willa raised her eyebrows at Simon who shrugged and

turned to do as Char instructed. Once all the herbs and salt were in place, and the candles lit, Elliot waved them all to stand behind the table near the star. He held out his hands and opened his mouth to say something, but was interrupted by a loud crash from the front of the house.

WYNTER EXHALED, TRYING TO CALM her racing heart and the tension in her muscles. *How did Archard find us?* Fear circled in her stomach, churning up her nerves. Rowan threw open the front door and she followed him out into the cold night.

First, all she saw were the dark figures of the trees, but then the Dark witches stepped out from the shadows, a line of black bodies, threatening. Wynter held her breath and cut her eyes to Rowan. He narrowed his eyes at Archard's covens and said to her, "Do you feel that?"

She nodded, struggling to find her voice under the tight knot of anxiety in her throat. "I've never felt Darkness like that. What kind of magic is he using?"

Rowan shook his head. "I wish I knew." He exhaled a long breath. Then to the group, he whispered, "Be on your guard. Something is different about Archard."

Rowan led the way down the steps. Wynter's blood rushed in her head, pulsed in her ears, dulling all other sounds. Archard's cold-as-steel eyes were locked on her across the front grass. Her knees wobbled and she swallowed, searching for strength. She inhaled and called the hot magic to her hands, ready to fight. *You can't have me, Archard. I'll die first.*

THE PALE LOOK OF FEAR on their faces was like a sultry, euphoric drug in Archard's veins. Every inch of him pulsed with pleasure and power. This moment was everything he hoped for—watching the shock on their faces as he stepped into the yard, the delicious panic, the flavor of fear in the air.

An impish smile on his lips, Archard raised his arms and called to the fire. Eager, ravenous flames burst to life in his palms in two, large, rotating globes. It was a bit dramatic, but he enjoyed the effect; he had their full attention, just as he wanted. Rowan, in all his self-righteous goodness, stepped forward, partially blocking Wynter with his ridiculously broad body. Archard leered at her, inhaling the intoxicating scent of her distress, much stronger than the others'. She would be easy to break, easy to coax into his world.

"Archard," Rowan growled.

"Rowan," Archard answered back as cool as ice. "I've come for what is mine." His eyes slid to Wynter. Rowan's entire body strained and Wynter wilted behind him. Rowan's jaw tensed, his fists clenched and unclenched; the ground shook beneath their feet. Archard thought of throwing the fireballs, just for his own entertainment, but waited to see what Rowan would do.

Rowan didn't give him the pleasure of a rebuttal. Instead he nodded to a couple of his witches. Swiftly, their lifted hands sent a wall of water shooting forward. Archard laughed and tossed the burning spheres at the water. The two elements met in a hissing eruption of steam. The two groups stared at each other for a moment before both sides leaped into action.

Within seconds, the yard was a chaotic mess of wind, fire, and water. The gifts bashed at one another. Whirlwinds cut through walls of water; rocks and mud were slung and deflected with fire or wind. Cracks in the ground opened and closed; storm clouds formed overhead and dumped rain like a shower of bullets.

The lines stood firm, evenly matched.

Only Archard was aware of Rachel slipping around the back of the house.

THE NOISE FROM THE FRONT yard was now deafening. "What are they doing?" Simon yelled.

"Fighting," Elliot screamed back. "Using the elements and magic to fight. Basically what you did yesterday, only they are trying to kill each other with it." He shrugged and turned back to the star. "Hold out your hands. We need to call to the magic and say a spell of protection, Ready?"

Simon nodded, and so did Willa who stood next to him. "What will this actually do?" he asked.

"It'll put a wall up around us that will, hopefully, be hard for a Dark witch to get through. It'll help keep the others safe, sending strength to their magic," Elliot explained quickly. "Here we go." The four young witches raised their hands over the star. Simon felt his palms grow hot as he focused on the magic. Elliot said, "Repeat this spell: *Fair moon, protect the Light. Keep us safe from this Dark fight.*"

The room filled with energy, hot and potent. Simon closed his eyes like the others and repeated the spell. On the third repetition of the spell, they all suddenly stopped. The heat was sucked from the room in a quick breath and replaced with cold—icy, biting cold.

"What is that?" Simon hissed, lowering his hands. He moved around the table, leaving Willa with Elliot and Charlotte. The cacophony was still going on outside, but he sensed someone moving toward them. There was something fuzzy about the presence, something slippery; he couldn't tell exactly where it was.

"Char?" he said, taking another few steps forward toward the front hall.

"Yes, I feel it, but can't get a grip on it."

"Me neither. Do you think it's one of the Dark witches?"

"Maybe. Hold on, I'll keep trying."

"Rowan told us to run," Willa said, her voice shaking slightly. "Is it time to run?"

Simon turned back to look at her and froze in horror. A woman dressed all in black, as sleek, lithe, and lethal as a panther stood behind Willa. There was a streak of red smudged across her forehead. Her arm drew back and light flashed on a wickedly sharp knife.

WILLA SAW THE RIGID FEAR in Simon's eyes just before the

sharp, hot pain hit her back. She wanted to cry out, but the pain was too powerful, pulling the breath from her lungs. It seized her whole body and Simon's image blurred. She heard him cry out, yell her name, but then the pain came again, a jerking reversal of the first. A hot, wet sensation ran down her back. She thought she saw the flash of a knife moving toward Charlotte and Elliot before collapsing to the floor under the weight of the pain.

Charlotte hit the floor next to her and then Elliot. She tried to focus on their faces, tried so hard to push through the pain to understand what was happening. Simon's voice cut through the haze, "No! Willa!"

"Stay there, Mind," another voice said, female and chilling. "No, I said, *stay!*"

"What do you want?" Simon spit, anger trembling on his voice. Willa blinked, looked across the floor at his hiking boots. The brown leather was scuffed and dusty.

"Just you," the cold voice said. "Come with me now without a fight and I won't burn their bodies right here in front of you."

Simon's boots shifted. Willa waited to hear his voice, but it didn't come. Her mind was still struggling to understand, but all she wanted to do was close her eyes against the pain and sleep. It hurt to breathe, her chest was wickedly tight. The floor beneath her was wet, sticky and warm. *Did someone spill something? Simon, it hurts.*

Willa blinked as Simon's boots moved toward her and then passed her. She wanted to turn, see where he was going, but her body didn't obey her command. *Simon?* Panic rose inside her, a vague realization of what was happening breaking through the pain. *No. Simon, why are you leaving? Help me!*

Blackness edged into her vision, the pain pulling her down. She closed her eyes, ready to give up. Then Simon's fingers brushed her head and the pain was sucked away. His voice broke into her head. *Stay down! Don't move until she's gone! Do NOT follow!*

CHAPTER 25
WANING GIBBOUS

September 1991

Amelia blinked against the brightness. Her body felt as light as a breath. *Am I crossing over?* Golden happiness pulsed in her heart. The last thing she remembered was the rush of heat when the baby had pushed against her palm. *Did I die? Sun and moon, I died. I'm crossing over! Thank the earth!*

All the faces of her loved ones moved across her mind: Grandma Ruby, her mother, her father, her husband Peter, Grandpa Charles. Soon, she would see them, be with them again. Maybe even Lilly would be there to greet her mother.

The light finally dissipated and Amelia squinted, eager to see her family standing before her with open arms. The first thing she saw was the slate of the clear blue sky, marked with a few wispy clouds. A bird cut across the blue, crying out.

Amelia frowned and turned her head to the side to see a forest of aspens, their spade-shaped leaves the cheery yellow of early fall. She realized she was lying on the cold ground. A ripple of apprehension moved over her heart. *No, no this can't be right.*

Sitting up, she looked down at her body. She wore her white nightgown again, the same one she'd been dressed in when the Dark witches came. It was dirty and stained with Solace's and her own blood. She shook her head. *No!*

She lifted her hands in front of her face, her younger hands, and they shimmered, translucent. *I'm a ghost? No! No, I want to cross over!*

The feeling of eyes watching her prickled the back of her head. Her ghost-body grew cold and slowly—*so slowly*—she turned to her left, knowing and dreading what she would find.

The cave grinned back at her with its black, toothless mouth.

Amelia's scream startled the birds for miles around.

CHAPTER 26
WAXING CRESCENT

Present Day, October

A single ball of fire streaked upward, slicing the night sky above the house. Archard grinned. Rachel had the Mind witch.

Excellent.

He allowed himself only a brief moment of celebration; he needed his full attention to hold back the assault of the Light witches. They were strong, much stronger than he had anticipated.

Gavin stepped up next to him and yelled into his ear. "I'm sorry, Luminary, but I think we should get the other witch and go. Now."

Archard barred his teeth at the sniveling man.

Gavin put up his hands. "We risk losing one or more of us in this fight. They are strong. If one of us dies, we will be worse off than before and this would have all been in vain. We must get the woman and flee." He took a cautious step back. "It's the smart thing to do. For the Covenant."

Archard glanced at the man, the chaos reflected in the surface of his insufferable glasses. Most of all, he hated that the man was right.

"Fine. Yes. Tell them to be ready." He pointed to his line of witches.

Gavin nodded with relief and disappeared down the line.

Archard moved his attention to Wynter. She fought valiantly and was strong, even after five months of Holmes's abuse. Breaking her and forcing her to join him would be a sweet pleasure.

Movement from behind the Light witches, on the front porch, caught his eye. Three more witches came running from the house.

Why are they not dead?

Rachel's job was to kill any witches with the boy, then take him back to the cars. Rachel didn't screw up; her skills were refined, lethal. Archard squinted through the mess in the air. He recognized the girl who helped rescue Wynter from the basement, the one whose mind he'd violated. She and the other two were covered in blood.

Rachel doesn't leave survivors. What the hell?

The girl grabbed Wynter by the arm and gestured wildly. Wynter faltered, her hands dropping to her sides. No matter what had happened, he knew Rachel had the boy and this was the moment he needed.

This is it.

"Get ready!" he yelled.

Wynter yelled something to Rowan, and in that short moment of distraction, caused all the Light witches' powers to falter for just a split second.

"Now!" Archard called out.

The Dark witches combined their powers and sent a rush of wind and heat across the lawn, backed by one of Bartholomew's spells. It moved across the lawn with the speed of a diving falcon, knocking the Light witches backward, scattering their bodies across the yard and front steps. Archard was right behind it. Wynter lay on the ground, unconscious. He scooped her up into his arms. Rowan was ten feet to the left. He lifted his head and caught Archard's eyes. Fury and hatred flashed in his blue eyes; Archard savored it, let the moment linger. When Rowan moved to stand, Archard grinned wickedly and enveloped himself and his prisoner in a pillar of fire.

His coven-mates had already fled. Archard sprinted down the drive, laughing as Light spells bounced off his protective magic.

WILLA'S EARS WERE RINGING, HER head faint from the impact of being thrown back several feet. She pushed herself up, fighting the dizziness. The Dark witches had disappeared down the driveway. She took off after them, but made it only as far as the first maple trees. Slamming into an invisible wall of magic, she fell to the ground, stunned. She crawled back, placed her hands on the cold barrier, just as she'd done in her dream.

No! Not this dream. No!

"Simon!" she screamed. Having him ripped from her side was like having one of her lungs collapse. It was worse than the pain of being stabbed in the heart only moments ago. She couldn't breathe right, her heart didn't beat right, and things inside her started to die. She called out in her mind, *Simon, Simon, Simon,* but he didn't answer; she couldn't *feel* him anymore.

By the time she, Char, and Elliot had recovered from being stabbed—thanks to Simon's healing touch—the mystery woman had disappeared with him. All Willa could think about was his pale, bloody face in her dream and how she'd watched Holmes cut Wynter. *Is she hurting him? Please don't hurt him!*

Rowan was now at the wall, too, his hands lifted, pouring magic at it, but unable to break it. Frustrated and helpless he pounded at it and then dropped to his knees next to her, his shoulders sagging in defeat.

"I can't lose her again. *I can't!*" he sobbed. With a guttural growl, he lifted his fists and brought them down on the dirt, splitting open the earth in a crack that traveled down the length of the driveway. Prostrate, forearms on the ground, as if in prayer, Rowan screamed in frustration.

Startled, Willa looked back at the rest of the covens, who stood huddled together, watching Rowan with helpless expressions. Willa, feeling as lost and angry as he, reached out and put her hand on his shaking back. To her surprise, Rowan placed his head in her lap, like a child in distress.

"Five months," he said in a small, broken voice. "I thought she was dead and he was *torturing* her. Five months. She puts up a strong front, but she's not over it. How could she be? She has nightmares every time she falls asleep."

Willa put her hand on his head, not knowing what to say. She hadn't thought about how Rowan would be nearly as traumatized as Wynter by her kidnapping and the lingering effects it had on both of them.

He said, "She won't survive that again. He'll kill her trying to force her into his covens. *He'll kill her.*"

"Rowan, they took Simon, too," she said, her voice breaking. He finally sat up, swiping at the tears on his face. He looked at her with sympathy.

"They did," he nodded. "They need an Earth and a Mind. Oh, Willa, I'm so sorry. But listen to me," he knelt and took her hands. Willa fought the sobs rising in her chest. "We *will* get them back, both of them. Do you hear me?"

She nodded and he drew her into his arms. "I'm sorry. I shouldn't have broken down like that. I'm Luminary—I should be stronger." He pulled back and looked her in the eyes again. "This wall will fall as soon as Archard is too far away to sustain the magic, and then we will go after them." He stood and pulled her with him. "But right now, we have to figure out a way to find where they are going or we will lose them forever."

ARCHARD DUMPED WYNTER INTO THE backseat of his black SUV, next to the Mind boy. The boy was unconscious, under a spell Rachel put on him. Archard waved his hand over Wynter, administering the same spell, so that she, too, would stay unconscious until he woke her at the cave. Rachel came around the car to meet him.

He spun on her, "Why didn't you kill those other witches?"

Her blue eyes flashed defiantly. "I *did!* I punctured their hearts."

Archard frowned. "But I saw them—three of them. They came out of the house and spoke to Wynter."

"What?" Rachel folded her arms and narrowed her eyes. "But all three were there in the kitchen; I didn't miss. They should . . ." Her eyes popped open and she leaned forward to look at the boy slumped against the window.

"What is it, Rachel?"

Her mouth hung open for a moment. "He touched them!"

"What?" Archard grew impatient and grabbed her arm. "What are you talking about?"

She looked at him, blinking. "He *touched* them. He stepped past them to follow me out the back door and very briefly leaned down to let his fingers trail across them. It was barely a legitimate touch. Do you think . . ."

Archard inhaled with realization. "Holy mother moon! Is

it possible?" Both witches leaned forward again to look at the boy's face. "You think he *healed* them?"

"What other explanation is there?"

Archard felt the eager, bubbly feeling of discovery rise inside him. "Unbelievable luck, Rachel! Not only do we now have two full True Covens, we also have a True Healer."

CHARLOTTE BROUGHT WILLA A CUP of tea and she took it numbly. She wore a fresh T-shirt, jeans, and jacket, her blood-ied clothes stuffed into the garbage. The buzz of the coven's frenzied conversation floated over her head. She couldn't focus on anything but the pain of Simon being taken from her and the fear of what might happen to him. *I can't survive without him. I don't want to. I need him.*

Char sat down next to her and touched her arm. "Willa, I know it hurts. I can feel how bad it is for you. What can I do?"

Willa looked up at her new friend's white, round face and broke down. Tears rushed to her eyes, a flash flood of emo-tions that she was not prepared for. It swept her away and overpowered her.

Clamping her hand over her mouth, she turned her head into the cool leather of the armchair. She drew her knees up to her chest and wrapped her arm around them, trying des-perately to stop the flood of emotion. But she was helpless. The levee was broken and she mere flotsam in the deluge.

Her crying echoed off the walls; she was only partially aware of her embarrassment. Charlotte moved forward, took the hot mug from her, and pulled Willa into her arms. She didn't talk, didn't try to tell Willa it would be all right; she simply and magnificently held her. Willa cried into her shoulder and let Char hold the pieces together for a moment until she could find the strength to do it herself.

After several minutes, Char said, "Simon is so strong. He's the strongest witch I've ever met, including the people in this room. He may be untrained, but he can handle himself."

Willa pulled back and wiped her face. She nodded. "I know. But Archard is so . . ."

"Scary," she gave a small smile. "Yeah, he totally is, but so are we when we want to be." Char reached back and retrieved the tea. "Here, this will help calm you. It has a potion in it."

Willa reached for the mug, but then hesitated. "A potion?"

Char laughed. "It's just herbs. Water infused with rose petals and a lot of honey."

Willa nodded and took a sip. The warm, sweet liquid moved down her throat, calm spread through her. She took a deep breath. "It's just hard not to worry when I had this awful dream earlier tonight . . ."

Char threw her hands out in front of her as if stopping traffic. "Wait! You had a dream? What happened?"

Willa blinked, surprised. "Umm . . . I was running in a forest, trying to get to Simon. He was in a cave and I couldn't get in. Then the sky broke and fell in pieces."

"Did you use your Dream Cradle?"

Willa nodded.

Charlotte spun around to the group who were still lost in discussion. "Rowan! Willa had a dream."

The talking paused, everyone looked up. Rowan's eyes widened. "Let's see it!"

CHAPTER 27
WAXING CRESCENT

Present Day, October

Amelia hadn't opened her eyes in days, possibly weeks. After realizing her afterlife was tied to the cave, the same as her life, she'd closed her mind off and simply drifted, the years meaning nothing. But then she sensed the Darkness. The stink of it beat against her senses, a long-forgotten terror welled up inside her. Amelia hid behind a tree, biting her lower lip, as she watched the witches arrive at the cave. There were two of them, a thin man and a blond beauty, both dressed in black. Between them walked two other people—a young man and a woman, hands bound and moving awkwardly, like sleep walkers.

A spell! They're under some sort of spell.

Amelia moved closer, her curiosity outweighing her fear. When she saw the Dark man's face, she almost collapsed to the ground. She gripped the closest tree, wrapping her arms around it. It was *him,* or almost him. The resemblance was horribly unsettling. The same cold, silver eyes and the same thin, oval face. The same potent evil oozing off him.

In that moment, looking at his face, the years compressed and broke through her icy walls. She was standing in the cave again, the Dark witch's strong hands gripping her upper arm. As though it were happening all over again, she remembered Solace's white, dead face looking up from the ground; the cold hardness of the chains biting into her skin; the crackling magic cloud above her.

Left for dead.

If her stomach had held food, she would have vomited it out on the tree. With effort, she pulled her eyes away from the man's face and over to his victims. The boy . . .

Impossible!

Amelia stepped through the trees, her eyes locked on his handsome face. She got as close as she dared, not sure if one of the Dark witches would be able to see her. It wasn't his physical features that she recognized, it was his powers. It was the energy flowing under her skin, the blue hum of it sang to her.

Is it really you?

Amelia wanted to run to the boy, put her hands on his face and look into his eyes, but she knew she needed to be patient.

The Dark man spoke to the blond woman. "We'll come back later. Tonight, I break them." The woman nodded and pushed the female victim forward. Amelia noticed her strawberry-blond hair, the dark crescents under her eyes, her too-skinny frame.

Poor thing!

A surge of pity and a strong desire to help moved through her.

But what can I do?

The witches moved into the cave, their footsteps echoing over the stone. She waited near the entrance, tucked into a crevice of rock, out of sight. A couple of minutes later, the Dark witches emerged and walked away. Amelia watched their backs disappear into the woods. Then she moved to the entrance of the cave, standing in the gaping, black opening.

In all her years of purgatory as a ghost, she had not once had the courage or desire to go in. The memories were too harrowing.

She closed her eyes briefly and then stepped in.

The memories and feelings flooded her almost instantly. Images flitted across her mind, and the echo of her screams moved through her ears, but she ignored them. The young man and woman were sprawled out on the floor next to each other. It was the same spot where she and Solace had waited.

Amelia shook her head. She glided over to the boy and crouched at his side. His yellow curls were smashed against the cold ground, and there was blood under his lower lip, but she didn't see an injury.

You put up a fight. Good for you.

She brushed her hand over his hair, enjoying the springy softness. Then she placed both her hands to his chest, pressing them flat against the solidness. Immediately she felt his power flowing inside him and she recognized it.

It is you! The baby who saved me!

"Oh, no! What are you doing here?" she whispered. "You can't be here."

She explored his powers further, reading his soul. There was something else inside him, something . . .

"What is that?" She pressed her hands harder. "Sun and moon! You have my powers, my magic. How is that possible?" She thought the curse of the Dark covens had killed her powers, taken them away. Could it be that the curse had only bound them? That her death had somehow released her gift into this boy?

But that wasn't all. Amelia cocked her head, closed her eyes and felt deeper.

"Impossible!" she whispered. "You have Solace's gift as well."

She gasped.

"And all this has turned you into a True Healer. How is that possible? How is *any* of this possible?"

Amelia sat back, tired from the effort of searching inside him. She gazed at the side of his face. *You have me and Solace inside you.* The cave walls suddenly seemed to press in on her. She looked around, panic in her stomach. "You can't be here. I can't let you die in this cave like we did."

She began to think, harder and longer than she had in years, her fear and sadness momentarily forgotten. At last, she had an idea. It would be difficult, probably impossible, but worth a try. Shifting forward, she put a hand to his chest again.

"Show me who you love," she whispered. The force of the love inside him hit her so hard that she rocked backward. She inhaled sharply. "And great love. Oh, my boy, we've got to get you out of here."

Amelia leaned down and spoke into his ear, "I will save you. I will find a way. No matter what it takes."

WILLA SPRINTED UPSTAIRS AND SNATCHED the Dream Cradle off the bedside table. She took a deep breath when Simon's scent filled her nose; he always smelled like the mountains and a touch of peppermint. To avoid another break down, she hurried out of the room and back to the covens.

"Here it is!" she called.

"Good!" Rowan said, moving to her. "Do you remember the spell Elliot taught you?"

"I have it written down." She was antsy with anticipation. Would her dream really be able to help them find Simon and Wynter?

"Good. Take out the moonstone, hold it out in your hand like this." Rowan put his hand out in front of him, parallel to the ground. "Think of the dream in your mind and then say the retrieval spell. Got it?"

"Got it," Willa tugged open the pouch and pulled out the cool, iridescent stone and the paper. She handed the pouch to Char who was attentive at her side. *Deep breath.* She held out the stone, glanced at the paper in her other hand and then said the words of the spell. "*Dream Cradle, reveal your nighttime keep. Moonstone, reveal what you hold deep.*"

Heat filled the room, the magic bouncing around her hand, sniffing at the moonstone. A moment later the stone burst to life with a brilliant white light. Willa blinked and turned her head away. Then, like an old-fashioned film projector, the moonstone threw out the scenes of her dream, masking the cozy, light room with the image of a forest in the dark of night.

Willa stared in wonder as the dream played out for everyone to see. When Simon's ghostly visage appeared in the cave, Char reached out and took Willa's hand; Willa was grateful for the anchor. With her scream of pain as the shard sliced into her leg, the dream scene flickered off, the moonstone stopped glowing.

Willa lowered her arm and looked expectantly at Rowan, who was frowning at the spot where her image had just been. "Rowan? Does it help?"

He turned to her and exhaled, brought a hand to his forehead. "Not enough."

The small balloon of hope in her chest deflated instantly. She dropped into a chair, slumped forward. "I'm sorry."

Rowan sat in the chair next to her. "Don't be sorry. It just isn't the solid clue we were hoping for. The forest looks like the ones we have in Colorado, but a lot of forests look like that. And that cave could be anywhere." He patted her leg. "We'll have to keep trying other things."

Rowan left and Charlotte dropped into his place. Willa leaned back, suddenly heavy with exhaustion, the pace and stress of the last few days catching up to her.

"Sorry, Willa. We'll find another way."

Willa nodded. "Do you think it'd be okay if I go lay down for a bit?"

Char nodded, "Of course. Go. I'll wake you if we find anything."

"Thanks, Char." Willa slipped discreetly out of the room and went upstairs. She closed the door to her room and leaned back against it, taking a long breath. "This is all my fault," she whispered. "Me and my stupid dreams! And now Simon is . . ." Fresh tears burned her eyes, but she pushed them back and crossed to the window. A colorless sunrise backlit the Tetons, accenting their sharp, rocky edges. She closed her eyes and tried to feel for Simon again. *Simon? Are you there?*

No answer.

She sighed. Her phone buzzed from the nightstand and she threw herself at it, thinking it might be him. But it wasn't. The caller ID read, "Mom's Cell." Willa sank to the bed, staring at the phone.

The ringing stopped. A moment later the phone vibrated indicating a new voicemail. Her thumb hovered over the phone. In the agony of missing Simon, her fight with her mother suddenly seemed so stupid. She pushed play.

"Willa, honey, hi. It's mom. I hope things are okay and that Wynter is helping you understand what I couldn't. I hope you are safe. Please call or text soon so I know." A pause. "Umm . . . Bertie called. She said you texted about not being able to come in to the museum for a while, but didn't leave a reason. You know how nosey she is. I wasn't sure what to tell her, so I said you and Simon got a last minute chance to go to New York for the weekend to see a show. I hope that's okay." There was a long pause. "Okay, well. I love you. Bye."

Willa sniffed back the tears and pushed the callback button. Her mom answered after only half a ring. "Willa! Are you okay?"

"No, mom," she cried. "I'm not."

"What's wrong? I can come get you."

"No, no, it's not that. It's . . ." she sighed. How would she explain? "Simon's missing. The Dark witches took him and I don't know what to do. What if . . . what if . . ."

"What? Oh, no! What can I do? Do you want me to call the police? The FBI?"

Willa couldn't help, but laugh. "No, Mom, they can't help, but thanks." A short pause. "I'm so scared. I'm scared I'll never see him again and I don't know how I'd live with that. He's . . . part of me. We shouldn't have come here. It's all my fault."

"Willa, it's not your fault. If it's anyone's, it's mine. I tried to hide who you are. If I'd told you about being a witch and helped you learn how to use the magic, maybe none of this would have happened. Do you know how sorry I am?"

"Yes," Willa whispered. "And I'm sorry I left so mad, but it really hurt."

"I know, and you have every right to be mad. Be mad as long you need, but please talk to me. I don't want to lose you over this."

"You won't."

Sarah sighed into the phone. "I can't tell you how glad I am to hear you say that."

A prickle of instinct moved up Willa's neck and she lifted her head, nearly dropping the phone. A ghost hovered near the window. She blinked at the woman, who was gesturing to Willa to come.

"Willa? Willa? Are you still there?'

Willa flinched and looked at the phone. "Mom . . . I'll call you later. I gotta go. Love you." Willa set her phone down and got up to walk over. The ghost, an attractive woman with auburn hair and bright green eyes, studied Willa as she approached. When she was close, the ghost asked, "Are you her?"

"Her who?" Willa asked.

"The girl who loves the boy in the cave."

Willa gasped, her heart suddenly pounding furiously. "Yes."

The ghost smiled, her face shimmering.

"I'm so glad I found you. It wasn't easy," she said, looking around the room with fascination. "It's nice to see some new scenery."

"I'm sorry, but do you know where he is?" Willa stepped closer, trying to regain the ghost's wandering attention.

The ghost shook her head and looked back at Willa. "I'm sorry. The boy. He's in the cave."

Willa's jaw dropped. "Yes. But *where?*"

"I can show you how to get there if you have a moonstone."

"Yes . . . yes, I do," Willa stuttered, and then ran over to get the Dream Cradle. She hurried back to the ghost. "Here it is."

The ghost fluttered closer. "I don't have all my magic anymore and I've exhausted myself finding a way to you. I will need your help to make the moonstone spell work."

Willa nodded. "Of course. Anything."

"Good. Hold it in your hands, call to the magic, charge it."

Willa did as she said, gripping the stone hard. "Now, say this spell: *Moonstone, keep this secret safe and sound. Moonstone, help make what was lost, found.*"

Willa nodded and then repeated the spell in a breathless whisper. Then she watched as the ghost placed her wispy hands on either side of Willa's head, touching her—Willa felt only a slight, cool breeze.

"I'm going to give you directions to the cave. Give you everything you need to know to help him and the woman. The moonstone will keep it for you and then guide you. Understand?" the ghost asked.

"Yes. I'm ready."

"Say the spell again."

"*Moonstone, keep this secret safe and sound. Moonstone, help make what was lost, found.*"

With a hard slap of pain, Willa felt the information move from the ghost into her own mind, then down her hands and into the moonstone. The stone grew burning hot in her hand, but she held it tightly.

A moment later, the process was over and the ghost stepped back. Willa reached out to steady herself on the wall. The last image—Simon lying on the hard ground of the cave—was burned into her mind. She looked up at the ghost, her white nightdress moving around her as if there was a breeze. "Thank you so much. How did you know? Who are you?"

The ghost smiled. "My name is Amelia. I was once trapped in that cave myself and have never been able to truly leave it. It is my endless hell. And the boy—what is his name?"

"Simon."

"Simon." She smiled again. "Simon is a part of me and a part of a very dear friend. I couldn't let him die in that cave like we did."

"Amelia? Are you Amelia Plate? Ruby Plate's granddaughter?"

The ghost blinked in surprise. "Yes, I am. How did you know that?"

"I'm from Twelve Acres. But wait . . . what do you mean Simon is a part of you? What happened to you in the cave?"

"Amazing," the ghost whispered, her eyes drifted away. She looked as if she was listening to something. Her face darkened, her expression suddenly very sad. "I'm sorry, but I must go. Hurry. Get to the cave as fast as you can. They don't have much time."

"Wait, Amelia. Wait!" Willa called out, but Amelia's ghost was already gone. She sighed and then whispered to the empty room, "Thank you."

She spun around and charged downstairs, bursting into the living room, holding the moonstone out in front of her. "I know where they are!"

CHAPTER 28
Waxing Crescent

Present Day, October

The air smelled of ancient dirt, stagnant water, and shadows of Darkness. Wynter didn't want to open her eyes. That would make it too real.

I can't do this again. I can't! I can't! I can't!

The hard ground of the cave pushed back against her, making sore, aching spots all over her body. The feeling all too familiar. But she didn't move to sit up. She just lay there, thinking.

I'm sorry, my love. I'm so sorry, Rowan.

In the darkness, Simon stirred next to her. Wynter couldn't decide if it was worse or better that he was with her.

"Wynter?" he whispered.

"I'm here."

"Are you okay?"

She smiled feebly. "No, sweetie, I'm not okay."

Simon shifted and soon was sitting next to her, leaning over her.

"Are you hurt? Did they hurt you?"

"No." Talking suddenly felt like a tremendous burden, so she didn't expound. Simon was quiet for a moment. She could almost hear his thoughts of how to escape, what to do, how to act. She had thought them many times herself.

"Wynter?" he said and then hesitated. "Why do you think we won't make it out?"

Wynter let the tears slip down her face to puddle on the cave floor. "They don't know where we are. This strange magic Archard is using—I don't know how they'll fight it. And he's going to ... I just ... I don't think I'm strong enough. I don't have it in me to fight again ... I can't."

"Yes, you can. You're not alone this time. I'll help you."

Wynter closed her eyes and fought her self-destructive thoughts. "You are an amazing young man. You remind me so much of Rowan." She paused to swallow, her throat parched and dry. "I hope you are strong enough for the both of us."

Simon's teeth glowed in the dimness, a tiny smile.

"I will be," he said.

A noise from outside the cave brought their heads up. Wynter scrambled into a seated position.

"They're back," she breathed, panic already rising inside her. Simon moved himself slightly in front of her. Two bobbing yellow lights appeared in the entrance of the cave, moving toward them. Archard and Rachel stood over them, lanterns in hand. Behind them, all the other Dark witches hovered, wraiths in the blackness.

Wynter's stomach turned inside out.

Archard grinned. "Good morning, Wynter."

His beady, icy eyes leered at her and she shrank away. Simon moved to block her more, which only made Archard's smile grow. "Welcome to our little retreat. This place has quite a history. Some very interesting things happened here about eighty years ago, but it's a long story and we simply don't have time right now. We have much more important matters at hand."

With a nod from Archard, Rachel, with cat-like speed, snatched Wynter under the arms and dragged her away. Simon scrambled to his feet and tried to dive after her, but two large pairs of hands clamped onto him, holding him in place.

"No! Leave her alone," he cried.

Archard stepped in front of Simon and looked into the boy's face. "What is your name?"

Simon glared down at the Dark witch, nearly a foot shorter and no match in physical strength.

"Simon," he said between clenched teeth.

"Well, Simon. I don't think you have any room to be making demands. In fact, I need to conduct a little experiment, so indulge me." Archard started to turn and then paused. "Oh, and magic won't work in here. The cave is enchanted against Light magic."

Wynter fought the urge to vomit and pass out. She watched Archard's smooth movements. There was something different about him, something . . . shifted. He wasn't like the others in his covens. He was more. Whatever the reason, it made her insides quake with fear.

What are you going to do?

Archard nodded and Rachel pushed Wynter toward the group of witches. A man secured one of her arms behind her back and took the other by the wrist. He forced her arm out from her body, parallel to the ground. She struggled in his grip, but was too weak.

Wynter met Simon's confused look. She tried to suppress the whimper building in her throat.

Rachel slid a long, sharp knife from one of her boots and held it up in front of Wynter's face. As Rachel stared at her, a half-cocked grin on her red lips, Wynter felt her spine of scars tingle. The memory of each and every pain flashed in her mind, fresh and stinging.

No, please, no.

Rachel, her platinum-blond hair glowing in the lantern light, waved the knife in front of Wynter's face, taunting. Archard cleared his throat and Rachel's eyes flashed annoyance. She quickly moved into action. She pressed the blade of the knife to Wynter's bicep near her armpit and held it there.

Wynter couldn't draw breath, her lungs fluttered with the attempt, but the anticipation of pain stopped the air from flowing in or out.

"Wynter!" Simon screamed. He bucked and pulled against

the hands that held him, kicking and jerking, his face red and sweaty with the effort.

"Leave her alone," he yelled. "Please don't hurt her."

Rachel and Archard grinned.

Then Rachel increased the pressure of the blade and pulled down in one swift motion.

Wynter screamed.

SIMON WATCHED IN ALARM AS bright red blood pulsed out of Wynter's arm. She screamed once and then went limp in the man's arms. He dropped her carelessly to the ground, backing away quickly to avoid the blood.

"Let me go!" Simon shouted. "LET. ME. GO!" He used all the strength he could find to pull against the arms holding him back, dragging them forward a few steps.

Archard leisurely crossed over, put his face in Simon's. "See how the blood pulses from the wound? That's her brachial artery. Her heart is pumping blood out of her body at an alarming rate. Soon, she will have lost too much to survive."

Simon knew that. Of course he knew that. And he also knew he could fix it, stop it.

"Let me go!" he pleaded. "Let me help her!"

Archard looked lazily at his fingernails.

"But what could you possibly do?" He cocked his head, raised a devious eyebrow.

Something in his tone made Simon stop fighting and look at him.

"Ah, that's right. I know what you can do, Simon." He stepped out of the way and swept his arm toward Wynter. "I must see this for myself."

The hands released Simon, but for a brief moment he hesitated.

What is this?

It felt like he was walking into some kind of trap, but it didn't matter. Wynter needed him. She would die if he didn't use his power.

Simon dove across the ground and knelt over Wynter's unmoving, blood soaked form. He turned once to look at Archard, who watched with hungry, unblinking eyes. Simon swallowed and took Wynter's freezing hand in his. Immediately, the blood stopped spurting and the skin closed itself. A few seconds later, Wynter's eyes fluttered open.

"It's okay, Wynter. I've got you," Simon whispered. He helped her sit up and put his arms protectively around her, tucking her against his chest.

Archard crouched down in front of Simon, the fine leather of his shoes squeaking.

"Very, *very* interesting, Simon. Not only that you can heal her, but you did it here," Archard gestured to the cavern, "where I've blocked the use of Light magic with a powerful spell. I wonder what that says about your rare power." Archard nodded and grinned. "Very interesting indeed."

Simon's stomach clenched at the implication, but he didn't have much time to think on it. Archard reached an open hand behind him and Rachel placed the dagger in his palm. He fingered the blade and looked at Wynter.

"All better now, Wynter?"

Wynter turned her face into Simon's chest and whimpered like a scared child. Simon wanted to hit Archard, a solid punch right on his pointed chin.

"Just amazing," the Dark witch continued. "Really. I've never seen anything like it. I think I would like to see it again." With a flinch of movement Archard pressed the dagger to Wynter's back, directly over her right kidney. Simon hissed and tried to pull away. "Don't move," Archard commanded.

Wynter sobbed into Simon's chest.

"What are you doing?" Simon spat.

Archard held the dagger in place, a grin on his lips. "Well, it's simple really. Either you agree to join my covens so that we might bind the Covenant, or . . ." he lowered his voice, "I will cut, burn, rip, and beat Wynter over and over again until you *do* agree. I know you will never let her die, so if you want to spare her all that pain . . ." He tilted his head to try to look at Wynter. "I don't think she can take much more anyway. Do you? Holmes was a . . . vicious creature. So don't belabor the decision."

When Simon didn't immediately respond, Achard applied a little pressure to the knife. Wynter screamed and clawed at Simon.

"Stop!" Simon yelled.

"You agree then?"

Simon's mind was reeling. He flipped through all the possibilities, evaluating each as quickly as possible. The walls of the cave seemed to press in on him.

What do I do?

There was only one thing to do.

"Yes," Simon whispered, not looking up. Wynter closed her eyes.

Archard smiled, tossing the dagger back to Rachel.

"Excellent! I'm sorry to tell you that you'll have to stay here, under guard, until the blood moon. Just a precaution in case you change your mind." He stood and brushed at his suit. "I will have food, water, bedding, and some clean clothes brought in. No need to treat our new coven-mates like animals, right?"

He spun on his heel and strutted away, the rest of the witches following. Just before he stepped out of site, he turned back.

"Oh, and thank you for the little demonstration. You're going to make me immortal, Simon."

WHEN ALL THE DARK WITCHES were gone, Simon released Wynter gently and stood. He grabbed the lantern left for them and brought it back to where Wynter sat, her head in her hands.

"Oh, Simon. What have you done?"

"I've bought us some time," he said, keeping his voice as low as possible. "Nothing more." He sat across from her, the lantern between them throwing light onto their faces.

Wynter looked up. "What?"

"Nothing happens until the full moon, right? We can either fight Archard for that time, or let him think we agree and use the time to find a way out. Or give the others time to find us." He shrugged. "It was the only thing I could think of." He averted his eyes. "I couldn't let him hurt you again."

Wynter reached out and put her hand on his arm. "Thank you for that, Simon."

Simon nodded. He looked at the blood smeared down the right side of her dress, the sound of her scream echoing in his head. He hated that Archard had caused her pain just to see him use his healing power. It was sick, twisted. It was the first time someone had manipulated his gift. It was a shock and an eye opener.

I'll have to hide it. Keep it safe. More than I ever did before.

"I'm sorry I couldn't stop that," he nodded to the crimson stain, still wet and sticky.

Wynter lifted her arm and examined where the cut had been. The skin was smooth, without even a scar.

"Don't be. You saved me."

Exhausted, she lay down and pillowed her head on her healed arm. "How did Archard know you are a Healer?"

The image of Willa, Charlotte, and Elliot's bodies on the kitchen floor popped into his mind. Willa's blood all over the floor. He looked at the bottom of his boots and the dark stains inside the treads. He fought a wave of nausea.

"The blond one, Rachel, I think, surprised us in the kitchen. She stabbed Willa, Charlotte, and Elliot." He shook his head. Wynter gasped. "I've never seen someone move that fast. I barely had time to call out Willa's name before all three of them were on the ground." He exhaled and ran a hand back through his hair. "I healed them as I followed her out—just a brief touch. She stabbed them because of *me*, to get me to come with her."

"Oh, how awful! Poor Willa, Char, and Elliot. I'm glad you were there." She frowned. "Archard saw them come out of the house to tell me you were taken. He and Rachel must have put two and two together, realizing you'd healed them." Wynter closed her eyes, then opened them again. "Were they dead when you healed them, Simon?"

Simon looked at her. "I don't think so, but it was close. Why?"

"Just curious about your powers—like everyone else."

Simon shifted to lie down as well, his hands under his head. "Do you think Archard thinks I can bring people back from the dead? Is that what he meant by that 'you're going to make me immortal' crap?"

"Not sure. It probably means he wants to keep you as his little pet to ensure that he can never be killed in the first place."

"Great."

Wynter yawned and they lapsed into silence.

In the cold quiet of the cave, with Wynter asleep across from him, Simon finally allowed himself to think about Willa. He'd been keeping his thoughts far away from her because the pain was overwhelming. But now he let the image of her pale blue eyes, chestnut hair, and pink lips fill his mind. Her floral scent, like lavender and ginger, filled his nose, and he imagined his hand on her bare, silky skin. His heart ached, a clenching, twisting feeling. There was no worse torture than missing her, needing her. It crept along the hollows of his bones and tore at his soul.

Willa, I'm trying to get back to you.

THE ONE AND A HALF hour flight on Darby and Cal's personal jet from Jackson to Denver had been agonizing, every minute a small torture. By the time they piled into the rented SUVs and started for Twelve Acres, Willa's fingernails were nubs.

She sat in the front seat of one of the cars, Rowan at the wheel. Char and Elliott were also there, the others following in the second car. The moonstone was alive in her hand, projecting a thick line of silver light out onto the road, bright enough even to see in the sunlight, showing the way.

It was midday and the sun shone brightly, the air slightly cool and scented with the smell of fallen leaves. They knew they were bound for the mountains outside Twelve Acres— she'd seen that much as Amelia passed her the information— and part of her hated that the cave was so close to her quiet, small town. That it had always been there, lurking, holding the secret of Amelia's death. Willa wished there'd been more time to talk to the ghost of Ruby's granddaughter and learn the whole story.

Rowan sped, and soon they were driving through

town, the light from the moonstone leading them toward the mountains. They passed Ruby's house and Willa's jaw dropped when she saw the police line tape. "Looks like they found Holmes's body," Rowan said darkly, his eyes fixed on the place of his wife's imprisonment.

Willa nodded, watching the house for as long as she could, memories replaying. Then, she set her eyes forward, impatient to get to the cave. She prayed they would arrive in time. Several hours had passed since Simon and Wynter were taken. Her only consolation was that Archard needed them both alive to form his Covenant. But that didn't mean he wouldn't hurt them in the meantime.

Halfway up the canyon the moonstone light turned down a dirt road leading back into the trees. Rowan parked. "We walk from here." Willa got out of the car and tucked the moonstone in her pocket to zip her jacket against the frigid mountain air. The air was thick with the scent of pine trees and rain. Willa tilted her head to the sky to survey the gathering clouds. Thunder rumbled in the distance.

I'm coming, Simon!

Willa wondered why she couldn't feel him yet, why he didn't answer her calls to his mind. Horrific scenarios taunted her, but she tried to push them away. *Maybe it's just some kind of spell blocking our connection.* She was certain that if it were something else, something worse, she'd be able to feel it.

The witches gathered in a tight circle at the edge of the trees. Rowan looked around at each of them. "I won't pretend this will be easy. Archard is using magic I've never seen before. Be cautious, but be aggressive." He exhaled. "We must not leave survivors. I know we hold life sacred, but sometimes there is no other choice. To let them live, especially Archard, only invites further war between us. Understood?"

Quiet nods offered consent. Willa bit her lower lip, a wave of nerves tightening her stomach. She didn't know how to fight with the magic, but she'd do anything and everything she could to get Simon back. So, even if all she could do was to throw a few rocks, she'd do it—and throw them *hard*.

"Willa?" Rowan said. "Lead the way. Go slow. I'll hide our approach with magic. When you see the cave, stop so we can survey exactly what we're up against."

She nodded and pulled the moonstone out of her pocket. The light snaked away from them and into the trees.

RACHEL, LEANING AGAINST THE RAILING of the cabin's balcony, said, "You do know he's just stalling?" She craned her head upwards to look at the gathering clouds.

Archard admired the long line of her pale neck, followed it down her body.

"Of course, he's stalling," he said. "That is why we'll go back in a couple hours and hurt her again."

He took a sip from the tumbler in his hand.

Rachel smiled, her red lips pressed together. "I still can't believe he can heal like that. It's unheard of."

Archard grunted in agreement. "Yes, it's the stuff of legends. The real question is *why* he can do it. Something had to have happened. He's no ordinary witch."

She shrugged. "Who cares why he can do it? Just think of the possibilities!" She ran a hand enticingly back through her long hair. As Archard took another sip from his drink, she crossed over to him.

"Oh, believe me, my dear, I have thought of *all* the possibilities. He's going to be a very valuable addition to my Covenant."

Rachel slipped her cat-like body into his lap and took the tumbler from his hand, knocking back the rest of the amber liquid. She set the glass aside and wrapped her arms around his neck. He placed a hand on her thigh as she lowered her lips to his ear. "Things are going very well for you, Luminary."

A little while later, a sudden noise tore Archard's attention away from Rachel.

"What was that?" she said, brushing hair out of her face. "Was it thunder?"

They sat up in the bed and listened. Thunder tumbled over the cabin, but it was different than the noise they'd heard. Archard catapulted out of the bed and threw open the French doors onto the balcony. A mile into the trees, a fight was rumbling to life. The rain, now pouring out of the clouds, spun around the tops of the trees above the cave. The sky flashed with lightning and the light of fire bursts.

"The cave!" Archard cried, charging back into the room, hunting for his clothes, angry heat erupting in his gut. He'd fortified the clearing and cave, but not with as strong of magic as he could have. He'd assumed there was *no* possible chance for the Light witches to find them.

Arrogance!

Rachel was already half dressed. "Do you think it's them? How?"

He clenched his jaw so tightly, sharp pains shot up into his head.

Not possible!

"Hurry," he yelled, regretting his few minutes of pleasure.

CHAPTER 29
WAXING CRESCENT

Present Day, October

Willa moved her eyes over the thin, spindly trees; she was reminded once again of the dream she'd had. The sky coughed up a low rumble of thunder as she looked up at the ghostly clouds. Several fingers of lightning streaked across the clouds, like cracks in a mirror.

She watched the clouds with growing apprehension.

She wanted to run, to race through the trees like she had in her dream, but the moonstone trail moved slowly, sliding over the ground methodically, sniffing out the way like an enchanted bloodhound.

A loud crack of thunder shook the trees. Lightning flashed. Willa flinched and lifted her hood onto her head as the first icy drops fell from the clouds. Behind her, Rowan chanted under his breath, casting spells to help mask their approach. The heat of magic moved around them, warming her cheeks, pushing away the chill.

The moonstone suddenly died in her hand, the light gone. "Rowan, it's gone," she whispered. They were still standing in the trees, but ahead, about twenty feet, gray light filtered down into a large clearing. Peering through the trees, she could just make out the black mouth of a cave. Goose bumps rose on her arms.

Rowan gestured to the rest of the covens, and the witches spread out in both directions. Willa squinted and watched for movement. Her heart began to beat a staccato rhythm against her sternum, punching at her ribs. She wondered what they would find when they made it to the cave. Too many scary images pushed into her mind, making her heart beat even faster. Suddenly, it was hard to breathe.

"Stay with me," Charlotte whispered, appearing at Willa's side. She looked at her in the darkness and Charlotte took her hand. "Push those thoughts away. Just focus on Simon. We're gonna get them out."

She swallowed the knot of emotion and squeezed Charlotte's hand.

Soon, all the other witches were gathered around, an eerie anticipation crackling in the air.

"There are only four Dark witches watching the cave and a few spells blocking it," Rowan said, addressing them all. "Remember what I said." He let out a long breath. "Let's go."

SIMON AND WYNTER SCRAMBLED TO their feet at the sudden onslaught of noise outside the cave. A burst of wind forced itself into the small chamber and the Dark witch standing only a few feet from them quickly moved to the entrance.

"What's going on?" Simon asked. The witch, stout and broad, ignored him. Simon glanced at Wynter whose eyes were pinched in fear. He rested a reassuring hand on her shoulder and then walked forward. Commotion was brewing outside—flashes of orange light, yelling, pounding feet.

Is it . . .?

Simon dared to hope, stepping up right next to the witch.

Wind churned the leaves, the spray of water hit his face. The three other Dark witches lined up in front of the cave, throwing back a defense to whatever was coming from the trees. Simon peered out into the dark trees.

Willa?

Finally, the guard noticed his progression forward. "Get back!" he hissed and wheeled around to face Simon.

Simon stood his ground. "What's happening?"

The man looked out into the fight, now escalating in intensity, and then back at Simon.

"I said, GET BACK!" The witch pushed his hand through the air and, with a flash of magic, sent Simon hurling backwards.

Simon hit the solid, rough rock with a grunt, his bones crunching and shifting with the impact. Pain shot outward through his chest and back. Wynter hustled over to him, placed a hand on his back.

"Holy moon! Simon, are you hurt badly?"

With his eyes squeezed shut against the pain, Simon forced a full breath back into his lungs. A spark of anger flared and expanded in his gut, raging hot up his throat. Despite the awful pain, he pushed himself up, Wynter watching with worried eyes. The pain would subside as soon as his power healed whatever damage was done.

Quietly, he moved toward the opening, ignoring Wynter's whispered pleas to stop. His chest heaved, the anger inside him suddenly seething. The guard had taken a few steps outward and was throwing his magic into the fight by levitating large rocks and hurling them at the trees. Simon came up behind him, ready to plow into the man. Since his magic was blocked by Archard's spell, he figured brutal force would work just fine.

Just as he was ready to lunge forward, Willa's voice broke into his mind.

Simon!

Power surged in his blood. The sound of her voice was enough to make every muscle tense, every part of him burn to be with her. He squinted into the trees, trying to see her through the chaos.

Willa! I'm here.

Simon! Are you okay? Wynter?

Yes, we are okay. Are you?

Yes, but the fight is hard. Archard has protected the cave with some spell. Rowan is trying to break it so we can get you out, but it's hard in all this chaos.

Simon took a few quick steps forward. The Dark witch spun around, again throwing Simon back against the hard rock. The pain was worse this time and he was sure he'd cracked a few ribs. Struggling for breath, he lay on the ground, the metallic tang of blood on his tongue. Wynter rushed over. "Simon, stop it! We can't use our magic in here. I can't protect you"

Impatiently, he waited while his ribs moved back together and healed. When he could draw a breath without his eyes watering, he sat up. The spark of anger inside him grew to a raging fire. Simon felt something shift inside him, felt a blitz of heat surge out from the center of his chest into his muscles. He glared at the back of the witch.

He jumped to his feet and moved forward, knowing exactly what he would do. When Simon was a step away, the witch spun, ready to strike him with more magic, but Simon was quick. He grabbed the man's wrist and looked him directly in the eyes.

"Stay out of my way," Simon growled.

The force inside him flowed into his words and moved out his mouth in a thick ripple of heat. It washed over the Dark witch, hitting him in the face like a punch. The witch cowered beneath the power of the words, collapsing to the floor and scrambling away from Simon as fast as possible.

Simon touched his hand to the stone of the cave and in a whoosh of cold air, the spell blocking Light magic shattered.

Simon stepped out into the clearing and peered into the trees again. He almost cried out when Willa's slender form stepped forward. All the light in the clearing converged in one radiant beam on her face. His connection to her blazed under his skin, sending more potent energy to every nerve.

Through the pandemonium, his eyes found hers.

Thunder split the sky and the rain fell faster, now in thick sheets. It fell like tiny shards of glass, each drop diamond-bright and sparkling. Through the glittering rain, Simon held Willa's eyes and a crystalline connection formed between them across the open space. It gathered all the power inside him into a burning ball and then it flashed to life, transformed, like a star being born.

Without dropping her gaze, Simon moved up behind the three other Dark witches. When they turned at the sound of his approach, he raised his hand and let out a blast of pure magic that catapulted them across the clearing.

They crumpled to the ground without a sound.

The Light witches emerged from the trees, staring at him with wide eyes and gaping mouths, but Simon didn't notice. He ran across the now silent clearing to sweep Willa into his arms. He lifted her off the ground and pulled her against his chest as tightly as he dared. Then, he set her down and took her face in his trembling hands. Her hair was heavy with water, flat against her head, tears running down her cheeks onto his fingers. Her eyes shone in the darkness.

"My Willa," he whispered, the words blurring together as his lips found hers. Sparks of magic fell from their joined lips, igniting little fires in the dried leaves, quickly extinguished by the rain.

FROM THE ENTRANCE TO THE cave, Wynter watched Simon with equal parts awe and concern. An odd blue power pulsed off the boy's body as he raced over to Willa. She turned her head to look at the Dark witches' unmoving bodies, sure they were all dead.

Did he mean to do it? How did he do it?

Her attention was pulled away from Simon by Rowan running full speed across the clearing. She fell into his arms, sobbing.

"I'm here, I'm here," he cooed. "You're safe."

"Rowan . . . he cut me . . . I thought . . ."

"I know. I'm so sorry I couldn't protect you," Rowan cried. "I'm so, so sorry."

Wynter sniffled. "Simon . . . He . . . stopped that witch with his voice. I've never seen . . ."

"What witch?" Rowan's eyes flashed. "The fourth witch! Where?"

Wynter saw the rock too late to warn him. It slammed into the back of Rowan's head with a sickening crack and he collapsed. Wynter screamed and tried to lift Rowan up, but the witch grabbed her and yanked her away, dragging her out into the rain.

"Rowan! No, let me go!" she screamed.

Wynter struggled against his hold, her eyes on Rowan, blood now seeping through his hair. When Wynter screamed his name, he rolled and forced himself as far up as his knees.

"STOP!" he commanded, and the Dark witch spun back around.

Wynter used her magic to push the witch. He landed hard in the mud a few feet away. Rowan thrust his hand out to open a crack in the earth under the man. With a chilling scream the witch fell into the earth and was swallowed whole. Rowan closed the fissure with a clenching of his fist.

Wynter hurried to him. The blood was soaking his shirt now and Wynter's stomach filled with panic. "Simon!" she screamed. Rowan collapsed forward into the mud. "No, no, no. Rowan!"

He didn't move when she called his name.

"Simon!"

Simon was at her side. "What happened?"

"His head," she said in a shaking voice.

Simon dropped to his knees and took Rowan's hand. A moment later, Rowan groaned and rolled over. Wynter scrambled closer to take his head in her lap. "Rowan?"

"I'm fine." His eyes rolled over to Simon. "Thank you."

Simon nodded. "What happened?"

"That guard was still by the cave," Wynter explained.

"Oh," Simon gasped. "I'm sorry. I forgot about him."

Rowan shook his head. "We all did. It's okay."

Darby, Cal, and the others all gathered around, some throwing sideways glances at Simon. The rain continued to pour down in heavy sheets. They were soaked and freezing.

"So where's Archard?" Darby said. "The other Dark witches can't be far away."

Rowan sat up. "He'll come," He turned to look at Wynter. "Can you fight?"

She smiled, pushed back her wet hair. "Oh, yes. He's hurt us enough. Let's end it."

He smiled as Wynter took his face in her hands and kissed him.

Simon helped Rowan to his feet and Wynter took her husband's hand. She heard a high-pitched whistling sound only a second before a fireball hit the center of the clearing and exploded.

CHAPTER 30
WAXING CRESCENT

Present Day, October

Willa saw the fireball descend out of the sky. Simon grabbed her and threw her to the ground covering her body with his. She clenched her eyes shut and waited for the fiery impact, but it didn't come. She and Simon looked up to see the Waters, Rain and Corbin, had acted impressively quick, using the falling rain to form a shield of water, protecting all the Light witches from the flames.

Rowan called out, "Simon and Willa, get back in the trees. This is going to get ugly."

Willa looked at Simon and saw the flash of defiance in his eyes. "Simon?"

"I'm not hiding in the trees. Archard is the whole reason we are here. He violated your mind, had one of his witches stab you in the heart and he almost killed Wynter just so he could watch me heal her." He pushed up and held out a hand to her. "I'm fighting. Stay with me and I'll keep you safe."

Willa took his hand, ready to argue, but stopped. Her own hatred for Archard welled up inside her, spinning into a burning need to fight. "Let's go."

He smiled and turned away.

"Wait!" Willa grabbed his arm. He turned back. "Simon, how did you do that?" she asked quietly, shifting her eyes to the Dark witches' bodies. The joy of having Simon back and the energy of their reunion were still racing in her blood, euphoric, but it was dulled slightly by what she'd watched him do. It had been necessary, but she didn't understand *how* he'd done it. The other Light witches hadn't demonstrated that kind of power.

Simon followed her gaze, his brows furrowed. "I have no idea."

Willa stepped closer to ask more, but Archard and his remaining five witches broke through the water shield. The water exploded and rocketed outward, hitting her and Simon like bullets. Then a hailstorm of rocks and whole trees ripped from their roots came at them. Simon grabbed Willa's hand and they dove out of the path of a falling pine tree. It crashed behind them. She blinked at it, breathless, body aching, turning her attention back to the clearing.

Willa searched the chaos for Rowan and Wynter. Rowan

suddenly broke out of the trees, charging forward like a bull to red, his hands lifted, spewing magic, aimed directly at Archard.

The rest of the Light witches were fighting the other Darks. One Dark witch was already lifeless on the ground, the victim of a swift cuff of air snapping her neck, courtesy of Hazel. A sound to Willa's right made her jump and lift her hands.

Charlotte and Elliot ran toward them. "It's just us!" Char yelled. "Simon! Can you sense Archard's intentions?" she asked breathlessly. "If you can read him, I can direct Rowan. Unless, of course, you can do that crazy thing you did before and just end this now."

SIMON FROWNED, IGNORED THE QUESTION, and looked out to where Rowan and Archard stood locked in a struggle of opposing flames in the center of the clearing. The ground bucked and shook under them, the quakes rippling out to shake the whole clearing. The power and heat Simon had felt inside him before that had enabled him to defeat the other witches was gone now and he had no idea how to get it back. Simon moved his eyes to the dead witches. *How* did *I do that?*

Shaking his head, he focused on Archard, cracking the door in his mind only to the Dark witch. First, there was nothing; it was too hard to break through all the raging energy and emotions, but then he felt a tenuous thread of connection. He grabbed onto it and held tight. "Archard is . . . angry. Whoa. I've never felt anger like this."

Charlotte closed her eyes. "I'll try to get a connection to Rowan's mind."

Simon watched Rowan closely. Archard was pushing him back, strain evident in the curve of his shoulders and trembling arms. Then Rowan flinched, his eyes flashed to the trees.

"I got it," Char said. "He's listening. What else you got, Simon?"

Simon tugged on the thread of Archard's presence. "He's very confident he can beat Rowan." Simon gasped. "Tell Rowan to duck!"

Rowan ducked, barely missing the aspen tree that came at him from behind.

Simon exhaled in relief and refocused. Elliot said, "They've killed two more Dark witches. It's just that blonde one who stabbed us and some guy with glasses left."

Simon narrowed his eyes, reaching further. He felt a shift in Archard's emotions. "His anger is getting out of control. He's . . ." *What is that?* Simon closed his eyes. A tremor of panic moved out of Archard. "He's panicking. He knows that most of his witches are dead. Tell Rowan to push hard. Archard will make a mistake."

"Good!" Char said, her eyes still squeezed shut. "Rowan says he has a plan, but he'll need our help."

OUT OF THE SIDE OF his eye, Archard saw two more of his witches go down. His covens were lost; there was nothing left. Even if he killed Rowan and all the Light witches, he still had no chance of binding a Covenant. He'd failed! Just like his grandfather. The blood moon would rise with his shame.

No! How did this happen? This can't be happening.

Anger, red and blinding, roiled inside him, his actions turned desperate. He threw anything he could think of at Rowan, but the damned Light witch was much stronger than he anticipated. Desperate, he growled and charged forward, tackling Rowan to the mud.

A foolish move; Rowan had the size and muscle advantage in a fistfight. His large fist slammed into Archard's ribs and he choked on his breath, sputtering at the lightning pain. Like a rabid animal, he lashed out, biting, scratching. Rowan tucked his head, spun, and kicked, putting the force of his magic into the movement. Archard sailed through the air to crash near the entrance of the cave.

His anger overcame his pain and he was on his feet in seconds, just in time for Rowan to plow into his middle, sending them both tumbling into the cave. The stone tore through his suit and chewed up his skin.

He pushed fire into his hands and dug his fingers into Rowan's back. The witch yelled as the flames burned the flesh on his back. Archard cackled in Rowan's ear. Rowan threw Archard off and he hit the wall of the cavern, slumping to the ground. His vision filled with black spots.

When Archard managed to get to his feet, Rowan was nowhere in sight. Archard threw his head from side to side and spun, looking for his opponent, waiting for the next attack. Only a sliver of light entered the cave and he quickly lifted his palm to ignite a small flame, which flickered to life, suspended over his skin, to illuminate the cavern.

He was alone.

Moving cautiously, his breath heaving, his anger seething, Archard approached the entrance of the cave. Wynter stood there, her hands lifted. He laughed, loud, the sound echoing off the stone. He straightened up and sauntered forward.

"So, Rowan runs away to let his woman finish the job, huh?"

Wynter didn't move, didn't react; she stood like stone, glaring back at him. Archard stopped only a foot in front of her—him still in the cave, she just outside it.

"Go ahead, Wynter. Take your revenge. Take your revenge for those two coven-mates I killed, slowly and painfully. Take it for every time Holmes touched you, cut you, every time he ravaged your mind. Take it for last night when I almost let you bleed out all over this cave."

Wynter's jaw twitched and Archard knew he had her. "You know each time you kill another human being you touch the Darkness," he hissed. "And I see you had *no* problem killing Holmes or my coven-mates." He narrowed his eyes at her. "You have more Darkness in you than you think, Wynter. You should have joined me. We would have made a great team."

Wynter flinched again, and this time he lunged forward, only to crash into a magical barrier, a wall of Light magic. With a growl, he lifted his hands and sent a blast of cold Dark magic at it, certain it would crumble. He tried again and again, his growls of anger escalating into bone-rattling shrieks. He tried the few spells he could remember from Bartholomew's grimoire, but still he was trapped.

Wynter smiled, a slow, satisfied smile. The fire raged out of control inside him, looking for an outlet. His skin flushed red and then began to smoke. "No!" he screamed. "How are you keeping this wall up? You're not strong enough!"

Wynter shook her head. "Not alone, no." The eleven other Light witches stepped out of the gray rain, hands lifted. Wynter crouched down to get closer to where he had collapsed on the stone floor, leaning against the magical barrier. "Your coven-mates are all dead," she hissed. "Well, almost all. Rachel ran off into the woods like a coward. But the rest lie dead in the mud." She leaned closer, her eyes tearing into his. "Whatever strange magic you've been using is not enough for you, alone, against two True Covens. You are beaten, Archard, and your talk means *nothing*. I'll kill you, taking my revenge, and then Rowan and I will bind a Light Covenant."

His whole body shook with anger, boiling, lava-hot fire inside him. He clawed at the wall, hoping at least to make Wynter flinch away, but she only glared. His skin was smoking fiercely now. He dragged off his suit coat and tore at his shirt, trying to release the unbearable heat inside him.

Wynter stood, lifted her hands. The ground trembled and heads of thick, rope-like vines burst out of the cracks in the rock and slithered toward him. He crawled back, appalled.

No! Not like Holmes!

The first vine twisted around his leg, sharp thorns tearing at his flesh—a feature Wynter had not included in Holmes's death—and moved upward. His fire raged behind his heart, bursting into flames, licking outward, ready to consume him.

WYNTER WATCHED AS ARCHARD'S SKIN smoked, thick fingers of black rising from his pores. He thrashed against her thorny vines now coiling around his whole body and screamed louder and louder. She backed away. Rowan stepped next to her.

"What's happening to him?" she whispered, eyes unblinking.

"His fire is out of control."

Suddenly, Archard's whole body burst into flames. She and all the Light witches stepped back from the hot shock wave. Wynter released her control of the vines. Archard howled in agony, the pitch cutting through the rain, filling the clearing. Flapping his burning arms and throwing his body in all directions, Archard got to his feet and ran to the back of the cave, crashed into the wall and collapsed in a heap of orange-red flames.

Wynter turned away. "Time to go," she said quietly. Her coven-mates turned with her and followed. Willa pulled a moonstone from her pocket and they followed its milky white light away from the cave and out into the wet forest.

THE RAIN STOPPED, WEAK AFTERNOON sunlight found its way

through the clouds. Willa walked hand in hand with Simon at the head of the group, the moonstone reversing their course back to the cars. She looked up at the sky, glad for the light after all the darkness. The numbness of shock settled over her mind and body. She didn't know what to think or how to feel. Only one thought cut through the shock: *I have Simon back.*

She looked over at him. His face wet and muddy, hair full of dirt and leaves, and his hoodie ripped in a few places. Simon returned her stare.

I have you back, she said to his mind. *There were moments . . .*

He smiled and pulled her closer, putting his arm around her. *I know, but I'm here. And I promise nothing will ever pull us apart like that again.* Then out loud he asked, "How did you find us?"

"Amelia Plate's ghost."

"What?" He furrowed his brow.

"She came to me, told me how to find you." Willa stopped. "Oh!" She turned. Amelia's flickering form stood back in the trees near the clearing. Willa lifted her hand and waved. Amelia waved back before disappearing. "Amelia?" Willa called out, but the ghost didn't return. She still had a hundred questions for the dead granddaughter of Ruby Plate, but knew they would have to go unanswered.

"Come on," Simon said, pulling her forward. "Let's go home."

CHAPTER 31
WAXING CRESCENT

Present Day, October

Two SUVs pulled up in front of Willa's house and the twelve tired, dirty witches piled out. Willa stood on the lawn looking up at the familiar sight of her home, thinking she'd never seen a more beautiful place. It'd only been a few days, but she felt like she was coming home after a long and arduous journey.

The front door flew open and her parents ran out, her mom's arms open wide. Willa ran to her, barely noticing the flow of tears from her mom's eyes.

"Oh, my baby girl," Sarah said into her ear. "What on earth happened to you?" She pulled back, a brilliant smile on her face. She pushed at Willa's tangled hair and brushed at the dirt on her face.

Willa laughed. "You wouldn't believe it if I told you." Simon stepped next to them, and Sarah released Willa and flung herself at him.

"Oh! You're okay. Willa said something had happened."

Simon smiled and awkwardly returned Sarah's hug. "I'm okay."

Ethan stepped forward. "Glad you're home, Willa," he said quietly. Willa threw her arms around him and he squeezed her tightly. She stepped back to tell him how good it was to see him, but bit her tongue at the look on his face. His eyes were narrowed at the group of witches milling on the lawn, muddy and ragged-looking. "Who are these people?" he whispered.

Willa briefly closed her eyes. "These are our coven-mates, Dad. Our friends. They are all witches."

Contempt and instant hatred darkened his face, his jaw tensing.

Sarah grabbed Willa's arm, breaking the tension she was oblivious to. "I'm *so* glad you're home," she repeated. She then turned to the group. "Everyone come in. I've got hot tea and a pot of soup. And two showers."

Willa smiled at her mom and then looked back at her dad. He was stepping away from the group, arms folded, face closed. Simon joined her and placed his arm around her shoulders. When she looked up at him, she saw the understanding on his face. She shook her head, wishing there was something she could say to make her dad understand.

"Let's go in," she said quietly. She and Simon walked past Ethan, into the house.

LATER, WHEN THE SUN DIPPED low in the sky and painted the clouds with sunset colors, Simon slipped away from the chaos in the house to the reprieve of the quiet backyard. Not even his mind-lock could keep out all the joy and excitement being passed around the kitchen as the triumph was relived. He needed some peace to think.

He sat in a lawn chair and dropped his head back with a heavy sigh. The gravity of what he'd done at the cave was finally settling in. *I killed three people.* The fact sat uncomfortably in his head. His whole life had been about healing.

How did I let that happened?

The incident was a blur in his head. He tried to move back through exactly what had happened, but a fuzzy, blue film covered the memories. All he could remember was the potent exhilaration of his power and Willa's brilliant eyes through the rain. A portion of that power still tingled inside him. It had never subsided completely, and he knew something had changed—permanently. In a way it was thrilling, knowing such power lived inside him, but if he were honest with himself, it was also frightening.

The image of the Dark witches' lifeless bodies lying in the mud rose up before him, haunting, taunting.

I killed three people.

It was easy to rationalize, but it still didn't sit well with him.

He wanted to talk to Willa about it, but that scared him, too. She was the only thing that brought peace to his confused heart, yet the words wouldn't form on his tongue. He feared what she might think if he confessed to how he had enjoyed the surge of power, and how a portion of it still lived inside him. The others were already uneasy around him, looking at him differently. He couldn't bear to see that look on her face.

The back door creaked open and the hum under his skin told him who it was. Willa sat in the chair next to him and stared out across the lawn for several quiet moments. Then, she turned to him and said, "My dad left. Didn't even bother to sit down with them, talk with them. Just left. Can you believe that?"

"I'm sorry, Willa," Simon said, as disappointed in Ethan's actions as she was.

She shook her head and sighed in frustration, then turned to him, "Well, what do we do now?"

He rolled his head and met her eyes. "What do you want to do?"

Willa bit her bottom lip, her eyes dropped to her hands. "I almost died. You could have died. When you were first taken, all I wanted was to run away from all this, get away so we'd be safe, but now . . ."

Simon sat forward and took her hand. He kissed the cool

skin on the inside of her wrist. "Now, we know who we are and what we are capable of. How could we ever go back to how things were before?" He swallowed, feeling the weight of decision in his chest. "We are witches and we will join the covens." Saying the words aloud lifted the weight from his chest, leaving behind a light sense of freedom. He knew it was the right choice, even if it wasn't the logical one.

She raised her head and nodded, a slow smile forming on her lips. "It sounds crazy, but I think that is what we are supposed to do. And with Archard and his covens dead, we'll be safe." She smiled. "Did you hear Wynter and Rowan talking about moving here? They are sure Archard destroyed their cottage, which is really sad. I liked it there." Willa looked out at the sinking sun. "Wynter has most of them convinced they should move here, too. She says this was once a town of witches, and it should be again."

Simon laughed. "Well, that will certainly make things a little more interesting around here."

Willa laughed, and then her face fell serious. "In a few days we will be a part of a Covenant, Simon. It's for life."

Simon exhaled. "For life." He nodded. "Sounds about right." He smiled at her as she shifted, bringing her face close to his. She smiled and then pressed her warm lips to his. The concern and worry he'd felt before melted away with her passion. Without breaking the kiss, he pulled her into his lap, enjoying the sparks in his blood and the stir of magic around their close bodies.

NEVER HAD A SCENT SMELLED SO wonderful. Willa stood in the entrance of the Twelve Acres Museum and drank in the smell of history. That dusty, intricate smell unique to time. She smiled as she gazed around at the small reception desk, the bulletin board of faded notices, the simple chandelier overhead, and the shiny tile floor.

But her joy was lessened by the reason for the visit, her stomach clenched with nervous energy.

"Can I help you?" a plump, friendly woman with coiffed blond hair asked. She leaned forward from the reception desk, a welcoming smile on her coral lips.

"Hello, Bertie!" Willa answered with a small wave.

Bertie gasped in surprise. "Willa?" Bertie, in her mid-sixties and suffering from two bad knees, wobbled forward. "Oh, my goodness! You look different." She stopped in front of Willa and looked her up and down. With a beaming smile she added, "Yes, there is a brightness in you. You look older and even more beautiful, and it's only been a few days! New York really agreed with you."

Willa laughed, blushing. "Thanks, Bertie. How are things?"

"Oh, fine, fine." she said. "So, how was the trip to the Big Apple? Did you have fun?"

Willa smiled, certain the word *liar* was about to pop into place on her forehead. "Yes, it was great."

Bertie sighed and looked Willa up and down once more. "New York is so fabulous, especially if you're young."

Willa smiled back, but was out of things to say. "Well, I've got to catch up on the dusting." She took a step toward the exhibit entrance.

"Oh, sure," Bertie said, waving her hand toward the interior of the museum. "Go catch up.

Willa laughed politely. "Thanks, Bertie. See you later."

As soon as Willa wandered into the main exhibit her stomach flopped with anxiety and excitement.

Solace. Willa couldn't wait to tell her friend everything, but worried that Solace might be too mad to talk, too hurt by Willa's sudden, unexplained departure.

It didn't take long to find the ghost-girl. She sat in an antique rocking chair in the *Life of Early Twelve Acres* exhibit room. A book rested open on her lap, but her eyes were closed, head laid back. Her body appeared thin and translucent, like a sheer curtain. Willa's stomach clenched with a new kind of pain. She didn't realize the strength of how much she had missed Solace. She wanted to run over, throw her arms around her friend and talk about everything that had happened in the past few days.

Suddenly, Solace sat forward, her eyes wide. "Willa! You're back!" The ghost flickered out of sight and reappeared in front of Willa. She threw her not-there arms around Willa. "When you came that night—the way you talked—I thought I would never see you again."

Willa wished there was something to hug back. Instead, she sighed in deep relief. "I know. I'm so sorry I made you worry. I really missed you."

Solace moved back. "It was only a few days!" She smiled

mischievously and then smoothed her features. "I missed you, too. Now, tell me what happened. I've been cooking up all kinds of crazy scenarios."

"Solace, you are never going to believe this—we are witches!"

Solace looked up, her brow furrowed. "Excuse me?"

"You and I, your parents, the town founders, Ruby, Simon—all of us are witches. We have *magic*. That is why I can see and talk to you. And why you can see my soul. It's also why I had to leave—to become a part of a legacy left by Ruby Plate and your parents."

Solace blinked once and then twice, gazing at Willa with critical eyes. "Are you playing some kind of Halloween joke, Willa? I know it's almost Halloween.

Willa shook her head. "No, no. It's *not* a joke. Look," she shifted her bag around and flipped back the flap. She pulled out the three yellow cloth-bound books. "These belonged to your mother. They are her grimoires, or spell books. Basically her journals." Willa held them out and Solace took them warily. "I also have Ruby Plate's grimoire." She pulled out the large red book. "She was an amazing witch."

Solace's face relaxed, her eyes finally softening. She looked longingly at the grimoires in her hands. "These were my mother's?"

"Yes," Willa smiled, "and she loved you *so* much. She waited her whole life for you. There's so much more to tell you. It all solves the mystery about Ruby and the names in her candlestick. And guess what?"

Solace looked up, intrigued.

Willa said, "I have a new one for us. It starts with a girl named Lilly whom your mom was trying to protect."

Solace's face broke into a smile. "Well, let's sit down then, and get to work."

CHAPTER 32
Blood Moon

Present Day, October

The blood moon reigned magnificently in the sky, full and bright. Its pearly, supernatural light penetrated the veil between this world and the Otherworld, drawing it aside for one glorious night. Power radiated from every surface, and magic sparked as easily as tinder, all charged by the full moon's one-night endowment.

Tonight Twelve Acres was a witch town again.

The Light Covenant gathered beneath the branches of Ruby's willow tree. The lithe arms of the tree trembled with joy to once again have the magic glowing around it. It was only right that the Binding happen in this place, where it had first happened a hundred and twenty years earlier. It had been Willa's suggestion, after she read about the original Binding in Ruby's grimoire, but Wynter had insisted on it, surprising them all.

The yard was completely changed, all signs of neglect vanished. Wynter and Rowan had made sure of that using their Earth gifts. The grass was lush and green, the bushes bursting with leaves, the flowerbeds overflowing with fragrant offerings. Especially for the ritual, Wynter had added moonflower vines and night-blooming jasmine in abundance. Soaking up the moonlight, the flowers glowed like twinkle lights strung for a nighttime party.

The twelve witches were immaculately dressed for the ritual. The women wore long, glittering, metallic-white dresses, the color of the moon, embellished with silver thread and beads. The men wore crisp, black-as-night Oxford shirts, open at the collar, black slacks, and elegantly tailored black frock coats.

Willa carried Ruby's beautiful silver candlestick—clandestinely borrowed from the museum for this night—and set it on the small round table next to Ruby's grimoire. She placed a tall black taper into it and then, after a few attempts, snapped the wick to life with her fingers. Smiling, she watched the flame grow. Tucked inside the stem of the candlestick was the original note, but there was also a new one. Willa had written the twelve names of the new Covenant members on a sheet of fresh parchment and rolled it up with the original.

Her eyes fell to Ruby's grimoire. It'd been a pleasure and

a thrill to read it from cover to cover over the last week. Now, more than ever, Willa admired Ruby for all she'd accomplished and hoped to follow valiantly in the witch's footsteps.

Life had quickly returned to normal. At first, it'd been hard to focus in class or while doing homework, her mind so full of the newness of the magic. But now, life had settled into a comfortable routine with a few thrilling changes. She and Solace spent hours poring over the grimoires, the ease of their friendship more comforting than ever. Every night, she and Simon met with the covens to learn, practice and prepare for the Binding. The strength of her connection to Simon grew deeper with each passing day.

Willa ran her fingers over the smooth, worn leather of the grimoire, laughing quietly at the sparks of heat in her fingertips. Then she opened it to the page where Ruby had written the Binding spell. In a few moments Rowan would read it.

"Are you ready?" Simon's deep voice whispered into her ear, sending pleasant chills down her body. She turned. He looked stunning in his black attire, the long frock coat accenting his broad shoulders.

"Ready," she said with a smile and took his arm. The difference was subtle, but to her it was impossible to miss. Something had changed inside him, something rooted in what had happened at the cave. It was hard to decide on the nature of the change. His powers were more potent than ever as he'd demonstrated in training every night, but he wouldn't talk about it. She'd tried to bring it up so many times, but he'd smoothly change the subject. Willa didn't understand why, but something about this was untouchable, forbidden.

No one else talked about what he'd done at the cave either. It had been swept under the rug, ignored like a mistake, but certainly not forgotten. She saw the way Rowan and Wynter watched him with narrowed eyes and the exchange of whispers.

It'd only been a week, though. Perhaps time would mend the awkwardness.

The other witches gathered around as Rowan stood at the table. He cleared his throat and the group quieted.

"First, we present Willa and Simon with their Gift Necklaces." He smiled at them and gestured for them to step forward. This was a surprise; no one had mentioned anything to Willa about necklaces. Wynter joined Rowan and held out two small black boxes, handing one to Willa and one to Simon.

"These are your Gift necklaces," Rowan explained. "This is a new tradition Wynter and I chose to begin with our Covenant. Each necklace is infused with magic and tied to the Covenant Binding. We'll use them in our Covenant rituals. They also act as a form of protection to us." He reached into his shirt and pulled out a long silver chain from which dangled a triangular symbol. Willa recognized it from Ruby's book as the Earth symbol. "We've given them to each person who has joined our covens. You are the last two to receive them."

Wynter gestured to the boxes. "Open them," she whispered excitedly.

Together they lifted off the tops. Inside, on a swath of black silk, lay Willa's necklace. The platinum chain was long, thin. From it hung a quarter-sized pendant shaped in the Dreams symbol, an upside-down triangle with two interlocking circles inside. She touched the pendant and gasped at how warm the metal was to the touch, heated by magic. Her hand tingling, she lifted the necklace from the box and lowered it over her head. It fell to the center of her breast bone. Immediately, a rush of magical energy moved through her from head to toe. Her pulse quickened and a smile spread on her lips.

Simon was also wearing his necklace now, the chain slightly thicker, more masculine, but the Mind symbol, a triangle with a dot just under the apex. He fingered the symbol and then looked up at her, his eyes dark with thoughts. She took his hand.

Wynter gestured for them to join her in the circle of witches now formed around the flickering candlestick. Rowan rested his hand on Ruby's open book and sighed contentedly.

"It's been a long, hard road, but here we are." He reached out and took Wynter's hand. Happy tears balanced on the edges of her eyes. "Our patience and sacrifices are about to pay off.

"Tonight our gifts come together in a way we have never experienced. Within our circle of twelve, the magic will have endless power, and the Powers of the Earth, the origin of all magic, will have a faithful group of stewards." His gaze moved affectionately around the circle. "Let's begin by joining the symbols."

Wynter leaned close to Willa and Simon. "This is where we separate into covens—female and male—and then join our necklaces together. Willa, come with me. Simon, Rowan will show you what to do."

Willa looked up at Simon, touched his arm and then moved away with Wynter. Charlotte grinned as Willa approached and pulled her into the spot next to her. When Char and Wynter and the other three women took off their necklaces, Willa followed.

"Now hold it out like this," Char whispered and gripped her pendant between her finger and thumb, lifting it to the center of their small circle. Willa did the same, meeting her coven-mates in the middle. "Now let go." Char grinned excitedly.

Willa let go and her necklace, along with the others, hovered in the air, chain hanging down from the suspended pendant. Amazed, she watched as the pendants came together, fused into a circle of six parts and spun to life. She moved with the other women back into one large circle. The two hovering, spinning circles of Gift symbols, one for the female coven and one for the male, moved to hang above the candle's flame.

"Join hands," Rowan called.

Willa took Simon's hand in her right and Char's in her left. Charlotte smiled and lifted her eyebrows.

"Here we go," Willa whispered. A twist of nervous anticipation turned Willa's stomach, her heart beat madly in her
chest. *Here we go!*

Simon squeezed her hand and she squeezed back.

Rowan inhaled deeply and then read from Ruby's grimoire, his voice solemn and thick with his accent:

> *"Silver light of the sacred Blood Moon*
> *We call to your strength, our magical cocoon.*
> *Grant us the power to carry the Light,*
> *To protect the magic with all our might.*
> *All the gifts we join this day,*
> *The Powers of the Earth, the one true way.*
> *A Covenant of Light, now forged for good,*
> *We bind forever, our true path understood."*

All heads turned upward. The blood moon glimmered in
the dark sky, sending a stream of pearly light down from the
heavens. It snaked and undulated, moving through the air
down to the Covenant. When it reached the willow it splin-
tered, falling over the tree's canopy like a firework's sparks,
raining down in brilliant bands of moonlight.

The light continued to move, seeking out the witches.
Awestruck, Willa watched a band of light spiral around her,
starting at the crown of her head and moving downward. The
temperate thread felt like the brush of wings on her skin,
kissing, caressing, and then seeping in to rest in the space
behind her heart—her soul. When it reached its home, a
pleasant burst of energy shot through her body.

Willa gripped Simon and Charlotte's hands tighter. A tangible, palatable vigor moved through her. It felt glorious, like every part of her was more awake, more alive, brighter. Power filled her, strength so shocking in its potency that she drew in a sharp breath. Magic hummed along every nerve and the earth called out to her. For a moment, she felt connected to every tree, every blade of grass, every flower, every animal nearby, but also to the moon, the stars, and the sun in the firmament. She inhaled the crystalline connection of all things and knew that she was forever changed.

In a burst of magic, she felt the heartbeat of everyone in the circle, felt hers match theirs.

"We are now bound to each other, body, soul and magic. We are a Covenant," Rowan announced, his voice rising triumphantly. He snapped his fingers and the black candle flame extinguished. Then the necklaces broke apart and floated through the air to their rightful owners. Willa pulled her own necklace from the air and dropped it over her head, the symbol hot against her chest.

A huge cheer rose from the group. Charlotte pulled Willa into a hug. "We did it! We did it! That was amazing!" She yelled.

Willa laughed, sharing in the feeling of triumph. She turned to Simon. "We did it."

He laughed and pulled her into a hug. "We did it." He kissed her hair. Over his shoulder, she caught the shimmering form of a ghost.

"It's Ruby!" Simon turned, but didn't see what Willa saw. "I'll be right back."

Willa ran over to Ruby, standing in the field of weeds behind the willow. "Ruby! You're here. When I didn't see you earlier I worried something had happened."

Ruby smiled. "Something did happen. After you left, I crossed over into the Otherworld, finally able to rest and be with my family and ancestors. The spirits of the dead are not supposed to stay here."

"Then how are you here?"

Ruby looked up at the sky. "The power of the blood moon thins the barrier between the worlds. I was able to come back to see the Binding. Thank you for helping make this happen, Willa. You've made the right choice."

A knot of emotion formed in Willa's throat at the words. "Thank you, Ruby. It was an incredible experience and I hope we do your legacy justice."

Ruby smiled, her face flickering out of focus. "I have no doubt."

"I saw Amelia, Ruby. She's a ghost at the cave."

Ruby frowned and sighed. "I know. My poor Amelia. I was able to help arrange her meeting with you, but she didn't cross over after as I had hoped. The Otherworld has its own schedule."

"I'm sorry."

"Thank you." She smiled again and then looked away. "I must go now, Willa. Goodbye."

Ruby was gone before Willa could say her goodbye.

Instead of immediately returning to the group, she stood alone for a moment, looking back at the happy sight of her friends, of her *coven-mates*. Her body still pulsed with the energy of the Binding, her heart hummed happily. She turned her head to the bright moon and felt a caress of warmth on her face. Smiling, she closed her eyes.

I'm a witch.

EPILOGUE
New Moon

The Near Future

Amelia left the cave and hurried through the forest, as she'd done every night for the last several weeks. The cabin was dark and quiet, a sleeping beast tucked under the trees. She put herself just outside the second-story balcony doors. No matter how many times she saw it, she couldn't stop the grimace at the hideous scene beyond the glass. A flash of memory crossed her mind, something she tried so hard not to remember—herself, old, twisted, and deformed. Waiting and wanting to die. She shook the memory away, refusing to compare herself to or have any compassion for the man in the bed.

Movement in the dark room caught Amelia's attention.

The blond woman moved around the bed, adjusting tubes and wires, trying desperately not to look at the creature in the bed. Amelia didn't blame her. It was painful to look at the deformed features, hairless head, and melted skin that festered and oozed. White bandages spotted with red blood and yellow pus covered almost all of the body; and so many tubes and instruments protruded from the form that Amelia was reminded of nightmarish sea creatures.

The creature in the bed stirred slightly, a gurgle of sound came from his throat. Amelia had seen the firestorm in the cave, heard his inhuman screams, and was amazed that the witch had survived. She watched the woman bend over and turn her ear to the lipless mouth. He was trying to speak. Amelia moved closer and noticed the door was slightly ajar. Without hesitating she slipped in, trying hard to ignore the sting of Darkness still so strong despite the witch's injuries.

The woman leaned closer as more gurgling noises came from what was left of the man's throat. Amelia moved next to the woman, so close she could see the small lines around her eyes. The man struggled to push the words from his fire-ravaged body. At first there were only a few soft clicks and grunts, but then the words took form on his tongue, moving into the room like noxious vapor.

"Get . . . me . . . Bartholomew's . . . book."

ACKNOWLEDGEMENTS

Sometimes, even for a writer, there are no better words to express gratitude than to say THANK YOU. The following people deserve thanks in abundance, rewards in heaven, and lots of homemade brownies.

First, my little family. My husband, Matt, who is everything I ever dreamed of, and more. I couldn't do this without you. My three babies who keep life interesting, chaotic, and wonderful. You are the best kids in the world. Thank you for helping me discover and accomplish my dreams. I love you forever.

To my parents. There are never enough words to thank my incredibly supportive and amazing parents. Thank you for believing, for babysitting, and for pretty much everything! I love you so much.

My five siblings: Carol, Kenneth, John, Paul, and Maren. You are my best friends and the most fabulous people I know. Thank you for always being there and for always understanding. To Austin, Teri Mae, and Maddie: I'm so glad that each of you have joined the craziness and fit right in. I love you all!

To Matt's family: Jill, Brett, Marci, Ryan, Jana, Scott, James, Erin, Mary, and McLean. Thanks for being the best second family anyone could ask for and for all the incredible support. Love you much.

Fran and Jenn, of Literary Counsel, my rock star literary

agents. Thank you, Fran, for believing in me from the first, and Jenn, for being a champion of my work. You are both so wonderful!

To the talented people at Jolly Fish Press, especially Christopher Loke and Kirk Cunningham. Your tireless efforts and enthusiasm are deeply appreciated. Thank you for making my book so beautiful and for believing in my work. I'm so lucky to be swimming in the fish tank.

A special thanks to the designers at Pixology Design and my editor Chris for creating the most perfect and most beautiful book cover an author could ever dream of.

To my beta readers: Marci, Maren, Jill, Matt, Kenneth, John, and Teri Mae. I apologize for subjecting you to such awful writing, but thank you so much for the input and advice.

To my fellow author, Jennifer Griffith, I owe you so much thanks and truck loads of cold cereal. Without your expert advice, *Blood Moon* would not have found its full potential.

A shout-out to my book club ladies who share my love of good books, and once a year indulge my love of a good Halloween witch party. You were all there when this story began and I love you.

Thank you to all those who have read my blog, followed my social networks, read my KSL columns, and watched my Studio 5 segments. I truly appreciate your support.

Finally, a huge and resounding thank you to YOU, the reader. Stories mean nothing unless they are shared and loved by others. Thanks for being a part of this story.

TERI HARMAN HAS BELIEVED IN all things won-drous and haunting since her childhood days of sitting in the highest tree branches reading Roald Dahl and running in the rain imagin-ing stories of danger and romance. Currently, her bookshelf is overflowing, her laundry un-folded, and her three small children running mad while she pens bewitching novels. Utah is her home, but she often imagines living in the wild landscapes of the Pacific Northwest.

Come share in the magic and chaos at
www.TeriHarman.com.